STEVE JACKSON & IAN LIVINGSTONE

FIGHTING FANTASY

Fighting Fantasy: new Wizard editions

Also available in the original Wizard editions

STEVE JACKSON & IAN LIVINGSTONE

STORMSLAYER

By Jonathan Green

Illustrated by Stephen Player

Wizard Books

Published in the UK in 2009 by Wizard Books,
an imprint of Icon Books Ltd., Omnibus Business Centre
39–41 North Road, London N7 9DP
email: info@iconbooks.co.uk
www.iconbooks.co.uk/wizard

Sold in the UK, Europe, South Africa and Asia
by Faber & Faber Ltd., Bloomsbury House
74–77 Great Russell Street, London WC1B 3DA or their agents

Distributed in the UK, Europe, South Africa and Asia
by TBS Ltd., TBS Distribution Centre, Colchester Road,
Frating Green, Colchester CO7 7DW

Published in Australia in 2009 by Allen & Unwin Pty. Ltd.,
PO Box 8500, 83 Alexander Street, Crows Nest, NSW 2065

Distributed in Canada by Penguin Books Canada,
90 Eglington Avenue East, Suite 700, Toronto,
Ontario M4P 2Y3

ISBN: 978-1-84831-078-0

Typesetting by Hands Fotoset, Nottingham

Printed and bound in the UK by
Clays of Bungay

To William

CONTENTS

HOW WILL YOU START
YOUR ADVENTURE?

The book you hold in your hands is a gateway to another world – a world of dark magic, terrifying monsters, brooding castles, treacherous dungeons and untold danger, where a noble few defend against the myriad schemes of the forces of evil. Welcome to the world of **Fighting Fantasy**!

You are about to embark upon a thrilling fantasy adventure in which **YOU** are the hero! **YOU** decide which route to take, which dangers to risk and which creatures to fight. But be warned – it will also be **YOU** who has to live or die by the consequences of your actions.

Take heed, for success is by no means certain, and you may well fail in your mission on your first attempt. But have no fear, for with experience, skill and luck, each new attempt should bring you a step closer to your ultimate goal.

Prepare yourself, for when you turn the page you will enter an exciting, perilous **Fighting Fantasy** adventure where every choice is yours to make, an adventure in which **YOU ARE THE HERO!**

How would you like to begin your adventure?

If you are new to Fighting Fantasy ...
You probably want to start playing straightaway. Just turn over to the next page and start reading. You may not get very far first time but you'll get the hang of how Fighting Fantasy gamebooks work.

If you have played Fighting Fantasy before ...
You'll realise that to have any chance of success, you will need to discover your hero's attributes. You can create your own character by following the instructions on pages 331–340, or, to get going quickly, you may choose one of the existing Fighting Fantasy adventurers described on pages 328–330. Don't forget to enter your character's details on the Adventure Sheet which appears on pages 342–343.

Game Rules
It's a good idea to read through the rules which appear on pages 331–340 before you start. But as long as you have a character on your Adventure Sheet, you can get going without reading the Rules – just refer to them as you need to.

STORM WARNING

'And that's how I bested Gog Magog, chief of the Giant tribe, and rescued Duke Ervane's daughter,' you say, concluding your tale and downing the rest of your flagon of ale.

For a moment The Traveller's Rest is silent and then its gathered clientele burst into a spontaneous round of applause, whoops and cheers ringing in your ears.

'Another story!' someone shouts from the other side of the bar.

'Yes, tell us another story!' an eager barmaid enthuses, obviously awed by being in the presence of a genuine hero such as yourself.

'Very well then,' you reply and gradually an expectant hush descends over the packed pub again. 'But which one do you want to hear?'

You have been adventuring throughout the Old World for more years than you care to remember. In that time you have faced countless perils and completed numerous quests. You have built up quite a reputation in the process, earning yourself the title Hero of Tannatown after you saved the town from the Crimson Witch and her vampiric swarm.

'Tell us again how you found the fabled sword Wyrmbiter,' a mop-haired youth calls out, suddenly finding the courage to speak up. Unconsciously, you put a hand to the wondrous weapon sheathed in the scabbard hanging from your sword-belt.

'No!' someone else overrules him. 'I want to know how you snared the Basilisk of Bonebarrow.'

'I want to hear how you recovered the Wraith Dragon's hoard!' a grey-bearded Dwarf bellows, his voice drowning out all the others.

'The Wraith Dragon's hoard it is then,' you accept.

You are about to begin your next tale when the door of the tavern bangs open and Varick Oathbreaker – who you know of old – enters The Traveller's Rest, followed by his band of cut-throats. He scowls on catching sight of you, the livid purple scar that splits his face in two – the memory of an injury you once dealt him – curls his top lip into an ugly sneer.

Picking up your flagon of ale – that someone has seen fit to refill for you without you noticing – you toast your rival's latest defeat. 'Bad luck, Varick, but you just weren't quick enough – again. Better luck next time, eh?'

'You want to keep an eye out behind you,' the bounty hunter warns you with a snarl. 'There's a storm coming. Mark my words, there's a storm heading your way!' Your rival turns to the bar, the ruffians accompanying him throwing you what you suppose are meant to be intimidating glances, but you're not bothered. It takes a lot to intimidate the Hero of Tannatown.

It seems that for as long as you have been adventuring, Varick Oathbreaker has been there at your heel, trying to beat you to the next bounty and yet never quite managing to get there first. The two of you are bitter rivals and there is no love lost on either side.

Most recently you beat him to the reward put up by Duke Ervane for the safe return of his daughter whose cavalcade had been ambushed by a tribe of Hill Giants led by the infamous Gog Magog. You came away from that escapade richer by one princess's ransom and with another story to share in that old adventurers' haunt, The Traveller's Rest in the village of Vastarin on Femphrey's southern border. Varick came away with nothing to show for his troubles.

That was some days ago now and much of the money has gone already as you celebrated your recent success with your friends and took some time to recover from your latest wearying adventure, hiring the best room at the inn for the duration of your stay. The place is even busier than usual, crowded with visitors who have come from far and wide to see the travelling Menagerie of Monsters that has stopped off here for a few days.

'I'm sorry,' you say, addressing your admiring audience, 'where was I, before I was so rudely interrupted?'

'You were going to tell us the tale of how you recovered the Wraith Dragon's hoard,' the adoring barmaid begins when her words are suddenly cut short by a crash of thunder that explodes right over the pub.

There is a second clap of thunder that shakes The Traveller's Rest to its very foundations and a glaring flash of lightning bathes the tavern in its searing light. The barmaid screams in panic and joins other members of the inn's clientele in taking cover under the tables.

'What, in Sukh's name, was that?' you hear Varick Oathbreaker swear in shock and surprise.

What indeed? The sound of the storm breaking overhead seemed to come from nowhere. One minute outside it was a pleasant, sunny day, the next a storm, the like of which you have never witnessed in all your days as an adventurer, is tearing the sky apart and turning day to night.

The smashing of tiles joins the roar of the storm as a hailstorm, the like of which you have never known before either, lashes the roof of the tavern.

Turn to paragraph 1.

1

You fling open the door of the tavern and gaze upon the mayhem engulfing the village of Vastarin. The sky is black with threatening thunderheads and gale-force winds are racing over the rooftops of the village, tearing the thatch from houses and sweeping helpless villagers off their feet. At the same time, forked lightning streaks down from the heavens, leaving smouldering scorch marks wherever it hits, while hailstones the size of grapefruit bombard the panicking Vastariners.

On the other side of the village square, the carriages and caged wagons of the Menagerie of Monsters stand parked. The roars and screeching cries of the fabulous beasts that make up the travelling zoo echo around the square as lightning lashes the tethered wagons too.

What can possibly be causing such a bizarre storm? Where one moment there was a calm and pleasant day, there are now howling winds, vicious lightning strikes and a devastating hailstorm.

People are in trouble out there, but how can you fight the elements themselves? Will you:

Stay inside the inn to shelter from the storm?	Turn to **16**
Run to help those people under siege from the lightning strikes in the middle of the square?	Turn to **37**
Make for where the storm appears to be worst, in the thick of the hailstorm?	Turn to **59**

2

You click your heels together three times and set off. Towns, villages, forests and fields hurtle past you in a blur, and you cross rivers in a single bound, barely breaking your stride. In no time at all, you reach your intended destination (cross the Seven League Boots off your *Adventure Sheet*), but where were you travelling to? (Remember, you can only visit each location once.) Was it:

The Eelsea?	Turn to **64**
The Witchtooth Line?	Turn to **250**
Mount Pyre?	Turn to **189**
The Howling Plains?	Turn to **83**

3

You skid to a halt in front of one of the caged wagons of the Menagerie. You hear a roar of animal anger and a paw lashes out at you, a paw that belongs to something with the face of an old man, the body of a lion, the wings of a huge bat, and a deadly scorpion's tail, but you're unharmed. The terrified Manticore is still trapped inside its cage.

Suddenly there is an explosion in the air in front of you that leaves behind the tang of ozone. As you blink the searing after-image of the lightning strike from your eyes, you see the heat-fused lock that had been holding the Manticore's cage shut on the ground at your feet. The twisted metal pings as it cools, having borne the brunt of that last lightning strike. The cage door yawns open before you and, as you look on in horror, the Manticore steps through it and pads towards you.

Its fear in the face of the storm has made it angry and the monster is ready to take its anger out on the nearest living thing – and that's you! You hastily unsheathe your sword, Wyrmbiter, and prepare to defend yourself.

CAPTIVE MANTICORE   SKILL 9   STAMINA 10

The tail of a Manticore carries a deadly sting but fortunately for you the poison glands have been removed by the Menagerie's owner. The creature is also weak from its long years in captivity but it is a formidable opponent nonetheless. If you survive your battle, there are still people who need your help, so turn to **59**.

4

One day from Chalannabrad it starts to rain, and doesn't stop. Another day later you enter a pleasant valley of managed woodland and green wheat fields. (Move the Day of the Week on 2.) At the end of the valley, lying in the shadow of a huge dam, is an equally pleasant-looking village. You are surprised that the river that runs through the fields isn't higher.

Passing between the soaking fields, the road a quagmire beneath your feet, you soon enter the village of Tumbleweir. Your arrival soon attracts the attention of the local headman. Your legendary deeds are known of far and wide in this part of the kingdom, and the concerned-looking headman requests the pleasure of your company at the local inn. Out of the incessant rain, over a tankard of ale he tells you the reason for his anxious state.

'It's the rain,' he says. 'It's been like this for a week and shows no signs of stopping. It's like the weather's all out of kilter.' Obviously Balthazar Sturm's Weather Machine has had an effect on the weather in this part of the kingdom too. 'Anyway, all this excess rainfall has filled the lake on the other side of the dam to near overflowing, and the dam can barely hold it back.'

'But aren't there sluices built into the dam to relieve the pressure?' you ask.

'There are, but the dam was built by Dwarfs centuries ago and there's no-one left here who knows how to open them. The sluices are connected to a series of valves, but we daren't try opening any of them in case we make a mistake and flood the village. I've heard that you have a cunning mind that's saved the day on more than one occasion. Will you help us now and stop the dam from bursting?' If you think you can help, turn to **85**. If not, turn to **52**.

5
You follow the right-hand tunnel into the dank darkness. You have not gone very far when the bobbing nimbus of your lantern reveals another tunnel turning to the right. Do you want to go this way (turn to

27), or will you keep to your present course (turn to 310)?

6

Standing at the edge of the fissure you peer down through the deepening gloom into the rift. You can just about make out the bottom. The rift opens out like a valley onto another level of sea-floor. On the other side of the rift, the shelf of rock you are on at present enters a narrow ravine between two rising walls of the reef before ending at a vast cave mouth. Do you want to descend into the Devilfish Rift (turn to 146) or will you keep heading towards the cave (turn to 46)?

7

'You have answered correctly,' the Keeper informs you. 'Now, how may I help you?' You briefly tell the mysterious Keeper about your quest to stop the mad weather-mage and overcome his bound Elementals.

'Ah, yes,' the Keeper of the Four Winds replies, 'I know of this Balthazar Sturm. He has gained magical supremacy over the elements and has Boreas, the North Wind, to do his bidding. To counter the threat this poses, I give you temporary command of his brother Zephyrus, the West Wind. To call on him, you need only intone his name, but you may only do so once – so choose the moment wisely.' (Write down the name Zephyrus on your *Adventure Sheet* and regain 1 LUCK point.) 'And now you must be about your quest.' Turn to **159**.

8

You have no other option but to fight the Colossus.

COLOSSUS   SKILL 9   STAMINA 12

If today is Earthday, add 1 point to the Colossus' SKILL score and 2 points to its STAMINA. If you are using a crushing weapon, such as a Warhammer or a Mace, every blow that connects will cause the Colossus 3 STAMINA points of damage. To swap Wyrmbiter for a crushing weapon, if you have one, you must forfeit one Attack Round, during which time the transformed mage will get in an unopposed strike. If you reduce the Colossus' STAMINA score to 3 points or fewer, turn to **29**.

9

If you have a Rope and Grapple, you are able to let yourself down into the darkness and all you suffer is a cold shower from the cascade, before finding yourself at the edge of a large natural chamber deep below the earth (turn to **80**). If you don't have a Rope and Grapple, *Test your Luck*. If you are Lucky you still make it down safely (turn to **80**), but if you are Unlucky, you slip (turn to **38**).

10

With the mined-out tunnels continuing to fall in on themselves behind you, you race back through the mine as quickly as you can. You finally find yourself stumbling along the tunnel by which you entered the mine, exhausted and gasping for breath, but alive nonetheless. You lurch from the mine into daylight, blinking against the sudden harsh glare. You collapse, gasping for breath, as a cloud of dust escapes from the mine entrance behind you; Fathomdeep Mine has been sealed for good.

It is time to continue your quest. If you possess a pair of Seven League Boots and would like to use them now, turn to **2**. If not, where do you want to travel next in your search for aid against Sturm's bound Elementals? Remembering that you can only visit each location once, will you make for:

The Eelsea?	Turn to **360**
Mount Pyre?	Turn to **343**
The Howling Plains?	Turn to **36**

Or, if you feel that you are ready, do you want to attempt to reach Balthazar Sturm's Weather Machine – the *Eye of the Storm* (turn to **350**)?

11

The fleeing villagers succeed in driving the rest of them back into their underground burrows. The farmer thanks you for your help and asks you which way you're headed. 'North-east,' you tell him.

'Like I said, you'll find nothing but a wasteland that way,' he says. 'Look, we're heading west to Chalannabrad. We want the authorities there to learn of our plight. Why don't you come with us?' If you want to take the farmer up on his offer (and you have not yet visited the Eelsea), turn to **93**.

If not, you continue on your journey alone. The farmer was right; this part of the kingdom has practically become a desert. (You may not recover STAMINA points for the days you spend on this leg of your journey as you would normally.) After two more days of trudging along beneath a sky the colour of beaten copper (move the Day of the Week on 2), you get your first glimpse of the welcome sight of the waters of Lake Cauldron. Turn to **189**.

12

It is said that if you hold a shell to your ear you can hear the sound of the sea from within. You wonder if the same is true of the Shell of the Seas. Taking it out you put it to your ear and listen. You hear a distant susurration, as of the ebb and flow of the tide, and waves breaking on the shore. It is as if you can hear a name being whispered: *Oceanus*. Return to **318** and keep reading the rest of that paragraph.

13

It is the end of the second day since you left the southern limits of Femphrey when you settle down for the night at the edge of a small wood. If you have the codeword *Detnuh* recorded on your *Adventure Sheet*, turn to **131**. If not, if today is Moonsday, turn to **95**; otherwise, turn to **40**.

14

Dropping through the air, buffeted by gale-force winds, you struggle to see where you're going. The great ship looms large beneath you. You throw out a hand and grab hold of the metal rail of the balcony in front of the craft's access hatch. You crash into the side of the vessel and, for a moment, look down. All you can see is a whirling maelstrom that surrounds the giant brass fish. And then you are heaving yourself over the railing and onto the balcony. Grasping the wheeled-handle in the centre of the access hatch, you turn it, open the door and enter the *Eye of the Storm*.

The hatch slams shut behind you, the clang echoing through the metal interior of the peculiar vessel. You make your way along a grilled walkway into the craft and stop when you come to a central stairwell. A cast iron spiral staircase leads both up and down, through holes in floor and ceiling, and you shoot a glance in both directions to see where it leads. As far as you can tell, you are on the bottom deck of the vessel. Below you the metal stairs lead down to the bilges of the ship: you can hear water sloshing down there. The stairs also lead to another two decks above this one.

One way of putting paid to Balthazar Sturm's plans would be to do as much damage to the *Eye of the Storm* as possible. While you are on board you will need to keep a running total of the destruction you cause in the form of a DAMAGE score, which currently stands at 0.

If you have a set of Blueprints and would like to consult them now, triple the number associated with them and turn to this paragraph. If not, where would you like to explore first?

The bilges?	Turn to **302**
The bottom deck (where you are now)?	Turn to **54**
The middle deck?	Turn to **126**
The top deck?	Turn to **258**

15

Hearing heavy clanging steps behind you, you turn to see the hulking golem-automaton you left in the bilges, forcing its bulk through the door to the Engine Room. The steel-cased figure stomps past you and sets about punching the metal sphere with fists like sledgehammers. You have no idea whose will is controlling the mechanical man but, whoever it is, Dreadnought seems set on destroying the Engine. There is a sharp *crack*, followed by a shrill whistling sound, and a torrent of raw elemental energy pours from the fractured shell of the containment unit. A second later, the Engine explodes. Shards of scalding hot metal hurtle across the room, embedding themselves in the walls, floor and ceiling. Fortunately you remained unharmed. The automaton's body shielded you from the blast, but in the process it too was destroyed. (Add 3 to your DAMAGE score, regain 1 LUCK point and strike the codeword *Notamotua* from your *Adventure Sheet*.) It seems that with the destruction of the Engine, the Elementals have left the chamber too. Leaving a scene of utter devastation behind you, you return to the landing. Turn to **126**.

16

Slamming the door shut against the wind, you return to your seat amidst your admiring fans, only rather than offering you beaming smiles they are now glowering at you in anger.

'Call yourself an adventurer?' one of them says in disbelief.

'There are people in trouble out there, people who need your help,' says the mop-haired youth.

The previously fawning barmaid scowls at you before adding, 'And I thought you were a hero, when really you're nothing but a coward!'

The Dwarf looks at you disparagingly. 'I suppose all your stories about slaying dragons and wrestling giants were just lies too.'

The crowd start to boo and jeer, calling you names like 'Liar!' and 'Coward!' You have lost their respect and dealt your reputation a damaging blow by behaving in such a cautious manner. (Lose 1 LUCK point!) You are going to *have* to do something now.

Returning to the door of the tavern you wrench it open again and decide on your next course of action. Will you:

Run to help those people under siege
from the lightning strikes in the
middle of the square? Turn to **37**
Make for where the storm appears to be
worst, in the thick of the hailstorm? Turn to **59**

17

The key slips easily into the lock and, with a click, the strong box opens. Inside is a startling sight. Sitting atop a pile of treasure is a human skull, wearing a marvellous crown made from bright red coral. (If you want to take the Coral Crown, and put it on, add it to your *Adventure Sheet*.) Bearing in mind Captain Katarina's fee, you scoop up handfuls of gold and gems. Roll one die to discover what you manage to pilfer from the coffer.

Dice roll	Treasure
1–2	A Silver Necklace (worth 6 Gold Pieces), a Bag of Gems (worth 12 Gold Pieces) and a handful of Gold Pieces (roll one die and add 6 to find out how many).

3–4   A valuable hoard of Doubloons (roll two dice and add 12 to find out how many Gold Pieces they are worth).

5–6   A Ruby Ring (worth 5 Gold Pieces), a Large Diamond (worth 15 Gold Pieces) and a purse of Gold Pieces (roll two dice and add 6 to discover how many).

Having loaded your pockets with treasure, regain 1 LUCK point and turn to **163**.

18

'Do not enter,' Brokk reads, translating the runes for you. 'Well I don't know why this stretch was blocked off but it must be for a good reason. I'm sure what you're looking for won't be found by going that way. I'd leave well alone if I were you.' Now turn back to **68** and decide what to do next.

Your weapon is seized, your hands roughly bound with rope, and only then are you dragged before the warrior-leader of the marauder tribe. The Battle-Khan regards you with open contempt.

'Who are you to infiltrate the camp of the mighty Khaddan Khan, Master of the Thundering Horde, greatest of all the marauder tribes?' He fixes you with a steely stare, his long moustaches twitching. There's only one way out of your predicament now.

'I am the Hero of Tannatown,' you throw back, 'slayer of the Bonebarrow Basilisk, Giant-killer and conqueror of the Crimson Witch. And I challenge you to a test of mettle by single combat.'

For a moment the Khan is silent. Then he bursts out laughing. That was not quite the reaction you had been expecting.

'Are you mad? I am the greatest of all the Khans of Lendleland. Other tribes pay fealty to me!' The Battle-Khan stops laughing and looks suddenly serious again. 'But a challenge is a challenge, and I accept yours. And when I am done with you, I shall feed you to my dogs that they might be as bold as you when facing imminent death.'

You soon find yourself at the centre of a circle of jeering Lendlelanders as their Battle-Khan prepares to prove himself in battle once again. This is one battle that you can only hope you will live to remember.

KHADDAN KHAN   SKILL 10   STAMINA 12

As soon as you reduce the Khan's STAMINA score to 4 points or fewer, turn to **48**.

20

'Now they were my idea,' the old man explains. 'All this messing about with heavier than air flying contraptions, I thought you'd need some escape mechanism should the precious thing ever go wrong. I call it the Portable Self-Releasing Drop-Arresting Sail – catchy name, don't you think? All you have to do to activate it is pull the cord when you're falling through the air, and it'll slow your fall, at least in theory. Never did get around to testing it properly though.' Return to **335** to ask another question or, if you're done, turn to **365**.

21

You do your best to avoid the gouting flames and showers of molten rock, but they are totally unpredictable. Roll one die and add 1; this is the number of STAMINA points you must lose as your body is burnt by the fiery eruptions. However, if you have a Dragon Tattoo, or you drank a Potion of Fire Protection before entering these tunnels, you may reduce this damage by 1 point. If you have a Dragon Shield you may reduce the damage by 1 more point, and if you are wearing a Wyrmskin Cloak, reduce it by 2 points. All of these reductions are cumulative, so if you drank the potion, have the shield and the cloak, you can reduce the damage by up to 4 points.

If you are still alive, you make it to the other side of the causeway only to find that you have reached a dead-end. (Lose 1 LUCK point.) You have no choice but to cross the cavern again to return to the tunnel to proceed. Roll one die again, but this time deduct 1; this is the number of STAMINA points you lose this time. Just as before, the tattoo, shield, cloak and potion can reduce the damage suffered accordingly. If you survive this second crossing, turn to **245**.

22

Your journey east eventually brings you to Femphrey's second largest settlement – Crystal City. (Move the Day of the Week on 3.) Many people believe that it is constructed from the crystals that its populace dredge from the lake, but that's about as accurate as saying that the streets of Chalannabrad are paved with gold!

As far as you can tell, the bizarre weather that has been afflicting the rest of the kingdom has not happened here; all is well. So what there is for you here is the opportunity to rest and recuperate from your exhausting adventure, although you can't hang around too long. Probably the best thing to do is visit the city's bustling markets.

Crystal City is one of the stops on the Pollua to Royal Lendle trade route that crosses the Old World and, as a result, you should be able to find a whole range of interesting and curious items for sale within its busy market hub. Do you want to look for practical equipment (turn to 41), or more unusual items (turn to 70)?

23

Although you run as fast as you can, the splintering crevasse catches up with you. The ground gives way and you plummet into the depths of the earth as tonnes of rock and earth come crashing down on top of you. Your adventure ends here, buried alive at the bottom of Fathomdeep Mine.

24

As you head for the hills you hear the whistle of arrows all around you. As you have already managed to put quite some distance between yourself and the horsemen, the Battle-Khan's warriors have taken up their bows against you. Roll one die and add 1. This is the number of arrows that find their mark (lose that many STAMINA points). If you are still alive, turn to 65.

25

'Meet the Mole,' Brokk says proudly, waving a hand at the incredible device. 'The most marvellous tunnelling machine this side of the Witchtooth Line. Now, if we can only get it to work, we'd make it to the deepest part of the mine in no time.' Do you want to see if Brokk can get the Mole working and use that to make your way through Fathomdeep Mine (turn to 124), or would you rather continue on foot (turn to 145)?

26

'Pesky, malicious things they are! Make my life a misery,' Inigo rants at mention of the lightning lab's guardians. 'They're Sturm's workforce, guards, gaolers all rolled into one. It was them that he put to work building the ship, along with that confounded steam-powered Golem of his. Want to know how he created them? They're Lightning Sprites bound inside sealed suits of leather and brass. Now, of course, if you come up against them again, and you probably will if you're going after Sturm, there is a knack to getting rid of them in a hurry, only you need to be a bit handy with a sword. There's a release valve, see? Where the brass helmet meets the suit at the back of the neck. Hit that and the Sprite will be released from its containment and banished back to the Elemental Planes.'

This is priceless information! (Regain 1 LUCK point.) If you ever find yourself fighting Sturm's Fulgurites again, to try to hit the release valve, if you win an Attack Round against one of the bound Lightning Sprites, *Test your Skill*. If you are successful you hit the spot and the Fulgurite effectively dies instantly. If you fail, you must continue the battle as normal, but can try to hit the valve again when you next win a round of combat. To ask another question, turn to **335**. If you're done with questions, turn to **365**.

27

This tunnel is significantly smaller that the main one and you have to crouch in places again to get through. You gradually become aware of a scratching, grating sound, as if something is trying to burrow its way out of the rock. Part of one tunnel wall suddenly cracks and collapses into the passageway. Emerging from the hole in the rock-face is a huge, armoured, beetle-like head. The huge insect has no eyes, but does have mandibles capable of chewing through the very rocks of the earth, and quite capable of chewing through your armour – and you! Monstrous mandibles clicking, the Rock Grub – bane of miners everywhere – attacks.

ROCK GRUB   SKILL 7   STAMINA 10

If you kill the huge rock-boring insect, wiping the Grub's viscous yellow blood from your blade, you consider which way to go now. The Rock Grub's bored tunnel has provided you with an alternative route into the earth. Do you want to keep to the Dwarf-cut tunnel (turn to 75), or do you want to crawl headfirst into the Rock Grub's tunnel to see where it leads (turn to 49)?

28

It looks like this is it! You've saved Femphrey from Balthazar Sturm's insane schemes, but at the cost of your own life. And then you remember the backpack. As you plunge towards the ground, desperate hands find the cord attached to the pack and give it a sharp tug. The top of the pack flies open, and a great mass of material unfurls from inside it, opening out to form a huge sail above you, still attached to the pack by a series of tensed lines. The sail slows the speed of your fall dramatically and you make ground-fall with hardly a scratch on you. You have never felt so glad to be on terra firma! Turn to **400**.

29

Sturm's rocky hide begins to craze and crack until his whole body is on the verge of falling apart. However, before it crumbles to dust completely, what is left of the Elementalist dissolves, as Sturm turns into water. In his liquid form, he swirls around the bridge, drenching you and sweeping you off your feet. A figure – humanoid from the waist up and a fountain of water from the waist down – rises from the surge, and its liquid features are those of Balthazar Sturm! If only you could boil the transformed Elementalist away, as a blazing fire turns water into steam ...

If you know the name of a Fire Elemental who you could command to help you now, turn the name into a number using the code A=1, B=2, C=3 ... Z=26. Add the numbers together and turn to this paragraph. If not, turn to **206**.

30

'What you're seeking lies through there,' Brokk says, pointing towards the fissure with his axe, 'but from here on, you're on your own. I'll wait for you, but I'll go no further myself. That place is cursed, I tell you.' Make a note of the fact that Brokk is no longer travelling with you (meaning that you lose any of the benefits that come from having him with you) and then return to 80 to decide on your next course of action.

31

Stepping warily, you enter the carcass of the dead sea monster through the split in its chest cavity. The creature's ribs rise above you like the vault of some bone cathedral. This really was a mighty behemoth of a beast. Suddenly something moves within, stirring up the sludge of liquefied flesh and rotting fish guts that has collected within the monster's guts. With a ripple of its repulsive body, a giant fluke worm slithers out of the slime towards you, as happy to eat live prey as it is to feast on dead flesh.

WHALE-WORM   SKILL 6   STAMINA 6

Flukes are usually tiny creatures, but the parasitic flatworms that inhabit the gut of giant sea creatures are orders of magnitude larger. If you slay the Whale-Worm, you find what you were hoping you might. Lying amongst the mess of the Bullwhale's last meal and its own decomposing flesh, is a shield bearing the image of a Red Dragon. It's not hard to imagine the fate of the previous owner. Taking the shield with you, if you want (adding the Dragon Shield to your *Adventure Sheet*) you quickly vacate the carcass again and proceed further into the rift. Turn to **179**.

32

With the hatchlings dead, you wipe your sword clean of their repulsive purple ichor. Certain that you have penetrated the lair of the Stormdrake, it is also apparent that the creature is not here. However, by disposing of the next generation of Drakes, if such monsters are responsible for creating climate chaos throughout Femphrey, then you have done the kingdom a favour. (Add the codeword *Mortsleam* to your *Adventure Sheet* and regain 1 LUCK point.)

You and Sylas between you decide that there is nothing to be gained by waiting for the Stormdrake in its lair – you have no idea how long it will be before it returns, and if the monsters you have just fought were only its young, imagine how terrible the parent must be. Besides, you have another quest to complete. Turn to 386.

33

The tunnel steadily widens and its roof extends away above you, until you find yourself at the end of a narrow causeway, which crosses the great lake of a magma reservoir. The lava bubbles and bursts, sending geysers of fire shooting into the scalding air of the cave. Do you want to risk crossing the causeway to get across the cavern (turn to 21), or will you return to the junction and go the other way (turn to 245)?

34

Doing your best to mimic the actions of the Fulgurites, that were tending to the machine when you first entered the Engine Room, you set about twiddling knobs here and closing pressure valves there,

hoping to cut the Engine's power feeds to other parts of the ship. *Test your Luck*. If you are Lucky, your actions have the desired effect (add 1 to your DAMAGE score). If you are Unlucky, you cause a glass dial to blow in your face, splinters of glass blinding you in one eye (lose 2 STAMINA points and 1 SKILL point).

If you are going to cause the Elemental Engine any greater damage, you are going to have to try something more dramatic. Will you:

Attack the Elemental Engine with your sword?	Turn to **47**
Take a Mace or a Warhammer to the sphere, if you have one?	Turn to **82**
Try using a Spanner, if you have one?	Turn to **63**
Quit the Engine Room and explore elsewhere?	Turn to **126**

35

The way you quickly scale the rocky path up the crag, anyone would think you were a mountain goat. In no time at all you are closing on the summit of the peak, clambering through a knotty stand of trees. You suddenly stumble and fall to the stony ground, grazing both knees (lose 2 STAMINA points). It felt like the ground itself bucked beneath your feet. While you are still picking yourself up, the ground in front of you heaves upwards and a monstrous creature bursts from the ground, dripping mud. It is massive, twice as tall as you with huge club-like arms, its bloated body sprouting disgusting, rubbery tentacles.

You have heard of such things before but never seen one in the flesh, as it were. The creature is an Earth Demon – not a true Demon, but one of a breed which earned that title for the alarming way they attack. Its feet still buried in the earth, trailing plants and tree roots, the monster lumbers towards you, arms and tentacles outstretched, ready to squeeze the life from you. Once again you are fighting for your life!

EARTH DEMON   SKILL 10   STAMINA 12

(If today is Earthday, increase both the Earth Demon's SKILL score by 1 point and its STAMINA by 2 points.) You have heard it said that Earth Demons draw their strength directly from the soil. Certainly, any blow you land against it will only cause it 1 STAMINA point of damage. But if you could separate it from the source of its power, you might be able to wound it more seriously. If you want to try this, after you win an Attack Round, turn to **71**. If you manage to kill the beast, turn to **51**.

36

A day since leaving the foothills of the Witchtooth Line (move the Day of the Week on 1) you come within sight of Tannatown. Just the sight of the place is enough to spur you onwards, and it is not long before you are entering the town once again. Inhabitants cheer and call to their neighbours when they see you, and you soon have a crowd of children scampering at your heels. By the time you reach the centre, the Mayor is there ready to welcome you, a

⊡ ⊡

crowd of well-wishers gathering outside the town hall, all trying to catch a glimpse of the Hero of Tannatown for themselves. The townsfolk have not forgotten what you did for them saving them from the Crimson Witch and as soon as you tell him of your quest, the Mayor invites you to stop and rest a while. If you want to take up the Mayor's offer of hospitality, turn to **161**. If not, bidding the people farewell, you set off once again. Three more days of travel through wind, rain, hail and even snow, eventually brings you to the desolation of the Howling Plains. Move the Day of the Week on 3 and turn to **83**.

37

Throwing yourself into the teeth of the terrible storm, your arm up across your face to shield your eyes from the incandescent explosions of the striking lightning, you dash across the square, dodging and darting to avoid being hit yourself. *Test your Skill*, adding 2 to the dice roll if today is Stormsday. If you are successful, turn to **3**. If you fail, turn to **74**.

38

Battered by freezing, rushing water, your limp body is thrown against jagged outcrops of rock and ancient rusted mine-workings. Roll one die and add 1; this is the number of STAMINA points you lose. If you are still alive, the tumbling torrent drops you into a freezing underground lake. Coughing the water from your lungs, half-drowned you drag yourself out onto the sandy shore at the edge of a large natural cavern. However, due to your dunking, half of your Provisions have been ruined and are now inedible. Cross off half the Meals you have remaining, rounding fractions down, and turn to **80**.

39

Unfolding the plans of Sturm's magical Weather Machine, you spread them out on the deck and study them properly for the first time. According to the Blueprints, to the fore of where you are now is a cabin labelled 'Wind Turbine' and another chamber after that one labelled 'Lightning Generator'. Aft of where you are now is an unmarked cabin and beyond that a room marked 'Rudder Controls'. The bilges below this deck are marked as just that. However, the two decks above are of much greater interest. On the top deck of the *Eye of the Storm* is an aft cabin marked 'Ice Maker' and a fore cabin labelled 'Burning Glass'. But it is the middle deck which would appear to be of the most interest to you. The whole aft section of this level is marked 'Engine Room' while the fore is marked 'Helm'. Now that you have a better idea of what awaits you on board the *Eye of the Storm*, return to 14 and decide where to begin your exploration of the vessel.

40

When dawn comes at last, you are more than ready to be on your way. You head north-west for two more days until the walls of the capital come into view on the horizon. Move the Day of the Week on 4 and turn to 50.

41

You find the following items for sale.

Item	Cost
Provisions	1 Gold Piece per Meal
Crossbow and 6 Quarrels	12 Gold Pieces
Breastplate	10 Gold Pieces
Potion of Fortune	6 Gold Pieces
Potion of Strength	4 Gold Pieces
Potion of Skill	5 Gold Pieces

Every day is market day in Crystal City, but if today is Highday, in a place where they worship the gods of trade and commerce above all others, you may knock 1 Gold Piece off the price of anything other than Provisions; as there are so many traders in town, competition is fierce.

You may buy as many Meals' worth of Provisions as you want, up to a maximum of 10; each Meal will restore up to 4 lost STAMINA points. You may use the

Crossbow once in each battle you fight before having to engage in hand-to-hand combat (as long as you still have quarrels to shoot); *Test your Skill* and if you succeed your crossbow bolt causes your opponent 2 STAMINA points of damage. On a roll of 1–4 the Breastplate will reduce any damage done against you by 1 point. When drunk, the Potion of Fortune will restore your LUCK score to its *Initial* level, the Potion of Strength will restore your STAMINA score to its *Initial* level, and the Potion of Skill will restore your SKILL score to its *Initial* level.

When you are done here, do you want to scour the market for more unusual items (turn to **70**) or will you leave Crystal City and continue on your journey (move the Day of the Week on 1 and turn to **189**)?

42

Not believing that there is any way you could best an Earth Elemental in combat, you run from the chamber, back into the mine. Behind you, the Elemental roars again, bringing its bunched fists smashing

down. At the force of the blow, the ground splits apart, a yawning crevasse opening in the floor of the chamber and chasing after you. Roll three dice. If the total rolled is less than or equal to your STAMINA score, turn to **10**; if it is greater, turn to **23**.

43

If the Ice Elemental injures you at all, the warming power of the Sun Talisman will protect you from its chilling touch to some extent. Reduce any damage caused by the Elemental by 1 point. However, if the Ice Elemental uses its Blizzard Breath attack against you, you may ignore the damage this causes altogether. Now return to **100** and prepare to fight!

44

Your blow connects with the sphere again, but not in the same place as last time. Instead, you strike the glass panel in the front of the Elemental Engine which fractures. You hear a sound like escaping gas and then suddenly there is a gale blowing within the Engine Room, and you have to draw your sword against the raging Greater Air Elemental you have inadvertently released from the containment chamber. Boreas, Elemental manifestation of the North Wind, is not pleased at having been bound within the device, and makes no distinction between his liberator and his captor. Screaming with elemental fury, Boreas attacks!

GREATER AIR ELEMENTAL SKILL 15 STAMINA 20

If you somehow manage to defeat the very essence of the North Wind, regain 1 LUCK point, add 2 to your DAMAGE score and write the codeword *Demlaceb* on your *Adventure Sheet*. You feel that you have done enough here, so you quit the Engine Room to explore elsewhere. Turn to 126.

45

As you plummet towards the ground, desperate hands find the cord attached to the pack and give it a sharp tug. The top of the pack flies open disgorging a great mass of material that opens out above you while remaining attached to the pack by a series of tensed lines. Your deployment of the sheet slows your fall dramatically and you land at the foot of the stack without a scratch. Regain 1 LUCK point. However, you will not be able to use this unusual property of the pack again, as you have to cut the ropes holding the sheet to prevent it dragging behind you as you go on your way. (Cross the Unusual Backpack off your *Adventure Sheet*, although you can still use it as an ordinary pack). Deciding it would be unwise to petition the Keeper of the Four Winds again, you retrace your steps, back through the Screaming Canyon and finally to the edge of the Howling Plains. Move the Day of the Week on 1 and turn to 394.

46

As you enter the narrow pass, you enter the domain of the creatures that make the reef their home – creatures that are always on the lookout for food.

Large-clawed crustaceans and needle-fanged eels strike at you from holes in the rock, while grotesquely large starfish and anemones sting you, intent on feasting on what the other Reef Dwellers leave behind. Fight the Reef Dwellers as if they were all one creature.

REEF DWELLERS   SKILL 7   STAMINA 10

You may escape from the Reef Dwellers after 3 Attack Rounds, if you wish, by backing out of the narrow pass and entering the fissure (turn to **146**). If you persist in fighting your way through and win, turn to **76**.

47

You lay into the shell of the iron sphere with your enchanted blade, expecting to slice it open like an apple, but somehow, the enchantments woven into your magical dragon-slaying sword are negated by the raw elemental energy being generated by the device. Rather than your sword harming the Engine, the iron skin of the Engine harms your sword, chipping its razor edge. (Lose 1 SKILL point and 1 LUCK point.) What will you do now?

Take a Mace or a Warhammer to
the machine, if you have one?   Turn to **82**
Try using a Spanner, if you have one?   Turn to **63**
Quit the Engine Room and explore
elsewhere?   Turn to **126**

48

As soon as it starts to look like you might actually win this fight, you also realise that you can't kill the Battle-Khan – not here, not in this way. If you do so, there would surely be another dozen or more pretenders to the Khan's title who would happily challenge you to single combat to win the leadership of the tribe for themselves.

Instead you seize the initiative and, having pushed Khaddan Khan back to the edge of the ring of horsemen with your next successful strike against him, rather than land a killing blow, you run at the downed warrior and use him as a step-up to vault yourself over the heads of the gathered marauders and out of the circle. You land in the saddle of an unattended steed and with a loud 'Yaah!' kick your heels into its sides. With a startled whinny the horse takes off in the direction of the hills. It does not take the horsemen long to set off in pursuit. *Test your Luck.* If you are Lucky, turn to **65**. If you are Unlucky, turn to **24**.

49

Hoping that the Rock Grub doesn't have a mate, still lurking within its burrow, you begin to crawl downwards on your hands and knees. The tunnel is lined with a sticky residue and you start to slip. Suddenly, the ground begins to shudder and shake all around you. Losing all grip, you slide down the twisting tunnel of the Grub's burrow until you fly out of the end into another prop-supported tunnel. Turn to **68**.

50

Your travels eventually bring you within sight of the walls of the capital of the kingdom of Femphrey – Chalannabrad! You have been here several times before, but the sight of the city's open, tree-lined avenues, stunning parks and monumental public buildings never ceases to amaze. But you're not here to see the sights – you have a quest to complete. As you make your way through the hustle and bustle of the city you could be forgiven for believing that nothing was wrong. The influence of Balthazar Sturm's weather-changing machine does not appear to have reached this far yet. You decide to make the most of this fact, and head for the city docks. As you do so, you consider what you will need for a quest that will take you to the bottom of the Eelsea.

Seeing as how you are not a fish, you are going to need to acquire some way of breathing underwater, just as much as you are going to need to find a ship to take you out to sea. Of course, Chalannabrad is also the perfect place to equip yourself in general. Do you want to visit the city's markets before doing anything else (turn to **91**), or would you prefer to press on with finding a way to breathe underwater (turn to **121**)?

Finally you reach the foot of the lonely tower. It has been built right on the edge of the rocky outcrop, where it overhangs the valley below. It appears to be of precarious construction, each level built on the one below in a higgledy-piggledy manner. Craning your head back, you see that the tower has a flat roof, with crenulated battlements open to the elements. A lightning conductor runs half the length of the tower, its spear-like tip projecting high into the sky above it. Coming off from the top of the tower is another turret, atop which stands a gleaming brass weathervane cast in the shape of a large cockerel. In front of you – not twenty metres away – stands the iron-bound entrance to the tower. There does not appear to be anyone on guard, so you step forward.

A harsh, grating cry halts you in your tracks, and causes you to look upwards again. The brass weathervane, stained green with verdigris from its exposure to the elements, has come free of its mountings and is swooping down towards you on wings of metal. The bird opens its brass beak and gives another screeching cry. Unsheathing Wyrmbiter once again, you prepare to meet the tower's guardian in battle.

WEATHERCOCK   SKILL 7   STAMINA 6
If you manage to destroy the Weathercock, turn to 94.

52

It is hardly befitting of a hero to abandon people who have openly asked for your help. Lose 1 LUCK point. With the headman's curses ringing in your ears, you leave Tumbleweir to its fate and continue on your way south-east. The rain eventually stops, the clouds part and the sun starts to beat down again. Two days later (move the Day of the Week on 2) you arrive on the edge of the wilderness known as the Howling Plains. Turn to 83.

53

Taking a deep breath, you step into the cloud. You can barely see your hand in front of your face, partly because the stinging gas is making your eyes water. You press on regardless but the cloud shows no sign of dissipating any time soon. And then you can hold your breath no longer and involuntarily take in a great breath of the noisome smoke. You start to cough, finding it harder and harder to breath. You stumble onwards, not knowing if you could make it back the other way before you pass out, and then suddenly, mercifully, you pass out of the gas cloud and fall to your knees taking in great lungfuls of clean air. You suffer no long term ill-effects from the gas cloud other than your streaming eyes. For the duration of the next battle you have to fight, you must reduce your Attack Strength by 1 point. Having recovered your breath, will you turn left (turn to 33) or right (turn to 245)?

54

Leading off from the bottom deck landing are two wooden doors, one on either side of the stairwell. The one aft of the stairs has no unusual markings, whereas the door to the fore has a spiral carved into it. Choosing somewhere you haven't already been, will you:

Open the spiral-marked door?	Turn to **86**
Open the unmarked door?	Turn to **184**
Leave the bottom deck and explore elsewhere?	Turn to **391**

55

Invoking the power of the God of Fire, you shout, 'I command you to help me, in the name of Filash, the Burning One!' The Fire Elemental roars in fury but is unable to attack you. 'Tell me,' you go on, 'how I might gain control over a Greater Fire Elemental?'

'You must know its name!' the Elemental roars, writhing in torment. You have no idea which Fire Elemental Balthazar Sturm has bound to his Weather Machine. But maybe there's another way.

'Then tell me,' you reply, 'what is *your* name?'

The Elemental screams its frustration to the walls of the magma chamber, but it has to answer. 'Vulcanus!' it howls. 'But you will never get the chance to use it!' Turn to **114**.

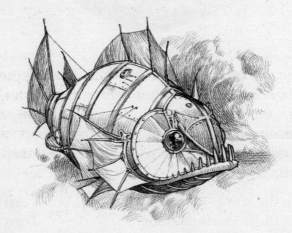

56

A huge explosion rocks the bridge, throwing you to the ground and blowing out the observation window-eyes of the fish in a hail of razor-sharp crystal shards. At the same moment Balthazar Sturm drops onto the platform in front of you, suddenly robbed of his incredible, storm-born powers. You grab hold of a handrail and hang on for dear life.

Sturm looks at you with disbelieving horror in his eyes as the entire platform breaks away and is sucked out through the front of the ship. The limp bodies of his minions and broken pieces of esoteric machinery follow soon after. The last you see of the insane Elementalist is his screaming face as he drops like a stone through the churning clouds surrounding the *Eye of the Storm*, arms and legs flailing.

With a scream of rending metal, the bolts holding the handrail to the wall shear through, and you find yourself hurtling through the shattered eyes of the fish after Sturm.

If you know the name of an Air Elemental who could help you now, turn it into a number using the code A=1, B=2, C=3 ... Z=26. Add the numbers together, double the total, and turn to this new paragraph. If you have the codeword *Susagep* on your *Adventure Sheet*, turn to **104**. If you have an Unusual Backpack, divide the number of *this* paragraph by the number associated with it and turn to this new paragraph. If you have none of these things, turn to **349**.

57

It takes half a day to reach Brokk's brewery. The copper and stone building stands nestled in a mountain valley pass where it is fed by a clear mountain stream, tumbling from the cold mountain peaks in a series of dramatic waterfalls.

Approaching the entrance via an ornate stone bridge that spans another roaring cascade, you knock on the door. It is opened by a silver-haired Dwarf with a plaited white beard, wearing a beer-stained apron. 'What do you want?' he says testily. 'Disturbing old Brokk when he's making beer is not to be done lightly.'

You tell him of your need for a guide to take you into the abandoned Dwarf mine. 'The Fathomdeep Mine, eh?' he says sucking at his teeth and looking at you thoughtfully. 'Yes, I used to work that seam, until the curse came upon that place. I've not been back since. But, yes, I'll be your guide, but it'll cost you – 10 Gold Pieces!'

You give a sharp intake of breath. 10 Gold Pieces is a lot of money. Do you really think it's worth it, when an adventurer like you could surely find your own way through the abandoned tunnels and mine workings? If you are willing and able to pay the necessary 10 Gold Pieces to hire the ex-miner, turn to **77**. If not, turn to **98**.

58

As you advance deeper into the cavernous gorges of the labyrinthine Screaming Canyon, you come under fire. Roll one die and divide the number rolled by 2, rounding fractions up. This is how many arrows hit you. (Each one causes 2 STAMINA points of damage.) And then the Birdman is on you, discarding his bow and arrows in favour of rending talons.

BIRDMAN   SKILL 9   STAMINA 8

If you kill the Birdman, you are able to continue on your way again, although you keep a watchful eye out for more of his kind, just in case. Turn to **166**.

59

You sprint across the square into the thick of the fantastical storm and right into the path of the hurtling hailstones. *Test your Luck.* If you are Lucky, turn to **100**. If you are Unlucky, turn to **87**.

60

Inigo reverently takes the glowing flask from you and gazes at the flickering ball of lightning in wonder. 'Arguably his greatest achievement,' the engineer says of his gaoler. 'He managed to harness the power of the storm, the life-giving force of electricity itself. Tricky procedure, you know. It's how he created the Steam Golem that I believe is still stomping about on the lower levels somewhere.' Return to **335** to ask another question or, if you're done, turn to **365**.

61

Weapon in hand you meet the colossal Elemental
head on, every sense heightened in the moment of
battle. (Remember to adjust the Elemental's stats to
reflect any damage it may have already suffered.)

EARTH ELEMENTAL   SKILL 14   STAMINA 22

(If today is Earthday, increase the Elemental's SKILL
score by 1 point and its STAMINA by 2). If you are
fighting the Elemental using a crushing weapon, such
as a Warhammer or a Mace, every blow that connects
will cause it 3 STAMINA points of damage. To swap
Wyrmbiter for a crushing weapon, if you have one,
you must forfeit one Attack Round, during which
time the Earth Elemental will hit you for 3 STAMINA
points of damage. If you lose an Attack Round roll
one die and then consult the table below to see what
damage you suffer. (You may use LUCK to reduce any
damage caused in the usual way.)

Dice Roll	Attack and Damage
1–3	Sledgehammer – the Elemental hits you with its massive stone fists. Lose 3 STAMINA points.
4–5	Seismic shock – the Elemental stamps its foot, opening a yawning pit in the ground beneath you. *Test your Skill.* If you are successful you avoid falling in and are able to keep fighting. If you fail, you fall into the fissure; lose 3 STAMINA points and you must fight the next Attack Round with your Attack Strength reduced by 1 point as you struggle to get out again.
6	Sent flying – the Elemental picks you up in one hand and throws you against the side of the cavern. Roll 1 die and lose that many STAMINA points.

If you incredibly manage to beat the Earth Elemental, turn to **10**.

62

At your killing blow, the Ice Elemental shatters into a million tiny shards of ice which are then carried away by the howling wind. A moment later the wind dies too, the lightning strikes cease and the pounding hail peters out. The storm has moved on. As you look to the skies, watching as the thunderheads drift away to the north, you fancy you glimpse a flash of gold – or is it brass? – within the departing storm clouds. There it is again. It looks just like … no, it can't be. You shake your head and look again, but the object has gone.

For a moment there you were convinced you saw a bizarre craft amidst the clouds, shaped like some huge brass fish! You can't shake the feeling that the bizarre vessel had something to do with the sudden appearance of the storm either.

The people of Vastarin start to emerge from all those places where they had sheltered from the storm, staring at you in awe. 'What happened here?' one woman asks in bewilderment. Much of the village is now little more than a storm-ravaged ruin.

'Have no fear,' you say addressing not only the woman but all of the gathered villagers, 'I shall discover who was behind this attack and make them pay. I swear it on my honour as the Hero of Tannatown.'

This meets with whoops and cheers from the people of Vastarin. You return to The Traveller's Rest to collect your backpack and set off soon after with their good wishes ringing in your ears. But where will you go? According to eye-witnesses the storm blew in suddenly from the south and, when it left, moved on again northwards, in the direction of the capital of Chalannabrad.

Having had some dealings with the College of Mages in the past, you could travel to Chalannabrad to find out if your contacts there know anything about this erratic weather or the curious fish-shaped flying machine. Alternatively you could retrace the path of the storm to see where it blew up from, in the hope that that might provide you with some answers.

So, what's it to be? Will you travel north, towards Chalannabrad (turn to **286**), or south, following the path of devastation left by the storm to its point of origin (turn to **111**)?

63

Using the tool, you start turning bolts and twisting valve wheels shut, hoping that in this way you might be able to stem the flow of magical energy being generated by the Elemental Engine from reaching other parts of the *Eye of the Storm*. And your actions do just that. (Add 1 to your DAMAGE score.) However, if you want to cause the device catastrophic damage, you are going to have to try something else. Will you:

Attack the Elemental Engine with your sword?	Turn to **47**
Take a Mace or a Warhammer to the machine, if you have one?	Turn to **82**
Quit the Engine Room and explore elsewhere?	Turn to **126**

64

Without further ado, you set off for the Chalannabrad docks. Making your way through the hustle and bustle of the city you could be forgiven for believing that nothing was wrong. The influence of Balthazar

Sturm's weather-changing machine does not appear to have reached this far yet. As you continue on your way you go over in your mind what you will need for a quest that will take you to the bottom of the Eelsea.

First of all, you are going to need to acquire some way of breathing underwater, if you don't already have such a thing. Secondly, you will need to find a captain of a ship willing to take you out to sea. Of course, Chalannabrad is also the perfect place to equip yourself in general. Do you want to visit the city's markets before doing anything else (turn to **91**), would you prefer to press on finding a way to breathe underwater (turn to **121**), or, if you don't need to worry about this, will you look for a ship (turn to **252**)?

65

Your head-start means that you have already put some distance between you and the pursuing horsemen. Once you are out of sight of them among the hills again you dismount, sending your steed back to the Khan's encampment with a slap to the rump, and take cover at the end of a rocky defile. You hear the bellowing horsemen gallop right past the mouth of the cleft but none of them stop to check your hiding place. When you are certain that the immediate danger has passed, you creep out of the defile again and continue on your way through the hills. Turn to **142**.

Not really sure how to get out of your new predicament, ignoring the rainmaker's protestations, you approach his rattling contraption and try installing the Spark within its inner workings, hoping that it might pep the machine up so that it will actually start to work. Having connected it up as best you can, you take a step back from the clunking machine.

There is a sudden loud crackling and arcs of actinic white light shoot from the core of the machine, enveloping every component in flickering lightning. But the best is yet to come. As you and the villagers watch in fearful wonder, the various parts of the machine detach from one another and then rearrange themselves. Standing in the middle of the village, is no longer a weird-looking machine, but a weird-looking golem-like creation. The three-metre tall giant of metal and wood gives voice to a grating metal moan and lurches towards you, intent, it would seem, on tearing you limb from limb. You must fight the haywire Gubbins Golem.

GUBBINS GOLEM   SKILL 8   STAMINA 10

The villagers flee in panic, along with the so-called rainmaker, leaving you to your fate alone. If you manage to destroy the machine, you waste no time in fleeing Quartz yourself, sure that the villagers will not be too keen on having you hang around after what just happened. (Lose 1 LUCK point.) You continue walking south-west for two days (move the Day

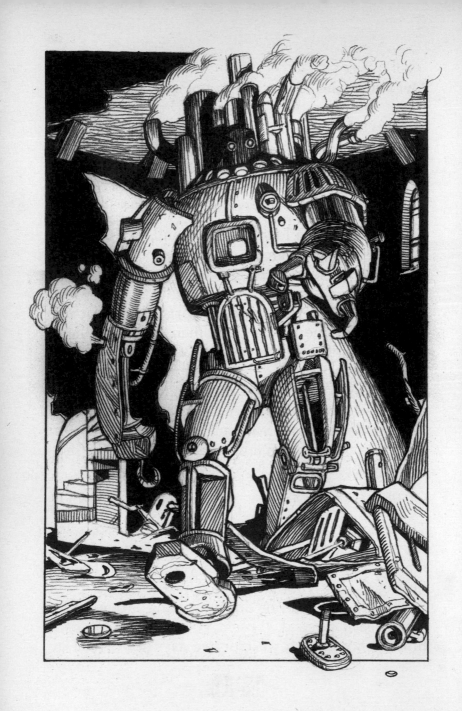

of the Week on 2), until you reach the desolate borderlands of the Howling Plains. Turn to **83**.

67

There is one final blast of steam and then the transformation is complete. Standing in front of you, an
impressive four metres in height, is a metallic,
humanoid figure. Its body is a rattling steam engine
and you can see the incandescent glare of chained
lightning behind a scorched glass plate in the middle
of its chest. The same furious light crackles within the
behemoth's glass eyes, while flaring metal chimneys
protruding from its shoulders puff smoke and steam
into the room. Steel-claw fingers reach for you as the
Steam Golem takes its first clanking step forwards.
Not for the first time you thank the gods that
Wyrmbiter is an enchanted weapon that can cut
through metal as easily as it cleaves through flesh.

STEAM GOLEM   SKILL 8   STAMINA 10

If you manage to destroy the colossal magical automaton, record the codeword *Rennaps* on your *Adventure
Sheet* and turn to **117**.

68*

The shaking subsides and you continue on your way,
feeling a little more anxious having been reminded of
the fact that this place has been a focus for earthquake
activity of late. Not much further on you find the way
forward blocked by a wooden barricade. Nailed to
the planks closing off this stretch of the tunnel is a

sign written in Dwarf runes, and you can't read Dwarf runes. Another tunnel turns left at this point, providing you with an alternative way onward. Do you want to pull down the barricade and keep following the main tunnel (turn to **186**), or would you rather turn onto the new tunnel to the left (turn to **310**)?

69

Honouring your agreement, you give half of the treasure you found beneath the waves to the avaricious captain (adjust your *Adventure Sheet* accordingly). Another day at sea returns you to the docks of Chalannabrad. (Move the Day of the Week on 1.) But as you are preparing to disembark from the *Tempest*, and continue on the next leg of your quest, Captain Katarina stops you at the gunwale.

'I wish I could do more to help you in your quest,' she says, looking almost shame-faced. 'If there is anything, just say it.'

Well, is there? If you are ready to seek out Sturm and his Weather Machine, and you know the name of an Air Elemental and want to call on it for aid now, turn its name into a number (using the code A=1, B=2, C=3… Z=26 and adding the numbers together) add 100 and turn to the paragraph with the same number as the final total.

If not, but you still wish to seek out Sturm, you bid Katarina farewell and prepare for the next stage of your adventure (turn to 350). Otherwise you will have to choose where you want to go next in your search for aid against the mad Weather Mage. Remembering that you can only visit each location once, will you head for:

The Witchtooth Line?   Turn to 157
Mount Pyre?   Turn to 22
The Howling Plains?   Turn to 4

70

It does not take you long to find a number of items that are a little out of the ordinary, but which could be of use to you on your quest? They are as follows:

Item	Cost
Glowstones	6 Gold Pieces
Crystal Mace	15 Gold Pieces
Luck Sprite	10 Gold Pieces
Wyrmskin Cloak	12 Gold Pieces
Blunderbuss	12 Gold Pieces
Bag of blackpowder and shot	2 Gold Pieces each
Potion of Giant Strength	7 Gold Pieces
Potion of Levitation	7 Gold Pieces
Healing Elixir	7 Gold Pieces

If today is Highday, when the merchants of Crystal City pay homage to the deities of trade and commerce, with there being so many potential buyers in town, you must add 1 Gold Piece to the price of anything other than bags of gunpowder and shot.

Glowstones are precisely that – stones that glow – and so can be used as a lantern. The Mace is carved from a single, massive piece of crystal, and is magical as well; if you hit an opponent with the Crystal Mace, roll one die and if you roll 4–6 it does 1 extra STAMINA point of damage. The Luck Sprite has been imprisoned within a crystal dodecahedron; the next three times you have to *Test your Luck*, you will be Lucky and you won't need to deduct any LUCK points either. On a roll of 1–2 the Wyrmskin Cloak will reduce any damage done against you by 1 point. You may use the Blunderbuss once in each battle you fight before having to engage in hand-to-hand combat (as long as you still have enough bags of blackpowder and shot), although the weapon's discharge is rather erratic; roll one die and on a roll of 1–3 the Blunderbuss will cause a non-magical opponent 3 STAMINA points damage. You may buy up to 6 packets of blackpowder and shot. If you drink the Potion of Giant Strength before a battle, it will raise your SKILL score by 2 for that one battle and the damage you cause by 1 point. The Healing Elixir will restore up to 6 points of STAMINA and 2 SKILL points.

When you are finished, do you want to search the market for practical equipment (turn to **41**) or will you leave Crystal City and continue on your journey (move the Day of the Week on 1 and turn to **189**)?

71

Roll two dice. If you roll a double, turn to 106. If you roll anything else, even with your prodigious strength you are unable to lift the hulking Earth Demon. Return to 35 and finish the fight.

72

You set the last tumbler, close the chest-plate and step back from the automaton again. The humming coming from within the golem rises in pitch and then, with a loud clattering bang, the thing falls apart completely, arms, legs and head disconnecting from the main body of the device and sinking beneath the oily surface of the bilge-waters. (Lose 1 LUCK point and remove the Spark of Life from your *Adventure Sheet*.) Disappointed, you climb back up into vessel above (turn to 54).

73

There is a nose-curling smell of rotten eggs coming from this passageway and it is getting worse the further you go. The air ahead of you starts to cloud with thick yellow smoke. The noxious-smelling gas soon fills the entire width of the tunnel. If you are to proceed any further, you are going to have to pass directly through the gas cloud. If you are happy to do this, turn to **53**; if not, you must return to the main passageway and carry on along it towards the lava river (turn to **141**).

74

You dodge and weave in an effort to avoid the bolts of raw electricity coursing down out of the sky but the storm seems to have a will of its own – and decides to make you the focus of its attacks. A searing bolt hits you, throwing you across the square trailing smoke and an unpleasant aroma of burnt hair. Roll one die, add 1 to the number rolled, and lose that many STAMINA points. Now turn to **3**.

75*

The secondary tunnel ends at a descending shaft and a ladder. Climbing down the ladder takes you into a larger Dwarf-made cavern, standing at the centre of which is the most incredible contraption you have ever seen. It is a construction of wood and metal, with large spiked wheels, caterpillar tracks and a massive drilling head at its prow. Impressive as the machine looks, you can't help noticing that it has also started to rust badly and you doubt that it's still in working order. Continuing on foot, you leave the chamber, entering another Dwarf-cut tunnel. Turn to **145**.

76

Cautiously you enter the gaping cave mouth, glancing up at the long, curving stalactites above you – trailing weed and alive with albino bottom feeders – as you do so. The floor of the cave has a curious, springy quality to it, as if you are treading on a bed of sponges. Suddenly the ground lurches beneath you, concussive waves within the water sending you whirling. And then the cave opening starts to close – only it's not a cave. It is really a mouth! Turning, you pull at the water with your arms, desperately kicking with your legs, as you try to stop yourself becoming a meal for some monstrous leviathan of the oceans. Roll three dice. If the total rolled is less than or equal to your STAMINA score, turn to **116**. If the total is greater, turn to **96**.

77

Cross the 10 Gold Pieces off your *Adventure Sheet*. Brokk ducks back inside the brewery and reappears some minutes later. He has exchanged his grubby apron for a coat of chainmail armour and is gripping a battle-axe in his ham-like fists. Slung over his shoulder is a coiled rope and iron grapple. He is also wearing a helmet which has the waxy stub of a candle stuck to the brim. You ask him what it is that awaits you in the mine, but he won't be drawn on the subject. 'You hired me to be your guide, that's all,' he says grimly.

When the two of you reach Fathomdeep Mine, if you find yourself reading a paragraph that has an asterisk (*) next to the number, subtract 50 from that reference and turn to the new paragraph to see what Brokk has to tell you. For as long as Brokk is with you, you may also assume that you have a Rope and Grapple (if you don't already). Brokk will also join in any battles you face underground. When faced with two opponents, you need only fight the first one to win the battle, as the Dwarf will do away with the other with his battle-axe. His attributes are SKILL 10, STAMINA 8. If you face only one opponent you will gain two Attacks, both of which can injure that opponent. In this case, if injuries are sustained they will only affect you on a dice roll of 1–3. Keep a careful note of Brokk's STAMINA score; if he dies, down there in the mine, you will have to continue alone (obviously losing the benefits gained by having the Dwarf fighting with you). Now turn to **98**.

Holding the conch shell above your head, you shout, 'Oceanus! Aid me now!'

With a rushing roar, water pours from the shell in an impossible torrent. It rapidly fills the chamber, causing electrical equipment to short out and sweeping Fulgurites from their stations. The waters surge together and rise from the floor of the bridge in a great column which gains crude arms and a face.

With a noise like waves breaking on a rocky shoreline, Oceanus, Spirit of the Sea, crashes into Sturm's stone body. Before your eyes, pieces of his colossal clay-like form break off and dissolve in the water. The Colossus bellows in rage but the tidal attacks of the Water Elemental continue to wash his body away.

But Sturm is not done yet. What is left of his rocky form dissolves as Sturm turns into water himself. The two watery creatures crash and surge around the bridge, dousing you and sweeping you off your feet. Then suddenly all is calm – until another watery humanoid figure rises from the roiling swell, only this time its liquid features are those of Balthazar Sturm! If only you could boil the transformed Elementalist away, as a blazing fire turns water into steam ...

If you know the name of a Fire Elemental who you could command to help you now, turn the name into a number using the code A=1, B=2, C=3 ... Z=26. Add the numbers together and turn to this paragraph. If not, turn to **206**.

79

The sandstone of the canyon here has been sculpted into all manner of strange shapes which, when the wind blows through them, produce the eerie wailing sound you heard earlier. Not for nothing is this place called the Screaming Canyon. Still a long way off, you make out a towering stack of wind-sculpted rock, rising many metres into the sky above the cliffs of the canyon. Something tells you that this stack of rock is where you need to be heading, but for the time being, the path ahead of you splits again. Will you follow the left-hand (turn to **119**) or the right-hand fork (turn to **99**)?

80*

You are standing on one side of a cathedral-like cavern. A waterfall cascades into a chill lake to the left and on the far side of the chamber you can see an ominously dark fissure leading, you suspect, to a network of caves beyond. Glowstones set into the walls and mats of phosphorescent lichen covering the vault of the water-worn cave illuminate pieces of discarded machinery – from piles of iron pit-props to experimental digging machines. In fact much of it looks like it has deliberately been wrecked.

As far as you can tell, Fathomdeep Mine ends here, at the entrance to the natural cave system beyond. If you want to proceed any further, you have no choice but to enter the crack in the cavern wall for yourself. Watching your footing on the uneven floor, you follow the fissure up into the cave network until the way onwards splits. From here you are going to have to go left, entering a high-roofed gallery hung with stalactites (turn to **152**), or right, following a low-roofed cleft which heads downwards again (turn to **387**).

81

Gulping down the potion you feel a warm glow permeate every part of your body – starting at your stomach and working its way to your feet and fingertips. Every nerve ending tingles with the sensation of raw power. (Restore up to 6 STAMINA points and for the duration of the battle to come, increase your Attack Strength by 2 points.) Feeling like you could wrestle a giant or take on a whole army single-handed, you stride towards the roaring Earth Elemental, ready to meet it in single combat. Turn to **61**.

82

With the heavy weapon gripped firmly in your hands, you take a swing at the iron sphere. The resulting clang reverberates around the chamber and along your arms. Hefting the weapon again, mustering all your strength, you take another swing at the Elemental Engine. Roll three dice. If the number rolled is less than or equal to your STAMINA score, turn to **135**; if it is greater, turn to **44**.

83

The Howling Plains lie to the south of Femphrey, beyond the expanses of fertile farmland, forming something of a barren no man's land between the kingdoms of Femphrey and Lendleland. Little grows here and much of the time howling gales blow across the plains, bringing dust-storms that harry merchant caravans stupid or desperate enough to brave this route across the heartland of the continent.

The sun beats down as you come to the edge of the Howling Plains. Ahead of you lies a parched and desolate land, home to wild animals and tribes of war-like Birdmen; behind, the rolling hills and lush green fields of your homeland. As you gaze south-wards, wondering what might await you within the bleak expanse of the Howling Plains, you see that the sky is coloured a dirty yellow. You feel a breeze on your face that soon becomes a powerful, raging wind, as the dusty sky resolves itself into an approaching sandstorm.

You are completely exposed out here. As you try to work out how much time you have before the sand-storm is upon you, you see a dancing silhouette before of it. This object is being blown towards you, ahead of the howling sandstorm. As it gets rapidly closer, swept towards you by the rising gale, you see that it is a huge balloon, stitched together from sheets of sailcloth, with a wicker basket hanging beneath it. You can hear desperate shouts coming from the balloon's pilot and it now looks more like he is actually trying to escape from the approaching sandstorm.

It is at that moment, when you feel the first stinging wave of sand particles hit your face, that an evil-looking face appears within the whirling cyclone of dust and sand, its mouth open wide as if ready to swallow the balloon and its terrified occupant. But what can you do to help the poor balloonist, or even yourself, in the face of this elemental sandstorm? Will you:

Blow a Hunting Horn, if you have one? Turn to **123**
Draw your sword, ready to defend
    yourself?   Turn to **173**
Take cover as best you can, in the hope
    that the sandstorm will simply blow
    over you?   Turn to **203**

84

The ore-truck hurtles over the end of the rails, and for a moment you feel a cold rush of air, in your face. And then the next stretch of track appears beyond the gaping hole and the cart crashes down onto the rails again. The truck continues on its way through the mine, descending deeper and deeper through a series of peaks and troughs in the track until it abruptly reaches the end of the line and bumps to a halt against a set of bumpers on one side of a large natural chamber, deep below the earth. Turn to **80**.

85

The headman, a farmer called Giles, takes you to the foot of the towering dam. He opens a grand set of wooden double doors, next to an ornately-carved archway – through which tumbles the churning outflow from the lake into the river – and leads you into a stone-built room. A series of large brass wheels are set into the far wall. They obviously need to be turned a particular way to open the sluice-gates and allow water from the lake to drain through the dam. Without further ado, you set about trying to solve the problem. *Test your Skill* and *Test your Luck*. If you are both successful and Lucky, turn to **150**. If you fail either test, turn to **180**.

86

As soon as you open the door, you are buffeted by a steady breeze. Shutting the door behind you, you look around. You are standing in a large room dominated by a massive set of bellows and the rotating blades of a windmill. The bellows pump up and down, powered by gear-driven machinery, causing the windmill fan to turn, which directs most of the airstream generated in this way out through a funnel in the side of one wall. On the opposite side of this windy room is another wooden door, this one marked with what is unmistakeably a lightning bolt. If you could somehow stop the fan from turning, perhaps you could weaken the power of the storm that is being generated by the Weather Machine. A large lever attached to the wind generator is currently pushed forwards. Will you:

Pull back on the lever?	Turn to 118
Attack the bellows with your sword?	Turn to 101
Leave this room and return to the landing?	Turn to 54
Open the door marked with a lightning bolt?	Turn to 133

87
Your body is bombarded by hailstones as heavy and hard as rocks. One hits you on the top of your head and sends you reeling. Lose 2 STAMINA points and for the duration of your next battle, reduce your Attack Strength by 1 point. Turn to 100.

88
Katarina gives you a disparaging look and then says, 'Call yourself an adventurer? But don't worry; I'm

not going to throw you overboard or anything like that. Let's just get back to land before that storm front catches up with us.' (Lose 1 LUCK point.)

Another day at sea brings you back to the docks of Chalannabrad at last and, taking your leave of Captain Katarina and the *Tempest*, you head out of the city to start upon the next leg of your quest. (Move the Day of the Week on 1.)

If you possess a pair of Seven League Boots and would like to use them now, turn to **2**. If not, remembering that you can only visit each location once, will you head for:

The Witchtooth Line?	Turn to **157**
Mount Pyre?	Turn to **22**
The Howling Plains?	Turn to **4**

Or, if you feel that you are ready, do you want to make your attempt to reach Balthazar Sturm's Weather Machine at the eye of the storm (turn to **350**)?

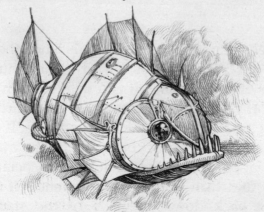

89

Your ploy works. Screeching with fury, the Blizzard-Wings turn their attentions on you and attack, talons outstretched.

	SKILL	STAMINA
First BLIZZARD-WING	6	7
Second BLIZZARD-WING	6	6

Unless you are wearing a Sun Talisman, you must reduce your Attack Strength by 1 point while battling the furious lizard-birds. If you kill them both, the Pegasus alights on the ground nearby. It trots through the snow towards you, snorting its appreciation, and nuzzles you with its nose. (Add the codeword *Susagep* to your *Adventure Sheet* and regain 1 LUCK point.) With a last whinny of gratitude, the Pegasus takes to the skies again, as the blizzard passes. The winged horse gone, you too continue on your way. Move the Day of the Week by 1, and turn to **250**.

90

You barely manage to reach the dais when the Keeper of the Four Winds raises her arms and hurricane-force jets of agitated air hit you with enough force to lift you off your feet and throw you back through the archway, and over the side of the stack. If you are wearing an Unusual Backpack, divide the number of the current paragraph by the number associated with the pack and turn to that new reference. If not, you plummet back down the side of the stack, your battered body bouncing off hard rock ledges, until you land at the bottom in your own private world of pain. Roll one die and add 2 to the number rolled. Lose this many STAMINA points. If you roll 3–4 lose 1 SKILL point as well, but if you roll 5–6, lose 2 SKILL points. You must also lose 1 LUCK point. Deciding it would be unwise to attempt to petition the Keeper of the Four Winds again, you retrace your route, back through the Screaming Canyon until finally you come to the edge of the Howling Plains. Move the Day of the Week on 1 and turn to **394**.

91

Chalannabrad's markets are just as busy as ever and you find plenty that could be of use to you.

Item	Cost
Provisions	1 Gold Piece per Meal
Rope and Grapple	3 Gold Pieces
Crossbow and 6 Quarrels	12 Gold Pieces
Chainmail Armour	8 Gold Pieces
Warhammer	10 Gold Pieces
Sun Talisman	6 Gold Pieces
Wyrmskin Cloak	12 Gold Pieces
Seven League Boots	10 Gold Pieces
Potion of Fortune	6 Gold Pieces
Potion of Strength	4 Gold Pieces
Potion of Skill	5 Gold Pieces

You may buy as many Meals' worth of Provisions as you want, up to a maximum of 10; each Meal will restore up to 4 STAMINA points. You may use the

Crossbow once in each battle you fight before having to engage in hand-to-hand combat (as long as you still have quarrels to shoot); *Test your Skill* and if you succeed your crossbow bolt causes your opponent 2 STAMINA points damage. On a roll of 1–3 the Chainmail Armour will reduce any damage done against you by 1 point. The Warhammer is not magical like your sword Wyrmbiter, but it is a crushing weapon; if you hit an opponent with the Warhammer, roll one die and if you roll 5–6 it does 1 extra STAMINA point of damage. On a roll of 1–2 the Wyrmskin Cloak will reduce any damage done against you by 1 point. When drunk, the Potion of Fortune will restore your LUCK score to its *Initial* level, the Potion of Strength will restore your STAMINA score to its *Initial* level, and the Potion of Skill will restore your SKILL score to its *Initial* level.

When you have made all the purchases you want, or can afford (and have recorded them on your *Adventure Sheet*), will you search the city for something that will let you breathe underwater (turn to 121), or, if you have already acquired such a thing, will you look for a ship to take you out to sea (turn to 252)?

92

As the Earth Elemental closes on you, you take out the flask containing the precious Spark of Life and hurl it into the creature's path. The flask hits some of the rusted machinery that the Dwarfs left behind, and explodes in a dazzling burst of lightning. Blue fingers of electricity crackle between the pieces of corroded metal and your mouth drops open in amazement as you watch it draw them together. The piles of scrap rapidly take on a semi-skeletal humanoid form – made entirely from the scrap littering the chamber – that then gets to its feet. Eyes that were once miners' lanterns crackle with bound lightning as the Golem you have created glares down at you. You point at the Earth Elemental and, with a grinding of rusted joints, the Golem turns and strides forwards to meet the Elemental in battle.

Conduct the battle between the Earth Elemental and your Rust Golem, as you would any other. This will be a titanic battle indeed! (If today is Earthday, increase the Elemental's SKILL score by 1 point and its STAMINA by 2 points.)

	SKILL	STAMINA
EARTH ELEMENTAL	14	22
RUST GOLEM	10	12

If your Golem somehow triumphs against the Earth Elemental, regain 1 LUCK point and turn to **10**. If the Earth Elemental destroys the Rust Golem (which is more likely), will you:

Quickly down a Potion of Giant	
Strength, if you have one?	Turn to **81**
Finish the Earth Elemental off	
yourself?	Turn to **61**
Run for it while you still can?	Turn to **42**

93

The journey to Chalannabrad takes four days. (Move the Day of the Week on 4.) During that time, the farming folk share what little they have with you and when you eventually leave the refugee caravan you have gained many more friends and 4 more Meals to add to your stock of Provisions. Regain 1 LUCK point and turn to **50**.

94

Leaving the mangled wreckage of the weathervane lying at the foot of the tower, you approach the large iron-banded door. You are just reaching for the iron door handle when you freeze, wondering what other sorceries could be protecting the tower. If you want to turn the handle to open the door, turn to **134**. If you would rather break the door down, turn to **164**.

95

You are woken in the darkest watches of the night, by a chilling cry. You are on your feet in an instant, weapon in hand, and just in time too. Crashing through the undergrowth, a hideous creature bursts from the wood. Its body is hairless, other than for a stringy black mane, its fish-white flesh marked by large blue-black blotches. It walks on two legs, but drags its knuckles along the ground and in one hand carries a crude flint axe. Its head is almost equine in form and as it advances it opens its malformed mouth again to moan at the moon. You have no choice but to defend yourself against the cannibalistic Mooncalf.

MOONCALF   SKILL 8   STAMINA 9

If you kill the Mooncalf, you settle down for what is left of the night, some way from where it attacked you, but sleep is slow in coming. Turn to **40**.

96

Despite swimming with all your might, you are unable to escape the 'cave' before the sea monster closes its mouth and swallows you whole. Your adventure ends here, as you become supper for some monster of the ocean depths.

97

As the Fulgurites' leathery bodies collapse in on themselves with a few last sparking flashes, you approach the massive metal sphere. You can feel the static electricity saturating the air skitter over your skin, setting every hair on your head on end. Cautiously you put your face to the glass pane of the porthole and peer inside the machine. What you see almost defies belief.

Four huge figures are trapped inside the sphere, each a pure embodiment of one of the four elements. They all have a semi-humanoid appearance despite being composed from solid earth, whirling air, raging fire and churning water. These must be the Greater Elementals that you were told Sturm had bound to his Elemental Engine to power the *Eye of the Storm*. The Elementals are trapped in a never-ending battle with one another, swirling and whirling around inside the containment sphere, their very essence and their constant conflict providing the Weather Machine with its magical means of propulsion.

You are certain that if you can damage the Elemental Engine, then you will deliver Balthazar Sturm and his Weather Machine a devastating blow. But how on Titan are you going to achieve such a thing? If you have the codeword *Notamotua* recorded on your *Adventure Sheet*, turn to **15** at once. If you have a set of Blueprints you could try using these to help you. If you want to do this, multiply the number associated with the plans by 30 and turn to the paragraph with the same number. If you have neither of these things, how will you damage the *Eye of the Storm*'s power source? Will you:

Attack the Elemental Engine with
    your sword?   Turn to 47
Take a Mace or a Warhammer to the
    machine, if you have one?   Turn to 82
Try using a Spanner, if you have
    one?   Turn to 63
Resort to fiddling with its controls?   Turn to 34

98

'Look,' the Dwarf says, as you prepare to set off, 'you're going to need to get your strength up before you head down into that mine, so why don't you sample one of my "special" brews?'

Brokk leads you inside the brewery, past huge copper cauldrons to his liquor store. He points out a number of earthenware jars lining a high shelf and tells you of their potential benefits. However, like anything the Dwarf has to offer, it's going to cost you. Take a look at the list of brews below. As long as you are willing to pay for them, you can choose to drink as many as you like. However, if you try more than two, for every one you sample after that, you must reduce your Attack Strength by 1 point (which is a cumulative penalty) while you are down in the mine, as you become intoxicated by the alcohol.

BROKK'S 'SPECIAL' BREWS

Dwarf Ale   3 *Gold Pieces*

Drinking this clear, honey-coloured ale has the effect of restoring 4 STAMINA points.

Trollbreath Beer   4 *Gold Pieces*

This muddy brown beer smells like a Troll's armpit, is the colour of a Troll's armpit but actually tastes quite good, restoring up to 4 points of STAMINA. It also leaves you with the worst case of halitosis you've ever had! For every battle you have to fight down in the mine, you may reduce your opponent's Attack Strength by 1 point if it is a living creature (so not Elementals, magical creatures, Demons or Undead) as they recoil from the noisome stench of your breath.

Skullbuster Spirit   4 *Gold Pieces*

Just a few swigs of this notorious Dwarf drink will leave you with a splitting headache (reducing your Attack Strength by 1 point for the first battle you have to fight down in the mines), but it also fills you with incredible strength. Every blow you lay against an enemy, while you are in the mine, does 1 extra point of STAMINA damage.

Cadwallader's 'Old Battleaxe' Cider   5 *Gold Pieces*

This powerful scrumpy has the effect of making

you even braver than normal, filling you with fighting spirit. For the duration of your time in the mine you may add 1 point to your Attack Strength (but still bear in mind that if you drink too much, you could lose this benefit again).

Wyvern's Wing   *5 Gold Pieces*

Brokk doesn't know what it is about this particular ale – whether it's the melt-water that comes down off the Witchtooth peaks or the hops he grows himself – but it works not unlike a Luck Potion. Every time you have to *Test your Luck* while you are down in Fathomdeep Mine, you may assume you are Lucky and you do not have to deduct any LUCK points for making the test.

Brokk's Blistering Brew   *6 Gold Pieces*

This one tastes like liquid fire and leaves you light-headed at the merest sniff (reducing your Attack Strength by 1 point for the first battle you have to fight down in the mines). However, it will also restore your SKILL score to its *Initial* level and up to half your STAMINA points.

When you are done sampling Brokk's wares, you set off for the mine. Move the Day of the Week on 1 and turn to **190**.

99

Hearing a raucous croaking cry, you look up to see two winged humanoid creatures coming at you out of the sun. You have unwittingly strayed into the territory of a tribe of war-like Birdmen and now you must pay in blood. Fight the Birdmen together.

	SKILL	STAMINA
First BIRDMAN	7	8
Second BIRDMAN	8	7

If you fend off the Birdmen's attack, you hurry on your way, not wanting to run into any more of their evil kind. Turn to **166**.

100

For a moment you are caught in a total whiteout as a blizzard of stinging ice flakes surrounds you. Then you break through into the eye of the whirling ice storm. There, at the very centre of the disturbance is a creature that appears to be entirely composed of ice. It stands one-and-a-half times as tall as a man, its humanoid body formed from slabs of blue-white ice. One arm ends in a huge fist of frozen water while its other hand bristles with spiky icicles. The Ice Elemental opens a frosted maw packed with frozen fangs and howls at you with a voice like the winter wind. Drawing Wyrmbiter, you prepare to battle the Ice Elemental. If you are wearing a Sun Talisman, turn to **43**.

ICE ELEMENTAL   SKILL 8   STAMINA 9

(If today is Fireday, reduce the Ice Elemental's SKILL score by 1 point and its STAMINA by 2 points.) If you lose an Attack Round roll one die and then consult the table below to see what damage you suffer. (You may use LUCK to reduce any damage caused in the usual way.)

Dice Roll	Attack and Damage
1–2	Blizzard Breath – the creature hits you with a blast of its freezing breath. Lose 2 STAMINA points.
3–5	Ice Hammer – the Elemental clubs you with its huge right fist. Lose 3 STAMINA points.
6	Icicle Strike – the Elemental fires icy darts from its left fist. Roll 1 dice to see how many hit you and lose that many STAMINA points.

If you manage to defeat the Ice Elemental, turn to **62**.

101

You hack at the leather of the huge bellows and have soon cut several great holes in the side. The bellows start to deflate and without the air that they were providing, the windmill spins to a standstill. You have successfully put Sturm's Wind Turbine out of action. (Add 1 to your DAMAGE score.) What are you going to do now? If you want to open the door marked with a lightning bolt, turn to **133**. If you want to return to the bottom-deck landing, turn to **54**.

102

Snapping the copper bands around the statuette, you call out, 'Arkholith! Defend me now!'

The figurine cracks open, and immediately begins to transform. It swells in size until it has become a hulking giant formed from great slabs of rock. With a growl like continental plates colliding, the Earth Elemental encircles the whirling Sturm in its massive arms. Sturm howls as the Elemental squeezes the very life from him.

The bridge is suddenly ablaze with brilliant white light as, in an explosion of lightning, Sturm transforms one last time. The Earth Elemental is obliterated by the lightning burst, searing bolts of energy striking the banks of machinery and exploding the bodies of fallen Fulgurites. You blink the grey afterimages from your eyes and gradually your vision clears. Turn to **397**.

103

In time you come to another junction; a new tunnel branches off from the main passageway at a right angle, and ahead you can see the tunnel you are following now ends at what you take to be the bank of the lava river you had to cross earlier. Do you want to follow the new branch to the left (turn to 73), or would you prefer to keep heading towards the magma flow (turn to 141)?

104

Caught in the maelstrom that accompanies the destruction of the *Eye of the Storm*, your plummeting body is buffeted by high winds as you drop towards the ground.

And then you hear the beating of powerful wings fighting the raging air currents and the wind is knocked from you as you land squarely across the back of the Pegasus! Giving a shrill whinny of triumph, the flying horse takes you away from the disintegrating ship and glides down to the ground. Its hooves hit the earth, throwing up a cloud of dust as it lands. You quickly dismount, having never been so happy to have the ground beneath your feet. Turn to 400.

105

The mine-cart hurtles off the end of the rails. For a moment you are sailing through cold air, wind whipping at your face. And then the next stretch of track appears ahead of you, but you already know you're not going to make it. The cart smashes into the scaffolding supports, throwing you out in mid-air. You drop through total darkness for a moment before you are met by the freezing embrace of an underground river. Before you even have time to catch your breath, you feel yourself being dragged over the edge of a thundering cascade. Turn to **38**.

106

Grabbing hold of the monster around its middle you manage to heave it off the ground – a phenomenal feat indeed. (Regain 1 LUCK point.) The Earth Demon howls in agony and great chunks of its clay-like body break off and drop to the ground. Decrease the monster's STAMINA score by 6 points. If this wound has finished it, turn to **51**. If not, return to **35** and finish the battle.

Here you stand, at the climax of your quest, and you have no means of reaching Sturm's flying machine (lose 1 LUCK point). Time is up for Femphrey too. You can feel the wind picking up and, looking up, see storm-clouds massing overhead. And there, amidst the oppressive thunderheads, no more than a distant golden speck in the darkening sky, you see the brass fish again. The *Eye of the Storm* approaches!

The wind becomes a gale and you struggle to stand as it continues to rise. All manner of debris is picked up by the whirlwind forming around you – from rocks and branches, to a startled-looking cow! – and then, suddenly, the whirling vortex plucks you from the ground and you find yourself hurtling skyward. The storm has caught you too! You are battered by the debris picked up by the tornado. Roll one die, add 2 and deduct that many STAMINA points. If you survive this battering, limbs flailing uncontrollably, you hurtle upwards, towards the *Eye of the Storm*.

The twister carries you higher and higher until you are actually over the flying machine. It is huge, bigger than a Bullwhale. Its sparkling glass eyes are large observation windows in the front of the vessel; its fins and tail, steering sails and a vast rudder. In the side of the vessel you can make out a round access hatch with a rail-guarded balcony in front of it. The wind suddenly drops and gravity returns, with a vengeance … Turn to **14**.

108

'Others have come seeking aid in their time, blown here by the winds of fate, but few have earned the right to receive it,' the Keeper intones. 'Seven sovereigns have sought my aid, and each sovereign sent seven sages, seven times, each sage accompanied by seven scholars. Tell me, how many have sought my aid?'

If you know the answer, add all the digits in the number together and then turn to the paragraph with the same number as the total. If the paragraph you turn to doesn't begin 'You have answered correctly', or you don't know the answer, will you attack the cloaked figure (turn to 90) or graciously admit defeat (turn to 159).

109

You climb higher and higher towards the summit of the volcano. The terrain gets rougher until you are scrambling through a landscape of nothing but black rocks and steaming volcanic vents. Sulphurous steam rises from holes in the ground which feels warm beneath your feet. Still far above stands the smoke-belching crater of Mount Pyre, a column of soot and ash continually rising from it high into the sky.

Rounding the side of a monolithic boulder, you find what you have been looking for – an incongruous, carved archway of black rock, set into the side of the volcanic peak – the entrance to the Fire Tunnels. The means with which to defeat Sturm's bound Greater

Fire Elemental lies within, you are sure of it. Having made any preparations you think are necessary, after making the strenuous climb to Mount Pyre's peak, you pass beneath the stone arch.

A long tunnel leads away towards the heart of the volcano, looking like it has been gnawed through the rock by some massive burrowing beetle. The walls of the tunnel glow with ambient heat, and in places flames break forth from the rocks strewing the sides of the tunnel, lighting the way ahead. The tunnel twists and turns until eventually you reach a T-junction where it joins another curving passageway. Will you turn left (turn to **169**) or right (turn to **219**)?

Will you turn left (turn to **169**) or right (turn to **219**)?

110

Opening the door, you find yourself at the threshold to a large chamber which must make up a fair amount of the rear of the *Eye of the Storm*. Taking up at least half the room is a huge sphere of riveted metal. It must be at least four metres in diameter and in the front of it there is a small glass porthole. The sphere shakes perceptibly as if great energies are barely restrained within. Leading from the huge metal sphere to every other part of the chamber and beyond are thick pipes and leather-sheathed bundles of wire. Smoke and steam vent from escape valves and dodgy seals, while the humid atmosphere is filled with a cacophony of clanking metal and resounding bangs, coming from inside the sphere. Tending to the sphere are a number of curious-looking creatures. They are short and squat – roughly the size of Dwarfs – and are completely contained within suits of stitched leather and brass helmets. From behind the tinted goggle-eyes of the helmets you can see blue sparks of electricity. They are Fulgurites – Lightning Sprites bound to Sturm's will. If you do not want to face the Fulgurites you can escape from the room, pulling the door shut behind you and turning its wheel-handle to trap them inside. (If you do this, turn to **126**, but remember that you won't be able to re-enter the Engine Room.) If you do not want to flee, you will have to face Sturm's minions in battle. Fight them two at a time.

	SKILL	STAMINA
First FULGURITE	6	5
Second FULGURITE	6	4
Third FULGURITE	5	5
Fourth FULGURITE	6	5
Fifth FULGURITE	5	4
Sixth FULGURITE	6	5

If you manage to defeat all the Fulgurites, turn to **97**.

111

You travel south for a day, following the trail of destruction left by the troubling tempest. (Move the Day of the Week on 1.) By midday of the second day you crest a rise and catch sight of the glittering reflection of sunlight on water. There, traversing the wide grassy plain ahead of you is the Siltbed River. The river marks the boundary between the kingdom of

Femphrey and its troublesome neighbour Lendle-land. Lendleland has long been the rival of Femphrey, jealous of the latter's fertile plains and the wealth it has dredged from Lake Cauldron to the east. But the trail of felled trees and mired roads left by the storm crosses the border and continues towards a line of distant hills over the border. You will need to be careful if you choose to cross the border and enter Lendleland. Do you want to keep following the trail south (turn to **158**) or would you rather turn round and head instead for Chalannabrad and the College of Mages (turn to **127**)?

112

His body fully ablaze now, Balthazar Sturm, in his guise as the Human Torch, reaches for you with hands alive with tongues of flame.

HUMAN TORCH   SKILL 10   STAMINA 9

If today is Fireday, add 1 point to the Human Torch's SKILL and STAMINA scores. If you reduce the Human Torch's STAMINA score to 3 points or fewer, turn to **267**.

113

You shout the name 'Vulcanus!' and a ball of furious flames explodes into being upon the bridge. The flames quickly coalesce into the shape of a fiery man. The searing heat given off by the Elemental causes beads of sweat to break out on your brow as you shield your eyes against the fury of Vulcanus' incandescent light.

Under the heat of the Fire Elemental's ferocious onslaught, Sturm's watery body begins to boil away to nothing. And then he is gone. (If you have the codeword *Demlaceb* written on your *Adventure Sheet*, turn to 397 immediately.)

For a moment you start to believe that Vulcanus has finished Sturm off, once and for all, but your relief is short-lived when a howling gale assaults both you and the Fire Elemental. Under the force of the raging wind, with a last fiery roar Vulcanus is snuffed from existence.

A cruelly smiling face appears within the tumult of the whirlwind before you now, but you already know who it is – Balthazar Sturm has drawn the power of the hurricane into himself. But what can withstand a howling gale, as mountains resist the relentless attentions of the wind?

If you possess a Clay Statuette, turn the name etched into it into a number using the code A=1, B=2, C=3 ... Z=26. Add the numbers together and turn to the paragraph with the same number. If not, turn to 284.

114

The Elemental vanishes in an explosion of incandescent flame. The magma immediately begins to boil, throwing out great splashes of molten rock. You watch in horror as the level of the lava lake visibly begins to rise until it is lapping at the sides of the spur. You have to get out of here and fast! You turn back to the two flights of stone steps. With a

cacophonous groaning crash the left-hand staircase splinters and topples into the rising lava. You take the right-hand stairs two at a time.

While you are making your escape, time really will be of the essence. You must keep track of how long it takes you using a TIME TRACK score, which starts at 0.

At the top of the rock staircase you sprint along the ruddy-walled tunnel beyond until you come to a junction. (Add 1 to your TIME TRACK). Will you go left (turn to **174**) or keep going straight on (turn to **144**)?

115

You have been travelling for two days (move the Day of the Week on 2), and are cutting through a forest, when you hear a loud crash, as of branches being broken, as something huge barges its way through the trees towards you. Before you can take evasive action, a lumbering Giant bursts from the trees ahead of you.

The Giant is as tall as a tree and carries a cow under one arm. At his waist hangs a huge barrel of beer and in his spare hand he holds a stripped tree trunk. The Giant's clothes are stitched together from animal hides and pieces of material – cloth that might have once been a tent or the canvas of a windmill's vanes, by the looks of things. He has a broken cart-wheel on a rope around his neck like a talisman. The Giant catches sight of you and an ugly grimace twists his lumpen features.

'Oo are yoo?' the Giant rumbles.

Confidently you call out your name. 'I am the Hero of Tannatown, slayer of the Crimson Witch, bearer of the dragon-slaying sword Wyrmbiter!'

'I know yoo!' the Giant booms. 'It was yoo what beat up Chief Gog Magog!'

'That's right,' you confirm cautiously.

'Then I challenge yoo to a wrestlin' match!' the Giant laughs.

A wrestling match? With a Giant? When you defeated the Giant Chieftain Gog Magog you did so with the help of staked pit and a concealed cannon. Will you:

Attack the Giant before he can attack you?	Turn to **176**
Accept the Giant's challenge?	Turn to **210**
Politely decline the challenge?	Turn to **194**

Forcing yourself through the water, fighting the great sucking draw of the current, you kick free of the monster's mouth just before its jaws close completely. You are lucky to have escaped with your life. Hoping that the leviathan hasn't actually realised that you've escaped, you swim towards the relative safety of the rift. Add the codeword *Retsnom* to your *Adventure Sheet* and turn to **146**.

117

Ducking through the smaller archway, you reach the spiralling staircase, but which way will you go – up or down? If you want to ascend the staircase, turn to **220**. If you would rather descend the stairs, turn to **160**.

118

The instant you pull the lever back, there is a metal-shearing grinding of gears and the windmill starts to turn the other way. As it does so, the wind being generated by the contraption is drawn back into the room. The force of the cyclone now circling the chamber flattens you against the wall. And that's not all that the machine has blown back into the ship. Capricious spirits of the air are drawn into the chamber too. Crackling with static electricity and pummelling you with their violent gusts of wind, screaming the Sylphs attack. Fight them all at the same time.

	SKILL	STAMINA
First SYLPH	7	4
Second SYLPH	6	5
Third SYLPH	6	4

If today is Windsday or Stormsday, increase the Sylphs SKILL and STAMINA scores by 1 point. If you defeat these air spirits, fighting against the gale still howling through the room, will you attack the bellows of the machine with your sword (turn to **101**), open the door marked with a lightning bolt (turn to **133**), or return to the bottom deck landing (turn to **54**)?

119

As you continue to make your way through the winding canyon, the cliffs begin to close in above you until it is almost as if you are making your way through a tunnel through the rock. *Test your Luck*. If you are Lucky, turn to **166**; if you are Unlucky, turn to **136**.

120

You hurl the bottled lightning at the monstrous creature, only for it to be batted away with the swipe of a tentacle. The flask tumbles through the water towards the reef, where it strikes an outcropping of coral and shatters. There is a blinding flash as the captured lightning is unleashed deep beneath the ocean. The monster emits an unearthly shriek and recoils. As your own vision clears, you make the most of the opportunity and attempt to make your escape into the open ocean. *Test your Luck*. If you are Lucky, turn to **222**; if you are Unlucky, turn to **282**.

121

It strikes you that there are three groups within the city who might be able to help you with this particularly tricky problem. Will you visit:

The Brotherhood of Alchemists?	Turn to **151**
The Guild of Artificers?	Turn to **181**
The Academy of Naval Sorcerers?	Turn to **221**

122

The cart hits the junction at speed and careens around the corner on two wheels. The tracks straighten out again and the truck crashes back down onto the rails, throwing up a shower of sparks. You grip the sides of the cart, knuckles white, your face set in a terrified grimace. But your rollercoaster ride isn't over yet. You see the track drop away beneath you as the cart rolls over the top of a steep curve. Suddenly the cart is hurtling down a near-vertical slope, plunging you into the all-enveloping darkness beneath the earth at a terrifying speed. Your bouncing lantern reveals nothing from this stygian abyss other than the precariously supported tracks as the mine-cart reaches the bottom of the dip and begins to rocket upwards again. Then you see it – a break in the line! Part of the track is missing, destroyed no doubt by some earthquake or other. *Test your Luck*. If you are Lucky, turn to 84. If you are Unlucky, turn to 105.

123

You put the horn to your lips and blow. A deep, sonorous note sounds across the dusty plain, growing in force with every metre it covers. By the time the soundwave hits the sandstorm the note of the horn has already drowned out the howling voice of the gale-force winds. The dust-formed face contorts, as in some hellish scream, and then the sandstorm breaks up, before your very eyes. Regain 1 LUCK point and turn to 223.

124

Brokk gives the machine a few judicious taps with his battle-axe and then climbs up into the tunneller's cockpit. You join him as he pulls at levers and punches buttons on a brass panel in front of him. And then, with a throaty roar, the Mole's engine roars into life. 'Just as I hoped!' Brokk chuckles in delight. 'There's still some juice left in the glowstones after all. Okay,' the Dwarf declares, tugging at another lever and gripping the steering control in his calloused hands as he pushes a wooden paddle on the floor with his feet, 'here goes nothing!'

And then you are off, the Mole rattling and clanking as Brokk steers it directly towards a wall of solid rock. The drill-head screeches as it runs up to speed and then, with a grinding roar, it connects with the rock-face. The machine chews through rock and mud with ease. There is nothing for you to do but sit back and enjoy the ride as Brokk directs the tunnelling machine through the earth, heading deeper and deeper into the mine.

Eventually, the mass of rock and earth in front of the machine collapses and, with a whirring scream, the drill-bit hits empty air. The Mole has ploughed through into a large natural chamber deep below the mountain. As the machine powers down, you and the Dwarf climb out of the cockpit to see where it has brought you. Add the codeword *Enihcam* to your *Adventure Sheet* and turn to **80**.

⊡ ⊡

125

You find your path descending again as the tunnel curves around to the right. The passageway pulses with a suffused orange glow. There is a sudden burst of blazing light, accompanied by a fiery roar. As you lower your hand from before your eyes, you see two ethereal figures hovering in the middle of the passageway in front of you. They look like burning human skeletons, their blackened bones clothed in a body of scintillating flame. Shrieking wildly, the Bone-Fires hurtle towards you, the bony fingers of their burning hands outstretched to grab you and tear your flesh. You must fight them both at the same time.

	SKILL	STAMINA
First BONE-FIRE	7	6
Second BONE-FIRE	6	6

(If today is Fireday, increase the Bone-Fires' STAMINA scores by 2 points each.) If you best these hellish spectres – the ghosts of other adventurers who died a fiery death within these tunnels – at your killing blow, their fires are snuffed out and their blackened bones turn to ash. The way ahead clear again, you press on. Turn to **103**.

126

You are standing on the middle deck of the vessel. Two steel doors lead off from the landing you now find yourself on, one to the aft and one to the fore, but neither of them have any distinguishing marks.

Will you:

Open the aft door (if you haven't done
so already)? Turn to **110**
Open the door to the fore (if you
haven't done so already)? Turn to **380**
Leave this deck and explore elsewhere? Turn to **391**

127

Not wanting to be responsible for a diplomatic incident between the two kingdoms, you turn back. After
another day's travel on foot, you pass the village of
Vastarin and keep on north towards the capital. Move
the Day of the Week on 1 and turn to **286**.

128

Hearing a shrill whinny, you look up to see the
Pegasus you saved – how many days ago now? –
galloping through the sky towards you, its huge
wings beating the air. The flying horse sensed your
need and has flown to your aid, ready to repay its
debt to you.

The Pegasus' hooves hit the ground. Grabbing its
mane, you vault onto its back. With another whinny,
your steed rears and then, with a powerful flap of its
feathered wings, leaps into the sky. You cling onto the
mane of the winged horse as it climbs higher and
higher with every beat of its wings, the wind buffet-
ing your face, the animal's hooves treading clouds
beneath it.

Peering through the wind you see a mass of churning, storm-black thunderheads. And there, amidst the tumult is the brass fish you saw for the first time all those days ago, after the devastation of Vastarin; Balthazar Sturm's Weather Machine! As you close on the vessel, you begin to really appreciate how huge it is! The fish's sparkling crystal eyes are observation domes; its fins, steering sails and its tail, a vast rudder. In the side of the bizarre craft you can make out an access hatch with a railed balcony in front of it.

If you have the codeword *Mortsleam* written on your *Adventure Sheet*, turn to **363**. If not, but today is Stormsday, you should also turn to **363**.

If none of these conditions are met, as the Pegasus flies as close as it can to the craft, fighting the hurricane-force winds, with a hasty prayer to the gods you throw yourself from its back … Turn to **14**.

A distant keening cry, from somewhere behind and above you, causes you to spin round and you are confronted by two horribly familiar winged shapes. Swooping down at you out of the sky, are two Aakor, like the winged wolves you fought in the hills to the south-west, on your approach to the Lightning Tower. They have been watching and waiting until the moment when your strength would be at a low ebb, and have decided that the time to strike is now!

	SKILL	STAMINA
First AAKOR	7	7
Second AAKOR	6	7

If you win, cross the codeword *Detnuh* off your *Adventure Sheet*. Free of your pursuers at last, will you continue south through the Screaming Canyon along the ravine to the left (turn to **99**) or the one to the right (turn to **58**)?

130

The aging engineer snatches the blueprints from you and pours over them eagerly. 'Ah, yes,' he says, 'these are the most up-to-date schematics for the craft. This is what we built!' he announces, stabbing a finger at the draughtsman's drawings of the flying fish vessel. 'You know what,' Inigo goes on, a mad sparkle entering his eyes, 'with these, if you could ever get on board the ship, you could really do some damage.'

'How do you mean?' you ask, intrigued.

'Well, there's the Elemental Engine for a start. That's what powers the whole thing – keeps it up in the air. Damage that and the *Eye*'s going down. And then there's the Burning Glass and the Lightning Generator. Damage either of those and you'll probably start a fire!'

To ask Inigo another question, return to **335**. If you're done with questions, turn to **365**.

131

You wake, on hearing a blood-curdling bestial howl. The cold silver orb of the moon is high in the sky above you, framed between the branches of the trees. And there, silhouetted against the moon, are three winged wolves. The Aakor pack have found you and this time have brought reinforcements. Snarling as they bare their fangs, the animals swoop towards you on their bird-of-prey wings. Fight the Aakor two at a time.

	SKILL	STAMINA
First AAKOR	7	7
Second AAKOR	6	7
Third AAKOR	6	6
Fourth AAKOR	7	6

This time the Aakor will fight to the death. If you manage to slay all of your attackers, strike the code-word *Detnuh* from your *Adventure Sheet* and turn to 40.

132

Your suspicions were correct. The water is rich in minerals which have a miraculous restorative effect on your fatigued body. (Roll one die and regain that many STAMINA points.) Turn to 171.

133

Opening the lightning bolt door, you enter another room containing a bizarre-looking piece of apparatus. Two brass spheres rotate from the blades of a spinning central column between two vertical pillars of crackling metal plates. The energy generated in this way is fed, via heavy bundles of cables, to a metal probe that protrudes from the craft through a hole in the front of its hull. Sparks fly from the spinning machine and you realise that your hair is standing on end. This contraption is obviously generating raw lightning, and on a massive scale. Looking at the machine, trying to work out a way of stopping it, you see a vertical lever, which looks like it can be pushed to the left or the right. Will you:

Move the lever to the right?	Turn to **154**
Move the lever to the left?	Turn to **170**
Leave the Lightning Generator and return to the stairwell?	Turn to **54**

134
Seizing hold of the doorknob, you give it a turn. Immediately a powerful electric shock passes up your arm and into your body. The door swings open, but you have been badly burned and are left with an uncomfortable sensation of pins and needles in your arm (lose 3 STAMINA points and 1 SKILL point). Cautiously you enter the tower, every hair on your head standing on end. Turn to **247**.

135
Your second blow lands in exactly the same spot as the first, and the stressed metal skin of the sphere fractures. You are hit by a raging torrent of raw

elemental energy and then, a second later, the Engine explodes. Scalding hot shards of twisted metal hurtle across the room as the blast throws you backwards to land against the door. Roll one die and add 2. This is the amount of STAMINA damage you suffer. (If you lose 6 points or more you must also lose 1 SKILL point.)

If you are still alive you pick yourself up from amidst a pile of *plinking* metal debris, relieved to discover that the Elementals appear to have left the chamber too. You stagger back through what is left of the door and onto the landing. Add 3 to your DAMAGE score and turn to 126.

136

The first warning you get that something is wrong is the light shower of dust and pebbles that precedes the landslide itself. As the collapsing cliff top crashes down into the chasm you are already running for your life, but you still suffer a number of injuries from falling rocks and bouncing boulders. Roll one die and add 1; this is how many STAMINA points of damage you suffer. If you are still alive, you run on through the choking clouds of dust thrown up by the rock fall. Turn to 166.

137

The door bursts open and two curious-looking contraptions hurtle through it. At first glance they appear to be animated suits of armour – not unlike the

Juggernaut, only considerably smaller – but they move along on wheels rather than legs and have great glass domes where their heads should be. One of these domes is full of sloshing water and the other, a whirling gas cloud. These are further examples of Sturm's melding of the magical with the mechanical, Elemental spirits bound within the devices to do his bidding. In this case they have been sent to put out the fire you started. Seeing you as another 'problem' to be dealt with, the Elemental-automatons trundle towards you, snapping pincer-claws outstretched. Fight them at the same time.

	SKILL	STAMINA
HYDROTOMATON	7	7
PNEUMATOMATON	8	6

(If today is Windsday, add 1 to the Pneumatomaton's SKILL and STAMINA scores, and if today is Seaday, add 1 to both the Hyrdrotomaton's SKILL and STAMINA.) If you destroy the machines, the Elemental spirits trapped inside are banished back to the Elemental Planes. Turn to **368**.

138

The cart hurtles round the bend; it is travelling faster than you realised. The precarious scaffolding beneath the rails gives way to solid rock again and the cart bumps to a stop at a set of bumpers. Dismounting from the ore truck, you set off along this new tunnel. Turn to 310.

139

The instant you flip the lens over, it collects the sun's rays that are entering the room through the crystal roof and beams this concentrated sunlight into the chamber. In only a few seconds, the wooden floor has caught fire, and from the rising flames leap two tiny Elemental creatures. If you are to escape from this room, you are going to have to get past these two first. Fight the Fire Sprites together.

	SKILL	STAMINA
First FIRE SPRITE	7	4
Second FIRE SPRITE	7	4

(If today is Fireday, increase the Sprites' SKILL and STAMINA scores by 1 point.) If you reduce the Fire Sprites' STAMINA to 0, they are forced to return to the Elemental Plane of Fire. (Add 1 to your DAMAGE score and make a note of the fact that you have started a fire on your *Adventure Sheet*.) Throwing open the door, you run back onto the landing at the top of the ship. Turn to 258.

140

'I'll tell you the way we ought to go,' Brokk tells you, 'and that's right. That's it, turn right here, then right again, down the pit shaft and that's where we'll find The Mole. It's an old tunnelling machine which would speed things up a bit and no mistake, if we could get it working, that is. But it would definitely be the quickest way through the mine, and probably the safest too.' Now return to 190 and choose which way to go.

141

You are standing at the crumbling edge of the lava river. Looking up, you can just make out pieces of the rock bridge you crossed earlier through the haze. The heat coming off the oozing river of magma is tremendous; you can feel your eyebrows starting to singe! But there is a way across. Several outcroppings of black rock emerge from the lava flow, effectively forming a series of stepping stones which lead to the other side, and another tunnel. If you want to risk crossing the fiery river using the stepping stones, turn to 312. If not, you will have to enter the passageway in the rock face behind you and look for another way through the volcano (turn to 73).

142

As you set out at dawn the following day (move the Day of the Week on 1) you see the tower for the first time. It stands on a distant outcrop, a twisting pinnacle of metal and stone, and the trail of devastation left by the storm is leading you right towards it. Keeping the tower in sight, you make straight for it.

By early afternoon, you have reached the bottom of the rocky crag on which the curious tower stands, an accusing finger pointing at the vast blue bowl of the sky. You can see three different routes by which to approach the tower. The first is a fast-flowing river that descends via waterfalls and churning rapids from the top of the peak to eventually meander away through this rugged landscape. The second is a steep, boulder-strewn path, up the side of the crag. The third, and longest route, is up the other side of the exposed escarpment. If you set off now, you should reach the tower before dusk, but which path will you take?

If you want to follow the river, turn to **182**. If you want to tackle the steeper climb up the side of the crag, turn to **35**. If you want to take the longer, but easier, route up the side of the escarpment, turn to **322**.

143

Two days from Lake Cauldron and halfway across the kingdom, as you head west towards the capital Chalannabrad, you enter a lonely wood. (Move the Day of the Week on 2.) Thankfully, Balthazar Sturm's influence does not appear to have touched this part of Femphrey, but that doesn't mean that there aren't other dangers to be wary of. If you have a Sabretooth Fang, turn to **329**. If not, *Test your Luck*. If you are Lucky, turn to **329**; if you are Unlucky, turn to **216**.

144

You come to the edge of another lava lake, crossed by a causeway. As you watch, this pathway breaks up and sinks into the rising magma. You are not going to be able to get out this way! You must add 1 to your TIME TRACK and sprint back to the junction, to go the other way. Turn to **174**.

145

Suddenly the ground begins to shake beneath your feet and you stumble, dust and tiny stones falling in a shower from the roof of the tunnel. *Test your Luck.* If you are Lucky, turn to **68**. If you are Unlucky, turn to **167**.

146

As you descend into the rift the surrounding light levels lower still further until you see everything through a twilit gloom. It is hard to make out much that isn't quite close already and everything else just appears as formless stygian shapes. You have not gone far when you find yourself approaching one of these dark silhouettes and see that it is in fact the carcass of a huge Bullwhale. Half of it has already been consumed by whatever killed it and the submarine carrion-feeders that have been picking at it since. Curved white ribs, the size of roof-beams, protrude from the rotting grey flesh of the whale's side. You have heard legends told of monsters such as this swallowing ships whole, and so having vast hoards of treasure hidden inside their bellies. It is just possible that there might be something worth having still lying in the guts of this decomposing brute. If you want to brave the innards of the Bullwhale, turn to **31**. If you would rather push on with your quest to find the Sunken Temple of Hydana, turn to **179**.

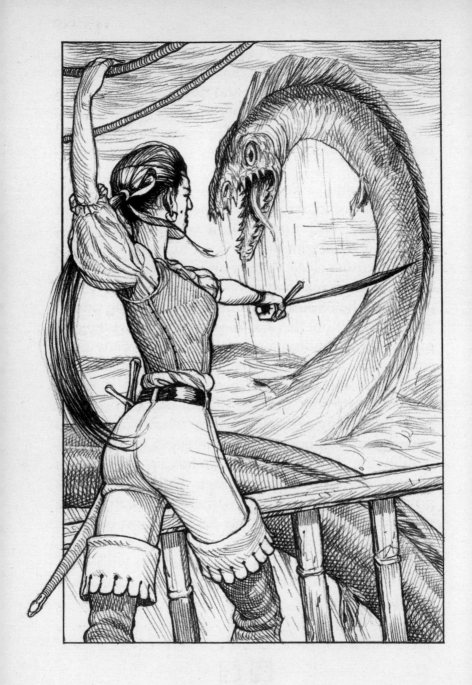

147

A shout from the crow's nest has you and Katarina running for the bulwarks. 'Over there, Captain!' the lookout bellows, pointing out to sea. 'Eel spoor!' The sea beyond the *Tempest* is in turmoil. As you watch, three great grey heads emerge from the churning white water, rising into the air on long, leathery-skinned bodies as thick as tree trunks. The Great Eels – from which the Eelsea gets its name – open fang-filled maws, ready to snatch any tasty morsel they can from the deck of the ship – and that includes you! With Wyrmbiter in your hands once more, you charge forward to meet the sea-serpents in combat, Captain Katarina at your side, scimitar drawn. The Captain takes on one of the fearsome sea monsters, leaving you to tackle the other two.

	SKILL	STAMINA
First GREAT EEL	9	10
Second GREAT EEL	8	9

If Prospero Seacharmer is with you, you need only fight the first of the monstrous Eels, as the wizard takes on the other with his potent magicks. If you win your battle, the Great Eels' loathsome bodies sink back under the waves, leaving the *Tempest* free to go on its way again. Turn to **359**.

148

You eventually reach a spot where several ravines converge. Still a long way ahead, you are now able to make out a towering stack of wind-sculpted rock, rising many metres into the sky above the canyon floor. You can't shake the feeling that ultimately this is where you need to get to. Two more gorges lead south from here, but neither appears to head directly towards the wind-carved stack. If you have the codeword *Detnuh* written on your *Adventure Sheet*, turn to **129** at once. If not, which way will you head now? Left (turn to **99**) or right (turn to **58**)?

149

Hearing a shout from above you, you look up and can't help but smile as you see Corbo Rundum's hot air balloon sailing overhead. 'Looks like you could do with a lift!' the balloonist calls down from the basket, and a moment later the end of a rope drops down beside you. 'Sorry, no time to land! Grab hold and hang on!' Not needing to be told twice, you grab hold of the rope as Corbo shouts, 'Up, up and away!'

The balloon rises steadily into the air, carrying you higher and higher over fields, towns and rivers that rapidly dwindle into miniature beneath you. Higher and higher you climb, travelling further and further over the storm-wracked landscape as the balloon is carried on the wind towards the middle of the kingdom.

'Thar she blows!' Corbo suddenly shouts over the rising gale. 'The one that got away!'

Ahead of the balloon you see a tempestuous mass of anvil-headed storm-clouds. And there, amidst the towering thunderheads, is the brass fish you saw all those days ago, after the devastation of Vastarin; Balthazar Sturm's weather-altering ship. It looks huge up close – bigger than an Arantian galleon! The fish's sparkling crystal eyes are observation domes at the front of the vessel; its fins, steering sails and its tail, a vast rudder. In the side of the vessel you can make out a round access hatch with a rail-guarded balcony in front of it.

If you have the codeword *Mortsleam* written on your *Adventure Sheet*, turn to **363**. If not, but today is Stormsday, you should also turn to **363**.

If none of these conditions are met, as Corbo's balloon sails over the top of the *Eye of the Storm*, with a hasty prayer to the gods, you let go of the rope ... Turn to **14**.

150

You open the sluice-valves so that they all feed the water backed up behind the dam through the outlet channel quickly and safely. With a great rushing roar, the outflow river becomes a raging torrent but it does not burst its banks and steadily the water level on the lakeward side of the dam begins to drop. You have relieved the pressure on the dam and saved the village as a result. Regain 2 LUCK points.

Giles and the rest of the villagers are full of gratitude for what you have done for them. They insist on rewarding you by giving you what little produce they can scrape together. When you eventually leave to continue your quest, you do so with 4 extra Meals in your Provisions, a Jug of Cider (which, when drunk, will restore up to 3 STAMINA points and add 1 to your Attack Strength for the next battle you fight) and 10 Gold Pieces.

Two days later (move the Day of the Week on 2), the incessant rain has stopped, and you reach the borders of the wilderness known as the Howling Plains. Turn to **83**.

151

After some asking around, you find yourself inside the establishment of one Mendelev Quicksilver. The crazed-looking pseudo-scientist – with his scorched robe and soot-smeared face – claims to have just what you need, a Potion of Underwater Breathing, but it will set you back a tidy 7 Gold Pieces. If you are happy (and able) to pay this, add the Potion of Underwater Breathing to your *Adventure Sheet* and turn to **252**. If not, you will have to visit the Guild of Artificers (turn to **181**) or the Academy of Naval Sorcerers (turn to **221**) instead.

152

The *tap-tap-tap* of your footsteps echoes around the gallery, the acoustics of the chamber having an amplifying effect on the vibrations. Before you know it, the stalactites are singing with strained harmonics, producing their own high-pitched whine. Hearing a crack, you immediately launch yourself across the chamber, determined to get to the other side as quickly as you can. Roll one die and add 1; this is the number of stone spears that break free of the roof and hit you (lose that many STAMINA points). If you survive, turn to **171**.

153

Making a series of peculiar gestures while muttering incomprehensible syllables under his breath, Matteus casts his spell. You half expect to feel different in some way or for your boots to show signs of having been enchanted, but nothing looks or feels any different. However Matteus assures you that the spell will have worked. 'To activate the enchantment, simply click your heels together three times,' the mage explains, 'and you will find that a journey that would normally take several days will take only a matter of minutes.' You will be told in the text when you can activate the enchantment, but for now add the Seven League Boots to your *Adventure Sheet*. Do you want to use the boots straight away? If so, turn to **2**; if not, turn to **193**.

154

You push the lever over and it locks into position, preventing you from moving it back again. You watch, slightly disconcerted, as the brass balls start to spin faster. The machine is generating even higher levels of static electricity now – you can feel it crackling from your fingertips.

There is a sudden crack, like a lightning strike, and a ball of scintillating energy pops into existence inside the chamber. Great arcs of static fly from its crackling outer corona. Tasting the enchantments bound to your magical sword, the Fetch glides towards you, intent on draining the blade's magical potential. You must fight this curious electrical creature.

FETCH   SKILL 11   STAMINA 6

If you are fighting the ball of scintillating electricity using Wyrmbiter and you win an Attack Round, both you and the Fetch suffer 2 points of damage as the creature shorts out! If you have another weapon with which to fight the Fetch (such as a Warhammer or a Mace) you will not suffer this damage, but to change weapons will take one Attack Round, during which the Fetch gets an unopposed strike against you.

If you win your battle, the Fetch disappears in a violent flash. Unable to do anything else to damage the Lightning Generator, you have no choice but to leave the room and return to the stairwell. Turn to **54**.

155

Not much further on, the tunnel runs to an end within a spectacular cavern that is thick with huge crystal-line growths. They are a myriad of translucent col-ours. One crystal stands out more than the rest. It glimmers with an inner flickering light. Looking closer you see the crystal's internal fire seemingly form the letter I. (If you want to take it, add the Fire

Crystal and its letter to your *Adventure Sheet*.) Retreating from the dead-end, you return to the last T-junction and take the other path. Turn to **125**.

156
Striding over the wreckage of the fallen automaton, you grasp the handle of the door in front of you. If you have started a fire, add 2 to your DAMAGE score. If your DAMAGE score is now 12 or higher, turn to **137**; if it is still less than 12, turn to **368**.

157
For three days you head north-east, under an almost permanently overcast sky. (Move the Day of the Week on 3.) Gradually, green fields give way to scrubby heathland, which in turn becomes the foetid mire that borders the shores of mist-shrouded Lake Eerie and the town that takes its name from the sinister mere.

The town lies under a dark cloud; threatening storm-clouds mass overhead, turning the day so dark that you could have sworn it was dusk. There is an air of anxious expectancy within the town of Eerieside, as if the building pressure of the storm was affecting the townsfolk in some way too. Arriving within the market square you come across a gathering hunting party. Approaching a lean-faced man with a wolfhound restrained on a chain, you ask him what has brought the hunters to Eerieside.

'Haven't you heard?' he asks in a conspiratorial whisper. 'Word is the Stormdrake has awoken and is on the loose.'

The Stormdrake – you have heard tell of this monster yourself. The legend goes that when the Stormdrake flies, apocalyptic storms will assault the land, leaving waste in its wake. Can it really be that such a creature actually exists? You had thought that the terrible weather was down to Balthazar Sturm's Weather Machine.

'So you're all planning on tracking it to its lair and putting an end to it,' you say.

'That's right. And put an end to this terrible weather,' the hunter says. 'Only we're not in this together. The mayor's offering a reward to whoever brings back proof that the monster's dead. Here, you look like you might be a bit handy with that sword of yours. Why don't we go after the Stormdrake together? I'll split the reward with you, fifty-fifty. What do you say?'

Do you want to join the hunter and go after the Stormdrake? If so, turn to **313**. If not, you see no point in hanging around the dour town of Eerieside – you've been here before and it's a grim, unwelcoming place – so set off again. Another two days of walking brings you into the foothills of the Witchtooth Mountains. Move the Day of the Week on 2 and turn to **250**.

⚄ ⚁

158

Having crossed the Siltbed River, not wanting to draw unwanted attention to yourself from the sallow-skinned Lendlelanders, you are grateful when the trail left by the storm leads you off the main highway and into a low range of hills to the south.

Cresting another rise amidst the scrubby hills you are surprised to see what looks like a fighting force massing in the valley below. Lendleland is known for the quality of its horses but many of them are employed by tribes of barbarian horsemen, and you are looking down on one such barbarian encampment right now. But why is an army of horsemen massing so close to the border of Femphrey at this time? Could it have anything to do with the strange storm that devastated Vastarin?

Do you want to try to infiltrate the barbarian camp by stealth, to find out what's going on (turn to 307), or would you rather steer well clear and go on your way through the hills (turn to 175)?

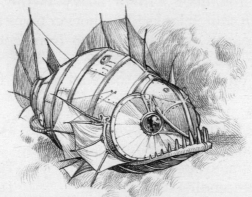

159

The Keeper raises one arm and points it straight at you. A spiralling vortex of air hits you, picking you up and carrying you backwards, through the natural arch. For a moment you think that you are going to be dropped back down the side of the stack but the conjured whirlwind carries you gently to the sandy floor of the canyon. Your audience with the mysterious Keeper of the Four Winds concluded, you set off again, making your way back through the Screaming Canyon, eventually reaching the borderlands of the Howling Plains. Move the Day of the Week on 1 and turn to **394**.

160

The spiralling staircase takes you deep into the rocky strata of the crag beneath the tower. The staircase is unlit, but just as the light from above is failing, a faint light appears at the bottom of the stairs. You come to a small iron door with a heavy-looking padlock securing it shut. It looks like whoever owns the tower doesn't want whatever is inside from getting out. However you notice that there is a large iron key hanging on a hook on the wall beside the door. Will you:

Unlock the door and open it?	Turn to **335**
Listen at the door before deciding whether to open it or not?	Turn to **285**
Keep descending the staircase?	Turn to **188**

161

For the rest of the day you are treated like a king. Healers tend your wounds, a notable physician plies you with restorative elixirs, the local blacksmith makes repairs to your armour, and that night you are guest of honour at a great feast. The next morning, having spent the night in the most comfortable bed you have ever slept in, in the finest hostelry in the town, you set off for the Howling Plains again. (Restore both your SKILL and STAMINA scores to their *Initial* levels and regain up to 2 LUCK points.) Three days later you find yourself in the baking scrub that becomes the dusty desolation of the Howling Plains. Move the Day of the Week on 4 and turn to **83**.

162

Turning the lens by 90 degrees, you wait to see what will happen. In only a matter of seconds, the huge magnifying glass has focused the sun's rays entering through the crystal dome of the roof, projecting a beam of concentrated sunlight at a point on the ground far beneath the Weather Machine. Curious to see the result for yourself, you peer through the telescope and are horrified to see that the Burning Glass has set fire to the thatched roof of a mill far below. (Lose 1 LUCK point.) What will you do now?

Smash the lens?	Turn to **192**
Flip the lens so that the concave side faces into the room?	Turn to **139**
Leave the Sun room before you cause any more suffering?	Turn to **258**

163

You are halfway across the hold when the ship's skeletal crew animate. You have trespassed within their galleon and must pay the price. As the skeletons come to life, you make a break for freedom, skeletal fingers clawing at your clothes and body.

SKELETON CREW   SKILL 6   STAMINA 12

Fight the skeletal sailors as if they were one creature, as you run the gauntlet of clawing hands and snapping skulls. If you reduce the Crew's STAMINA to zero, it means that you have made it through the hold, escaping through the hole in the ship's side. Thankfully the undead sailors do not attempt to follow you out of the ship but you decide against exploring the wreck further and so make your way back to the fissure in the sea-bed. Turn to 6.

164

Giving yourself a bit of a run up, you launch yourself at the door, your shoulder square on to the iron-banded boards. Roll three dice. If the total rolled is less than or equal to your STAMINA, the door bursts open under the force of your charge (turn to 247). If the number rolled is greater than your STAMINA score, the door resists your best efforts to break it open and you jar your shoulder badly (lose 1 SKILL point and 2 STAMINA points). You have no choice other than to try more conventional means to open the door (turn to 134).

165

You find a barge owner called Koll who, along with his wife and teenage son, is making the journey east, taking spices to sell in the market towns of Bathoria. (Deduct 6 Gold Pieces.) Travelling by boat along the incredible River of Fire is a very pleasant way to spend a day. (Move the Day of the Week on 1 and regain 1 STAMINA point on top of what you would anyway.)

During the journey, Koll tells you that he heard from another bargeman moored at Shard Wharf, that the south-west of the kingdom is suffering terrible floods at the moment, and that there is even talk of the mythical Stormdrake having taken to the skies once again.

Parting company with the barge owner and his family at last, you proceed again on foot and are soon scrambling up the black volcanic slopes of Mount Pyre itself. Turn to **109**.

166

You emerge from the winding chasms of the Screaming Canyon at the base of an imposing stack of sand-scoured and wind-carved rock. It rises vertically from the valley floor, a column of narrow ledges, treacherous overhangs and sheer rock faces, but you know, within your heart of hearts, that the mystical aid you have travelled all this way to find, is to be found at the top of this stack. If you have a Rope and Grapple or a Potion of Levitation (and you would like to use it now), turn to **256**. If not, turn to **196**.

167

The shaking continues, and gets worse. The mine must be suffering another earthquake. You sprint forwards as a pit-prop crashes to the floor behind you, bringing half the roof with it. Another prop, loosened by the seismic shocks, comes down on top of you. (Lose 3 STAMINA points). Pulling yourself free of the fallen beam, nursing a lump the size of a phoenix's egg on your head, you stagger onwards as the rumbling subsides again. Turn to **68**.

168

'Zephyrus!' you call. 'Zephyrus, I need you!' Suddenly the wind begins to rise, blowing from the west.

Hurtling towards you, carried on the wind, is an ethereal figure, with the upper body of a powerfully-muscled giant but who, from the waist down, is a whirling vortex of air. In fact – he *is* the wind!

'You called and I have come,' the Air Elemental says with a voice formed from the howling gale. 'Command and I shall obey!'

'Carry me to the Eye of the Storm!' you order Zephyrus, shouting to be heard over the gale. (Cross Zephyrus's name off your *Adventure Sheet* – you may not call on his help again.)

The Elemental manifestation of the West Wind lifts you high into the sky. Fields, towns and rivers fly by beneath you as Zephyrus carries you further and further over the storm-wracked kingdom of Femphrey, now far below you.

And then you see it! Zephyrus is carrying you directly towards a broiling mass of near-black storm-clouds – and there, amidst the towering thunder-heads is the brass fish you saw all those days ago, after the devastation of Vastarin; Balthazar Sturm's abominable Weather Machine. It looks huge – bigger than a Bullwhale! Its sparkling crystal eyes are observation domes in the front of the vessel, its fins and tail, steering sails and a vast rudder. In the side of the elementally-powered vessel you see an access hatch with a railed balcony before it.

If you have the codeword *Mortsleam* written on your *Adventure Sheet*, turn to **363**. If not, but today is Stormsday, you should also turn to **363**.

If none of these conditions are met, with one final breath of wind, Zephyrus sends you on your way towards the approaching vessel that lies within the eye of the storm (turn to 14).

169

The tunnel ascends in a tightening spiral until it emerges onto the inner face of the volcano's crater. Smoke and foul-smelling fumes rise from the bubbling lava that you can see far, far below you, making you gag and your eyes water. The path you have been following continues as a ledge that curves around until it reaches a nest – of sorts – apparently made from charcoal-black branches in a cleft in the rock. But what sort of creature would build its nest in the cone of a volcano?

That question is answered when you hear a screeching cry and look up. Blinking through the shimmering heat-haze you see a hideous, bat-winged creature flapping towards you. It has ugly, humanoid features, bat-like wings in place of arms and its stringy legs end in razor-sharp talons. Shrieking, the Blisterwing attacks!

BLISTERWING   SKILL 6   STAMINA 6

For the duration of this battle, reduce your Attack Strength by 1, due to the smoke and noxious vapours rising from the volcano's cone. If you kill the nasty creature, do you want to climb the ledge to search its nest (turn to 199), or will you re-trace your steps instead, returning to the junction to continue along the tunnel the other way (turn to 219)?

170

Cranking the lever to the left appears to cut-off the feed to the lightning conductor but the spheres are still spinning and electricity is still being generated. Small bolts of lightning leap from the crackling columns, striking at random the chamber walls. One finds your sword and gives you a jolt (lose 2 STAMINA points). Another spark finds a discarded oily rag which bursts into flame. (Add 1 to your DAMAGE score and record that you have started a fire on your *Adventure Sheet*.) Quickly backing out of the chamber as the fire starts to spread, you head back to the landing. Turn to **54**.

171

Leaving the cave behind you, you enter another tunnel that twists and turns until it finally emerges into another large, natural chamber, deep below the mountains. The arch of a natural stone bridge spans the centre of the cavern, the floor of which drops away below it, lined with the upward pointing spears of ancient stalagmites. The only way onward is over the bridge. You are halfway across when you are assaulted by a high-pitched, high-speed clicking sound, and two Giant Bats swoop down from their roost among the stalactites in the roof of the cave and attack.

	SKILL	STAMINA
First GIANT BAT	5	7
Second GIANT BAT	5	6

If you lose two Attack Rounds in a row, turn to **201**. You may choose to escape from the Bats by running across the bridge, but must forfeit one Attack Round in the process. (You may also drink a Potion of Levitation before this battle, if you wish, which means you can ignore the two lost Attack Rounds rule, but you also then forfeit the chance to escape from the fight.) If you leave this cavern with your life, turn to **273**.

172

The moment you set the last tumbler to the right position the Juggernaut grinds to an immediate halt. Steam hisses from the joints of its steel limbs, accompanied by a descending metal whine, as its sorcery-imbued mechanisms power down. You have stopped the seemingly unstoppable! Regain 1 LUCK point and turn to **156**.

173

Wyrmbiter begins to glow with its own esoteric energies. In response you see other features appear within the whirling cyclone of dust and sand as arms reach out of it, huge hands ready to pick you up and toss you into the air – all composed from abrasive sand and grit. The Sandstorm isn't going to give up the balloonist without a fight.

SANDSTORM   SKILL 8   STAMINA 10

(If today is Windsday, add 1 to the Sandstorm's SKILL score and 2 points to its STAMINA.) If you lose an Attack Round to the Elemental, roll one die and consult the table below to see what damage you suffer. (You may use LUCK to reduce any damage caused in the usual way.)

Dice Roll	Attack and Damage
1–2	Sand-blasted – the Elemental hurls itself against you, bombarding your body with abrasive sand. Lose 3 STAMINA points.
3–5	Fists of Fury – the Elemental hits you with its sandpaper rough fists. Lose 2 STAMINA points.
6	Swept off your feet – the Elemental lifts you into the air on a spiralling column of air and then lets you fall back down to the ground. Roll 1 dice and lose that many STAMINA points.

If you manage to defeat the Sand Elemental, turn to **223**.

174

You find yourself running through a cloud of venting, sulphurous gas but press on regardless. Moments later, you emerge on the other side and facing another junction. (Add 1 to your TIME TRACK.) Will you head left (turn to **204**) or right (turn to **224**)?

175

Now that you know there is a barbarian army gathering in the next valley, you start to feel uneasy. You may be a renowned hero, but a lone adventurer against the might of an army on horseback wouldn't stand a chance – not even you!

You are roused from your thoughts by the sound of horses' hoofs on the stony track ahead of you, and a moment later catch sight of two sallow-skinned Lendlelander horsemen coming your way. You have accidentally run into a patrol from the camp back in the valley. Will you:

Try to hide from the horsemen?	Turn to **235**
Prepare to face them in battle?	Turn to **264**
Run for it?	Turn to **205**

176

Shouting a battle-cry, you charge the Giant with your weapon raised high above your head. The Giant gives a bellow and prepares to meet your attack with his huge tree-trunk club.

GIANT   SKILL 9   STAMINA 11

If the Giant makes a successful strike against you, roll one die and consult the table below.

Dice roll	Effect
1–2	You suffer a glancing blow from the club. Lose 2 STAMINA points.
3–4	The Giant delivers a powerful strike. Lose 3 STAMINA points.
5	You are knocked down. Lose 2 STAMINA points and reduce your Attack Strength by 1 point for the next Attack Round, as you pick yourself up.
6	You are sent flying. Lose 3 STAMINA points and reduce your Attack Strength by 1 point for the next Attack Round, as you struggle to get to your feet.

If you slay the Giant, you are able to continue on your way again. You travel for another two days without meeting any other resistance. Move the Day of the Week on 2 and turn to **250**.

177

Kicking off from a sturdy oak joist, you launch yourself at the door. The sea-rotted planks crumble as you collide with them and break into the ship's strongroom, as you suspected you would. Standing there amidst the rotted remains of treasure sacks and crab-pillaged boxes is a treasure chest of much sturdier construction – it's made from solid iron. Although the surface is red with rust you are unable to force the strong box. The only way you are going to open it is if you have a Golden Key that fits its gleaming golden lock. If you do, turn to the paragraph with the same number of 'teeth' as the key. If not, you have no choice but to leave the sunken treasure room (turn to **163**).

178

You wend your way between the towering cliffs, under the merciless stare of the Sun Goddess, sweat dripping from your body. Your attention is suddenly caught by something flashing in the sunlight. Shielding your eyes from the sun, you see the Birdman just in time, the sun reflecting from the blade of the crude spear it is clutching in its taloned hands.

BIRDMAN   SKILL 8   STAMINA 8

With the Birdman dead you will be able to continue your journey again. Turn to **79**.

179

As you progress further into the rift, so the encroaching gloom increases. As the open ocean appears ahead of you, you find yourself standing at the edge of another underwater precipice. Cautiously you peer over the edge; the continental shelf drops away into abyssal darkness with no sign of ever ending. You dread to think what lives down there. Looking right you can see nothing, but then you look to the left. Could that be a fallen column? Is it just possible that you have reached the Sunken Temple of the Sea God at last?

Just as you're thinking that nothing's ever that easy, you feel a rumbling beneath your feet, a disturbance in the water around you, and then it appears. Rising from the abyssal depths of the ocean is some nightmarish demon of the deep. It looks like a hideous cross between a monstrous crustacean and a giant octopus – and it is huge! The monster pulls itself up onto the shelf with its coiling tentacles and starts to drag itself towards you, two huge pincer-claws snapping menacingly. From the mass of flesh that is its body, looming above you, you fancy you see a watery eye watching you intently. You sense that the monster is intent on devouring you, but how are you going to defend yourself against such a creature?

If you have the Spark of Life, and want to use it, multiply the number associated with it by 20 and turn to that paragraph. If not, will you draw your sword (turn to **242**), or attempt to flee (turn to **282**).

180

Perplexed by the problem of the sluices, much as you would like to help Giles and the people of Tumbleweir, you wouldn't have a clue what you were doing and might actually make things worse for them.

It is only when you are outside the sluice-house that you realise that the consequences of your failure to solve the problem could be catastrophic. Terrible creaking groans are coming from the dam and you can see trickles of water cascading from between the wooden struts and copper pipework that make up the structure. Time is running out for the people of Tumbleweir, but there is nothing you can do ... Is there?

If you have the codeword *Naromroc* written on your *Adventure Sheet*, turn to **355** at once. If not, turn to **372**.

181

Having stated your business you are ushered into the guild and taken before a tall, bespectacled man, wearing a heavy leather apron and impressive-looking tool-belt. When you enter his workshop he is busy putting the finishing touches to a large spherical contraption of brass, glass and wood, big enough to carry a man. 'It's a Submarine Conveyancing Carriage,' he explains, taking in the uncomprehending look on your face. 'Let me introduce myself. I'm Brindle Deep but most people call me Briny – as in Briny Deep. Get it? Well anyway, I'm something of a specialist when it comes to submersibles and submarine matters.' Briny gets very excited when you tell him what it is you need. 'Now that I *can* help you with,' he declares proudly. 'I've been working on my patented Breathing Helmet for some time now; I just need somebody to test it out for me.' He hands you a heavy brass helmet, with a glass viewing pane in the front, attached to two brass cylinders. 'The helmet goes over your head and the cylinders, which strap onto your back, feed a controlled stream of air into it, allowing you to breathe underwater. As it's still only a prototype, I won't charge you if you'd like to try it out for me at sea. Just try to bring it back in one piece.' If you want to accept Briny Deep's generous, if rather unnerving, offer add the Breathing Helmet to your *Adventure Sheet* and turn to **252**. If you would rather not risk your life trying out some untested new-fangled device, will you pay a visit to the Brotherhood of Alchemists (turn to **151**) or the Academy of Naval Sorcerers (turn to **221**) instead?

182

Clambering over mossy rocks and along the muddy paths that skirt the fast-flowing river, you make good time and soon see the tower more clearly above you, as the twisting watercourse curves around the peak from its summit. Rounding a bend you see that the path you are following comes to an abrupt end before a sheer rock face. The only way onwards is to cross the river where it surges between the slippery water-smoothed boulders of a course of rapids. Cautiously you set out across the precarious steppingstones formed by the boulders.

You are halfway across the river when the surging flow starts to quicken and white-crested waves begin breaking against the stones on which you are balancing. Suddenly a large wave rises up from the river, looking like it is about to crash right over your head, but then stops. You see an indistinct face appear at its crest, while two spumes of water separate from its sides and lash out at you. You are under attack from an Undine – a malicious water spirit – that is intent on knocking you off the rocks in the hope that it can then drown you in the river.

UNDINE   SKILL 7   STAMINA 7

(If today is Seaday, increase both the Undine's SKILL and STAMINA scores by 1 point. However, if today is Fireday, reduce the Undine's SKILL and STAMINA scores by 1.) Being made from the waters of the river, the Undine batters you with jets of water which will only cause you 1 STAMINA point of damage if the Elemental creature hits you. However, every time the Undine wins an Attack Round, roll one die; on a roll of 6 turn to **212** immediately. If you defeat the water spirit, you are able to continue on your way to the top of the peak (turn to **51**).

183

A savage snarl rips cuts through the tormented air, as cold and as sharp as the freezing talons that suddenly make a grab for you out of the snowstorm. You are caught across the shoulder. (Lose 3 STAMINA points, unless you are wearing a Sun Talisman, in which case you only lose 2.) Turn to **261**.

184

Opening the door you step down into a cramped and cluttered cabin. It is filled with all manner of curious paraphernalia. There are shelves crammed with books, a map-desk, and there may even be a bed in here somewhere. If so, it must be under all the maps and charts that cover nearly every surface. Among the papers littering the desk, you find a large map of the kingdom of Femphrey, a leather-bound journal that would appear to be the ship's log book, and a set of plans for some strange-looking apparatus. On the other side of the cabin is another plain wooden door. Will you:

Examine the map?	Turn to **198**
Take a look at the Log Book?	Turn to **215**
Study the plans?	Turn to **229**
Open the other wooden door?	Turn to **259**
Return to the landing?	Turn to **54**

185

You enter the tunnel beyond the archway and follow its twists and turns until you come to yet another T-junction. Do you want to turn left (turn to **155**) or right (turn to **125**)?

186

You pull down the wooden planks and advance warily along the passageway. Your lantern casts eerie, flickering shadows onto the enclosing walls, causing you to jump more than once at imagined phantoms. There is a loud pop as something suddenly gives beneath your foot. You immediately take a step back but hear another pop as you crush something beneath your heel. A cloud of grey-green spores erupts into the air around you from the burst puffballs covering the tunnel floor. So that is why the tunnel had been closed off – the place is infested with poisonous fungi! You start to cough uncontrollably as your body reacts to the toxins in the spores. (Lose 4 STAMINA points and 1 SKILL point as you become dizzy and disorientated.) You stagger back out of the tunnel, gulping down great lungfuls of clean, damp air, between convulsing coughs, as you stumble into the other tunnel. Turn to **310**.

187

Weakening under your relentless assault, Sturm's watery body evaporates and disappears. Can it be that you have beaten him at last? (If you have the codeword *Demlaceb* written on your *Adventure Sheet*, turn to **397** immediately.)

Your relief is short-lived when a howling gale assaults the bridge. You are pushed back by the force of the raging wind. A cruelly smiling face appears within the whirlwind before you, a face that is now horribly familiar – Balthazar Sturm! But what can withstand the awesome power of a hurricane, as the mountains resist the unrelenting wind?

If you possess a Clay Statuette, turn the name etched into it into a number using the code A=1, B=2, C=3 … Z=26. Add the numbers together and turn to the paragraph with the same number. If not, turn to **284**.

188

The light gets brighter with every descending turn of the stair until you finally reach the bottom. A strong wind whipping at your body, you find yourself standing at the edge of a stone platform which juts out over a precipitous drop down into the river valley below. You have passed right through the over-hanging cliff of the crag! You quickly take in the rest of your surroundings. On the wall behind you hang what appear to be a number of backpacks. A heavy-looking chain secured to the platform by means of a large iron ring trails over the edge of the drop. Will you:

Look at the backpacks more closely?　　　Turn to **202**
Pull on the chain?　　　Turn to **255**

Return to the locked iron door?	Turn to **285**
Ascend the staircase again and explore the upper levels of this strange tower (if you haven't done so already)?	Turn to **220**
Ascend the staircase and leave the tower?	Turn to **398**

189

And so you come in sight of Lake Cauldron. Also known as Crystal Lake, due to the fact that the minerals in the water, carried from the volcanic Mount Pyre by the River of Fire, react with hot springs in the latter to form crystals, it takes you the best part of a day to circumnavigate it but as dusk falls you see the twinkling lights of Shard Wharf ahead of you.

This trading post has grown up where the River of Fire empties into Lake Cauldron. Mount Pyre lies within the mountainous highlands of Mauristatia that stand at the heart of the Old World, and is still some days' travel further east. A number of boats navigate the steaming river trading goods between Femphrey and the principalities of Mauristatia. Passage upriver will cost you 6 Gold Pieces. If you would like to buy passage on one of these boats to speed your journey along (and can afford the money), turn to **165**. If not, you will have to continue on foot through the rugged terrain that borders the gently simmering waterway (turn to **232**).

190*

'Fathomdeep Mine' reads the peeling sign over the dark tunnel mouth cut into the foot of the mountain. When the Dwarfs abandoned this place, they left all the headgear behind. Winch systems have been left to rust where they stand, along with the mine carts they pulled, and the tracks the carts ran on. You approach the boarded-up entrance and prise off enough planks to allow you access. Lighting your lantern, you step into the dripping darkness beyond.

Water plops incessantly from the roof of the tunnel into the puddles that have formed between the sleepers of the rails, and you are reminded of the fact that this used to be a Dwarf mine when you are forced to bend almost double to pass along certain stretches. Thankfully, not much further on you reach a junction, where you find you are able to stand upright again. The mine cart tracks continue into darkness along the left-hand tunnel, while to the right is another passageway which looks like it was constructed solely for miners making their way on foot.

Do you want to follow the tunnel to the right (turn to 5), or would you prefer to keep following the mine cart tracks (turn to 290)?

191

As you prepare to fight the solidifying Magma Beast, another one rises from the oozing orange lava and slowly strides towards you. Start by fighting the first Magma Beast by itself. After three Attack Rounds the second lava monster will reach you and join the fray.

	SKILL	STAMINA
First MAGMA BEAST	8	9
Second MAGMA BEAST	7	8

(If today is Fireday, add 2 points to the monsters' STAMINA scores.) If you lose four Attack Rounds in a row, the Magma Beasts' relentless onslaught pushes you from the rock you are standing on and you plunge into the lava flow – there is no way you can survive that! If you defeat both of the Beasts, without being consigned to a fiery grave, turn to 251.

192

Only a Mace or a Warhammer will smash the lens. If you do not have either, turn back to 213 and make another choice. If you do, you bring the heavy head of the weapon down on top of the lens which shatters under the impact, sending shards of glass whickering through the air. Roll one die, divide the number by two (rounding fractions up) and deduct that many STAMINA points. If you survive, you may also add 1 to your DAMAGE score, and then turn to **258**.

193

'It's time you were on your way,' Matteus Charm-weaver informs you. 'I will petition the Council to work what magicks they can to lessen the impact of Sturm's weather attacks but it will not be enough to stop him and his craft – that will be up to you! May the gods smile upon your endeavours.'

And with that you depart the College of Mages. But where will you travel to first in your quest to find the means to defeat Balthazar Sturm's bound Elementals?

The Eelsea?	Turn to **64**
The Witchtooth Line?	Turn to **157**
Mount Pyre?	Turn to **22**
The Howling Plains?	Turn to **4**

194

'I fort you was a hero,' the Giant mocks you, 'but yoo ain't nothin' but a coward.' With that, he hefts the tree-trunk club in his huge hands and takes a swing at you, sending you flying. Your flight across the clearing is brought to an abrupt halt by a tall oak. (Lose 4 STAMINA points.) The Giant lumbers across the clearing to where you are lying, to see if you're still alive. 'Now, are yoo goin' ta wrestle me or wot?' Will you accept the brute's challenge (turn to **210**), or draw your sword and attack (turn to **176**)?

195

Your wanderings bring you to the edge of Lake Eerie itself. A forlorn curlew cry is the only sound that disturbs the unnatural stillness hanging over the lake, and then something breaks the water some metres from the shore. The wolfhound barks excitedly, pulling at its chain. Suddenly, something black and monstrous bursts from the lake in a spray of brackish water that drenches you, Sylas and the dog, cutting short the animal's cries. 'By all the gods!' is all Sylas can manage before a grotesque reptilian head shoots forwards on the end of a long neck and the hunter falls wounded to the ground. As you arm yourself once more, you realise that you are facing another creature from legend – the Eerieside Beast. With a croaking cry, the water monster attacks.

EERIESIDE BEAST   SKILL 9   STAMINA 12

If you kill the monster, its lifeless body slips back beneath the dark waters of the lake (no doubt there to become a meal for something else, just as terrible). Turn to 386.

196

With only your hands and feet to help you, you begin your ascent. *Test your Skill* and then *Test your Luck*. If you either fail the SKILL test or you are Unlucky, turn to 226. If you pass the SKILL test and are Lucky as well, turn to 256.

197

The metal spars and joists continue to reshape themselves into a towering figure as you sprint across the detritus-strewn chamber, desperately trying to make it to the smaller archway on the far side. *Test your Luck.* If you are Lucky, you make it unscathed (turn to 117). If you are Unlucky, a rusted pipe-work arm slams into you, sending you flying back across the chamber. Lose 4 STAMINA points and turn to 67.

198

The map has been covered with scrawled arrows and handwritten notes. The south-eastern extent of Femphrey is annotated with 'Burning Glass successful' while to the north-east are written the words 'Cryo-Engine used here'. To the south-west has been written 'Flooding due to increase in rainfall observed'. Just south of the border with Lendleland is a picture of a tower and above that, back in Femphrey the village of Vastarin with the words 'Trial run' above it. Interesting as all this may be it's not going to help you halt Sturm's plans of conquest. Do you want to:

Look at something else on the desk?	Turn to 243
Open the other wooden door?	Turn to 259
Return to the landing?	Turn to 54

199

Risking life and limb, you clamber up to the Blisterwing's nest, and come face to face with its squawking brood. As you search the nest, the young Blisterwings snap at your hands and arms. (Lose 2 STAMINA points.) You do not find anything of value within the tangle of fire-blackened branches and so carefully make your way back down the inside of the cone. Re-entering the tunnel, you return to the junction and carry on past it. Turn to **219**.

200

As the creature closes on you, so does another dweller of the deep – this time the sea monster that almost swallowed you whole! Having missed out on a tasty snack, it's been after you ever since. Only now that it's found you, it's also found the Abyssal Horror – which would make a much more satisfying meal! The Leviathan closes on the monster, angler-fish jaws stretching wide as the horror prepares to defend itself as best it can with its constricting tentacles and snapping pincers. As the two sea monsters engage in their titanic struggle, you make for the Sunken Temple. Regain 1 LUCK point, cross the word *Retsnom* off your *Adventure Sheet*, and turn to **222**.

201

Either due to sheer luck, or by somehow consciously coordinating their attacks, the bats swoop down at you together and buffet you with their wings. *Test your Skill*. If you are successful, you teeter on the edge of the bridge but manage to regain your balance just in time (return to **171** and continue your battle with the bats). If you fail, you lose your balance and slip from the bridge for your body to be speared on the stalagmites below. If this happens, your adventure is over.

202

Taking one of the packs from its peg on the wall you open it and discover that it is actually made up of two compartments. The bottom one is empty and could be used in the same way as the backpack you currently carry. However, the upper section is stuffed with a tightly-packed cloth of some kind and even has a cord trailing from it, allowing it to be opened quickly. If you would like to swap the backpack for your own, you hastily empty the contents of yours into it (and add the Unusual Backpack to your *Adventure Sheet*, making a note of the fact that it has two compartments). Now *Test your Luck*. If you are Lucky, turn to **233**. If you are Unlucky, turn to **255**.

203

You duck down on the ground, trying to make yourself as small as possible. A moment later, the sandstorm hits. Abrasive grit and hot sand scour your body, rubbing any exposed skin raw. Lose 4 STAMINA points. If it is Fireday you must increase this damage by 1 point, but if you have a Dragon Tattoo you may reduce the total damage by 1 point.

You hear a terrified scream as the balloon is swallowed up by the sandstorm and, once it has passed, you scan the skies but can see no sign of the balloonist or his balloon. Lose 1 LUCK point and turn to **263**.

204

The path runs out at the edge of the lava river you crossed earlier. This can't be the right way to go to escape from Mount Pyre. Without hesitation, you turn on your heel and run back to the junction, taking the other path. Add 1 to your TIME TRACK and turn to 224.

205

What chance did you think you'd have against trained warriors on horseback? The approaching Lendlelanders run you down after only a brief chase, one of them sending you flying with a kick. (Lose 2 STAMINA points and 1 LUCK point.) You are seized and dragged back to the barbarian camp as their prisoner. Turn to 19.

206

Once again you are fighting for your life, as the Deluge seeks to overwhelm you.

DELUGE   SKILL 11   STAMINA 11

If today is Seaday, add 1 point to the Deluge's SKILL score and 2 points to its STAMINA. Because you have been washed off your feet by the surge, you must fight the first Attack Round with your Attack Strength reduced by 1 point as you struggle to get to your feet. If you reduce the Deluge's STAMINA score to 3 points or fewer, turn to 187.

207

You down the potion and it takes effect immediately. However, the Potion of Levitation only allows you to ascend, not to fly, and Sturm's Weather Machine isn't even in sight. But then, as the ground drops away beneath you, you are caught by the wind and whirled away.

Looking up, you see storm clouds massing overhead, and there, amidst the oppressive thunderheads, no more than a glittering speck against the darkening sky, is the brass fish you saw after the devastation of Vastarin. The *Eye of the Storm* approaches!

The wind becomes a gale and you find yourself being drawn towards the flying Weather Machine by a whirling tornado. But the vortex has picked up other things too – fish from a lake, whole branches, ripped from the trees of a forest, and even heavy rocks! You are battered by this debris. Roll one die and deduct that many STAMINA points. If you are still alive, you hurtle upwards, limbs flailing.

The whirlwind carries you higher and higher until you are over the strange craft. It is enormous, bigger than a Bullwhale. Its huge sparkling eyes are large observation windows in the front of the vessel; its fins and tail, steering sails and a vast rudder. And in the side of the elementally-powered vessel is a round access hatch with a railed balcony before it. The wind suddenly drops and you discover that the effects of the potion have worn off ... Turn to **14**.

208

In time you come to another fork among the criss-crossing canyons. From the left-hand route you can hear a disconcerting wailing sound. In the distance, at the end of the right-hand path you can see what appear to be birds riding on the thermals rising from the sun-baked ravines. If you want to take the left-hand path, turn to **79**. If you would rather take the right-hand path, turn to **148**.

209

Opening the door to the turret you enter what are obviously the living quarters of whoever owns the tower, although there is no one here now. The small room is cluttered with furniture, including a bed and a large desk, but two things in particular grab your attention immediately. The first is the fact that almost every available surface – from the desk to the walls, and even the bed – is covered with large sheets of parchment covered in plans for what looks like the most incredible machine. The second is a large tele-scope which has been angled so that it is pointing out of an open window. Do you want to take a closer look at the plans (turn to **289**), or through the telescope (turn to **239**)?

210

Having shed your weapons and armour, you and the Giant face one another across the clearing ready to wrestle. If you have a Potion of Giant Strength, and want to down it before you have to wrestle, turn to

291. If not, roll four dice. If the total rolled is less than or equal to your STAMINA score, turn to **291**; if it is greater, turn to **305**.

211

'Turn back, stranger. Turn back!' the robed man says as he catches sight of you. He throws back his hood and you see that he is tonsured, his eyes wild and bulging. 'Only doom awaits you this way. Turn back, I say!'

You tell the man that you are determined to press on and when he asks you why, you see no reason not to tell him of your quest and who you are.

'The Hero of Tannatown, eh?' he says when you have finished. 'You were lucky with that Basilisk, weren't you?' You didn't think that luck had anything to do with it! 'Well, I suppose you know what you're doing, but if you ask me, you're doomed.'

You ask the pessimistic priest who he is.

'Muldwych,' he replies, 'but some call me the Mad Monk.' You can see why.

You suddenly become aware of movement within the reedy pools either side of the path and barely have your hand on your weapon when two loathsome creatures rise from the swamp. Dripping mud and slime, they moan horribly. In fact, their vaguely humanoid bodies are nothing but mud and slime! You recognise them at once; they are Marsh Wraiths, primal, elemental creatures of the swamp. Marsh

Wraiths are very territorial and both you and the mad monk have trespassed within their domain. As Muldwych makes a feeble attempt to defend himself with his staff, you are effectively forced to fight both of the creatures by yourself.

	SKILL	STAMINA
First MARSH WRAITH	7	5
Second MARSH WRAITH	7	5

Due to the insubstantial nature of the Wraiths' slimy bodies, hits against them will only do 1 point of STAMINA damage. If you defeat both of the swamp monsters, they flop back into the marsh and trouble you no more. Turn to 369.

212

The force of the Undine's attack unbalances you. Making the most of the opportunity, the water spirit crashes its wave-like body over you, sending you splashing into the river. Unable to fight the force of the current you are carried back downstream, over waterfalls and bruising rapids. It is all you can do to keep your head above water as you are hurled against rocks and jutting tree roots. You eventually manage to grab hold of one of these roots and heave yourself free of the river's clutches. (Roll one die, add 1, and lose that many STAMINA points.) Your dip in the river has also ruined some of your Provisions. (Lose half your Meals, rounding fractions down.) If you are still alive, you eventually find the strength to get to your feet and set off up the hillside again, but which route will you take this time? The steep rocky path (turn to **35**), or the longer, gentler path up the exposed slope of escarpment (turn to **322**).

213

The first thing you notice when you enter the sun room is the heat. The roof of the chamber is almost entirely made of glass and standing at the far end is what looks like a large magnifying lens – a full three metres in diameter – set within a semi-circular frame. Beside it is a telescope supported on a tripod frame, pointing out of the crystal dome at the front of the ship. You see that one side of the giant lens is concave and the other convex. At the moment the lens is at 90 degrees to its cradle, with the concave side facing upwards. Do you want to:

Smash the lens?	Turn to **192**
Turn the lens so that the concave side faces out of the ship?	Turn to **162**
Flip the lens so that the concave side faces into the room?	Turn to **139**
Leave the Sun room altogether?	Turn to **258**

214

The Fire Elemental roars towards you, its body a ball of incandescent flame. Once again you are forced to rely on your enchanted blade.

FIRE ELEMENTAL   SKILL 12   STAMINA 16

If you somehow manage to defeat the Elemental power that dwells at the heart of Mount Pyre, turn to **114**.

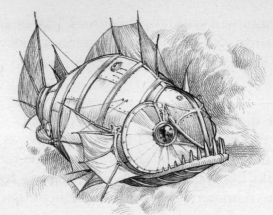

215

The book practically falls open at a page bearing a pen and ink sketch of an artificial man constructed from iron. Written in a column beside it is the following:

Activate ~ 270   Deactivate ~ 072

As you suspected, the rest of the book is merely a record of the various places the *Eye of the Storm* has already visited during Sturm's rampage of revenge across the kingdom. Intrigued by your discovery, you consider what to do next. Will you:

Look at something else on the desk?   Turn to **243**
Open the other wooden door?   Turn to **259**
Return to the landing?   Turn to **54**

216

The first you know of the waiting ambush is when you hear the zing of arrows slicing through the air towards you. Roll one die and add 1; this is the number of arrows that hit you. (You may reduce this number by 1 if you have a Dragon Shield, a Breastplate, Chainmail Armour or a Wyrmskin Cloak. These items have a cumulative effect, so if you are wearing a Wyrmskin Cloak and carrying a shield, you reduce the number of arrows that hit you by 2.) Any arrow that does injure you causes 2 STAMINA points of DAMAGE. If you survive the arrow attack, you hear the sound of bowstrings being pulled taut a second time. Turn to **329**.

217

Below decks, the ship looks like a mass grave. Everywhere you see the skeletons of the dead crew, still frozen in the positions they were in when the galleon was claimed by the sea. Some lie in hammocks, some are trapped by the rusted remains of the ship's cannons, while others lie tumbled in dark corners, rictus grins locked on their fleshless features. Making your way through this ghoulish graveyard you come at last to a heavy-looking door. You try the handle but it is locked. You are in the right part of the ship for this to be the entrance to the ship's strong-room. You try searching for a key within the muck of the hold but to no avail. Will you try breaking the door down (turn to **177**) or would you prefer to exit the hold without further delay (turn to **163**)?

218

The ground heaves again and this time cracks open, directly under you. You fall into the fissure, grazing your arms and legs on rocks buried in the ground. Lose 2 STAMINA points, and in the ensuing battle reduce your Attack Strength for the first two Attack Rounds by 1 point as you scramble free again. Turn to **346**.

219

The tunnel slopes downwards at a steep gradient, always curving round to the left. It is not long before you reach another junction; a new passageway leads off to your right. If you want to follow this new tunnel, turn to **319**. If you would rather keep to your current course, turn to **249**.

220

Climbing the stone staircase you arrive at the first floor. You are in another circular chamber, smaller than the last, with large arched windows that are open to the outside. Standing in the middle of the chamber, on top of a carved marble plinth, is a truly astonishing object. It is a large glass bell jar, within which have been trapped a kaleidoscope of striking blue and silver butterflies. What can possibly be the reason for them being kept in this way? If you want to enter the room and release the imprisoned insects, turn to **253**. If not, you continue up the stairs (turn to **281**).

221

Affiliated to the College of Mages, there are plenty of sorcerers at the Academy happy to help you with your problem – for a price! You manage to haggle one wizard – called Prospero Seacharmer – down to 10 Gold Pieces. For that fee he will travel with you out into the Eelsea and cast an appropriate spell on you when you wish to descend below the waves. Fully-qualified naval sorcerers don't come cheap! If you can afford his fee and you want to hire the wizard, deduct 10 Gold Pieces and add the name Prospero Seacharmer to your *Adventure Sheet* and turn to **252**. If you can't afford his fee, or you don't want to spend that sort of money on hiring a wizard, you will have to visit the Brotherhood of Alchemists (turn to **151**) or the Guild of Artificers (turn to **181**) instead.

222

The Sunken Temple is a magnificent building that would not look out of place among the sacred buildings that line the Street of Holies in Chalannabrad. It has a grand pillared entrance that supports a pediment carved with mermen riding seahorses engaging in battle with many-tentacled horrors. A grand cupola dome projects from the roof. Not wanting to remain out in the open ocean any longer, you enter the Grand Temple of Hydana, God of the Sea.

There, at the heart of the temple, beneath the golden cupola, inlaid with bejewelled tesserae, stands an imposing statue of the Sea God himself. It looks like it has been carved from jade and depicts Hydana as a four-metre-tall fishman – with a tail, scaly skin, the torso and arms of a man and a face that is somewhere between the two – holding a golden trident. On a plinth in front of the statue, is an innocuous-seeming sea shell. Something tells you that one of these treasures of the temple is the artefact you need to gain power over Sturm's bound Water Elemental, but which one? Will you try taking the golden trident (turn to 301) or the shell (turn to 321)?

223

The dust and sand dissipate on the wind until there is nothing left to suggest the dust storm had ever been there. A moment later, the balloon touches down close by. You run over to the basket to see if the pilot is alright. The swarthy-skinned man pushes a pair of goggles up onto his forehead and brushes the sand from his voluminous robes.

'Thank you so much!' he gushes. 'I was in real trouble there. In fact I'd go so far as to say that you saved Corbo Rundum's life! However can I repay you?'

You tell Corbo Rundum that he doesn't owe you anything – saving people's lives is all in a day's work for a hero like you! You do however ask that he tells you how he came to be pursued by a Sand Elemental.

'I'm an inventor from Quartz, a village to the east of here. A terrible drought is affecting the farmlands there and if they don't get some rain soon, the harvest will fail. Some of the farmers reported seeing a curious brass fish in the sky, drawing the rainclouds towards itself. At first everyone thought they'd had a drop too much cider, until the drought came, that is. Reports suggested that the strange craft came from the south, so I set out in my balloon to see what I could discover for myself. I was halfway across the Howling Plains when that evil sandstorm blew up and chased me all the way back to here.'

You ask Corbo what he plans to do now.

'Head back to Quartz I think, or perhaps to Chalannabrad, to petition the College of Mages for help. I swear there's nothing natural about either the drought or that sandstorm. How about you?'

You tell him that you are going to continue south across the Howling Plains.

'Well, if there's nothing I can do to dissuade you, watch out for Birdmen. I spotted some south of here, over the Screaming Canyon.'

You thank Corbo for this information and, leaving him to make repairs to his balloon, set off again south. Add the codeword *Noollab* to your *Adventure Sheet* and turn to **263**.

224

The tunnel walls rumble and heave around you, and you can feel the temperature rising. You run on up a steep incline, panting for breath in the unbearable heat, imagining that you can feel the flames of the approaching lava licking at your heels. And then you come to another junction. (Add 1 to your TIME

TRACK.) This time will you turn left (turn to 254) or keep going straight on (turn to 304)?

225

You just miss the lip of the ledge beyond the broken bridge and find yourself plummeting down the side of the fiery ravine. You scrape your arms, shins and back as you fall and land, battered and bruised, on the scalding rocks at the edge of the magma river. Roll one die, add 2, and then deduct the total from your STAMINA score. If you suffer 6 or more STAMINA points of damage, you must lose 1 SKILL point and 1 LUCK point too. If you are still alive, turn to 141.

226

You are halfway up when the ledge you are standing on crumbles under your weight and, although you stretch upwards for your next handhold, you miss it by a hair's breadth. And then you are falling, tumbling down the side of the stack, bouncing off the hard rock, grazing your arms, your legs and your back on the unforgiving stone surfaces. You land at the bottom in a heap and in a great deal of pain. Roll one die and consult the table below to see what state you're in.

Dice roll	Damage sustained
1	You have twisted your ankle and sprained your wrist as well. Lose 4 STAMINA points and 2 SKILL points.

2	You have skinned your knees and injured your back. Lose 4 STAMINA points.
3–4	Roll one die and add 2 to the number rolled. Lose this many STAMINA points.
5	You have jarred your shoulder and suffered a blow to the head. Lose 3 STAMINA points and 1 SKILL point.
6	Roll again on this table two more times to see what damage you have sustained. (If you roll a 6 again, ignore the instructions given here and simply roll again.)

If you are still alive, and you want to try scaling the stack again, turn back to **196** and make the same two tests for success. If you decide that such a course of action is too risky and you want to give up on your quest for finding something to help you beat Sturm's Greater Air Elemental, you set off again, trudging wearily back through the Screaming Canyon, eventually returning to the border of the Howling Plains. Move the Day of the Week on 1 and turn to **394**.

227

The tunnel enters a large square chamber where it comes to an end. The chamber is littered with the rusted remains of mining equipment – everything from pick-axes to gold-panning trays. Squatting at the centre of it all is a massive toad-like creature with skin the colour and texture of rusting metal. The chamber echoes with the sound of metal being ground between diamond-hard teeth. The monster stops mid-chew and waddles around on its claw-like feet to face you. It pauses, sniffing the air. Then it opens its broad mouth, emitting a strange croaking-growl, and you catch sight of row upon row of shark-like teeth. You have iron about your person, and the Ferrovore can smell it on you. Moving with startling speed the rust monster lurches towards you, deter-mined to feast on the metal you're carrying.

FERROVORE   SKILL 7   STAMINA 9

If you slay the Ferrovore, you retreat from the cham-ber – the monster having already consumed anything that might have been of use to you – and (choosing a way you haven't been already) go right at the cross-roads, along the slime-dripping tunnel (turn to 327), or straight on, along a damp passageway (turn to 399).

228

Having dealt with the vultures, you retrieve the adventurer's pack and have a look inside. Apart from a few spoiled provisions you find only a few Gold Pieces (roll one die and add 2 to find the total) along with a Rope and Grapple. Having taken what you want, you pause for a moment to cover the man's remains with rocks as best you can, to save it from the predations of other scavengers. Turn to **148**.

229

The plans are for subsidiary mechanisms operating within the *Eye of the Storm*. You find one labelled 'Lightning Generator' which bears the warning, 'Do not set lever in left position'. Another, which has a picture on it of something that looks not unlike a large magnifying glass, has written underneath it, 'Concave lens must be facing outwards for safe operation'. This might be of use when it comes to looking for ways to shut down the Weather Machine. Putting the plans to one side, will you:

Look at something else on the desk?	Turn to **243**
Open the other wooden door?	Turn to **259**
Return to the landing?	Turn to **54**

'Zephyrus!' you shout. 'Zephyrus, heed my call!'

The bridge is suddenly subjected to a raging gale. It howls around the chamber, sending Sturm's minions flying, and then coalesces between you and the Human Torch. The Air Elemental appears as a furious whirlwind with the upper body of a powerfully-muscled giant formed by fluctuations in the tormented air.

'You called and I have come!' the Elemental of the West Wind declares. Turning to the transformed Weather Mage it says, 'And now let me blow out this fire!'

Zephyrus circles the blazing Sturm, faster and faster, enclosing the Human Torch within a cyclone of unrelenting force. Through the whirling tornado you watch as Sturm's flames start to flicker fitfully until the very last tongue of fire is extinguished, leaving the wizard as a blackened cinder.

But then the mage begins to transform again, his body hardened and swelling in size until he stands before you as a three-metre-tall behemoth of earth and stone. Against the man-mountain, Zephyrus can do nothing and disappears with one last hurricane howl.

With a roar like a crashing landslide, the Colossus stomps towards you. But how can you fight something made of solid earth? If only you could wash it away, as the sea eats away at the land …

⚀ ⚁

If you have the Shell of the Seas and you know the name of a Water Elemental who could help you, turn it into a number using the code A=1, B=2, C=3 … Z=26. Add the numbers together and turn to the paragraph with the same number. If not, turn to **8**.

231

You launch yourself onto the next steppingstone as the Magma Beast makes a grab for you. The monster misses you by only a hair's breadth but then another Beast rises from the slow-moving lava flow, between you and the next steppingstone. With the two monsters closing on you from both directions, you are forced to fight them at the same time.

	SKILL	STAMINA
First MAGMA BEAST	8	9
Second MAGMA BEAST	7	8

(If today is Fireday, add 2 points to the monsters' STAMINA scores.) If you defeat both of the Beasts, turn to **251**.

232

You have been travelling for a day into the desolate wilds of Goblin Country, as it's known in these parts, when you run into a band of Hobgoblins. You spot the warning signs that tell you an ambush has been put into play from a good quarter of a kilometre away and so come at them from their flank, taking the Hobgoblins by surprise instead, before engaging them in battle. Because of this, you can fight the first two Attack Rounds against their chief before the rest of his robber band can join the fray and defend their leader.

	SKILL	STAMINA
HOBGOBLIN CHIEF	7	7
First HOBGOBLIN BANDIT	6	6
Second HOBGOBLIN BANDIT	6	6
Third HOBGOBLIN BANDIT	7	6

If you kill them all, searching their pockets reveals why they were preparing to ambush you – they possess absolutely nothing of value themselves. You continue on your way into the rugged landscape that lies at the foot of the volcano and after another day you are scaling the craggy slopes of Mount Pyre itself. Move the Day of the Week on 2 and turn to **109**.

233

What do you want to do now? Will you pull on the chain (turn to **255**), return to the locked iron door (turn to **285**), ascend the staircase to explore the upper levels of the tower, if you haven't done so already (turn to **220**), or leave the tower altogether (turn to **398**)?

234

Holding the shell high above your head, you shout 'Oceanus, aid me now, and call forth the waters from above!'

With the crowd on tenterhooks, you keep your eyes firmly on the cerulean bowl of the sky. And then it begins. At first they are only a few wispy threads of white but these scraps of cloud rapidly coalesce, changing colour to grey, and then almost black. The dusty wind that whistles through Quartz is joined by a distant rumbling, like the grumbling of Sukh the Storm God himself.

With a loud clap of thunder directly overhead, it starts to rain; not a light shower, or even a heavy downpour, but a torrential deluge. The downpour drenches the landscape from horizon to horizon, to the delight of the laughing villagers and the chagrin of the disgruntled rainmaker. Whoops and cheers rise from the assembled onlookers and some of the villagers start to dance, splashing through muddy puddles that weren't there moments ago.

While the villagers drive the fraudulent rainmaker out of Quartz, they heap praises upon you (regain 1 LUCK point) and reward you with gifts of money (a total of 8 Gold Pieces) and food (add 3 Meals to your total Provisions).

As you are leaving the village yourself, you notice that, in his hurry to leave, the rainmaker has left behind a large Spanner. If you want to take this with you, add it to your *Adventure Sheet*. You must also cross the Shell of the Seas off your *Adventure Sheet*; you will not be able to call on the Water Elemental's assistance again.

You continue walking south-west, and after two days, reach the baking borderlands of the Howling Plains. Move the Day of the Week on 2 and turn to **83**.

235

You throw yourself flat on the ground behind a scrubby bush and pray that the barbarians won't spot you. *Test your Luck*. If you are Lucky, the patrol trots right past without the Lendlelanders ever seeing you (turn to **142**). If you are Unlucky, the sharp-eyed horsemen see through your hiding place and prepare to run you down; you have no choice but to draw your sword and defend yourself (turn to **264**).

236

You enter a large chamber that takes up the whole of the rear section of the top deck, but the first thing you notice is the cold. It's freezing in here! The second thing is the ice. Everything inside the chamber is rimmed with frost and icicles hang from the ceiling. And the cause of all this cold?

At the centre of the room is a huge glass sphere, mounted within a brass cradle, containing what would appear to be a howling blizzard. The power of the snowstorm is channelled out of the globe through a pipe which connects to the roof of the vessel. You know immediately what you have to do to damage the magical mechanism here, but it really is bitterly cold, cold enough to … You cannot help chuckling to yourself even as the gorilla-sized automata that have been left to guard this delicate device knuckle towards you over the icy floor.

	SKILL	STAMINA
First BRASS MONKEY	7	8
Second BRASS MONKEY	7	8

While you are fighting the snowstorm's guardians, you must reduce your Attack Strength by 1 point, because the floor is as slippery as an ice rink. Also, unless you are wearing a Sun Talisman, you must reduce your Attack Strength by another point due to the sub-zero temperature of the room.

If you defeat the Brass Monkeys, picking up a broken-off metal limb, you hurl it at the globe which shatters on impact. The howling force of the blizzard escapes into the room as you make a sharp exit, slamming the door to the chamber behind you again. Add 1 to your DAMAGE score and turn to **258**.

237

You are very well-prepared for your final confrontation with the megalomaniacal Balthazar Sturm but the time you have taken will have also given him more time to prepare for his final conquest. (Add 1 LUCK point, even if this takes your LUCK score beyond its *Initial* level and add the codeword *Mortsleam* to your *Adventure Sheet*.) However, you have yet to reach Sturm's Weather Machine; how do you intend to achieve such a thing?

If you want to use a Potion of Levitation, turn to **207**. If you know the name of an Air Elemental and want to call on it for aid now, turn its name into a number (using the code A=1, B=2, C=3 … Z=26 and adding the numbers together), add 30, and turn to the paragraph with the same number. If you have the codeword *Susagep* written on your *Adventure Sheet*, turn to **128**. If not, but you have the codeword *Noollab*, turn to **149**. If you have none of these things, turn to **107**.

'Zephyrus! Zephyrus, heed my call!' you yell into the wind from the prow of the *Tempest*. The breeze coming off the sea immediately begins to pick up and the sails snap in the wind as the waves around the rocking ship crest white.

Approaching the ship is an ethereal figure, with the upper body of a powerfully-muscled giant but who, from the waist down, is a whirling vortex of air. Zephyrus, Elemental manifestation of the West Wind, heard your cry for help and has come to your aid! (Cross Zephyrus' name off your *Adventure Sheet* – you may not call on his help again.)

The sails suddenly blow full and before you really understand what's going on, the *Tempest* is lifted out of the water as the Air Elemental carries the ship, Captain Katarina, her crew and you into the sky. Before you know it, the *Tempest* is sailing into the maelstrom that is raging across the firmament.

'You called and I have come,' the Air Elemental howls with a voice that is the rising gale itself. 'Command and I shall obey!'

'Find Balthazar Sturm's Weather Machine!' you command the Elemental, shouting. 'Take us into the eye of the storm!'

Higher and higher you climb, the landscape dwindling beneath you until it looks like nothing so much as a wonderfully detailed map. Onwards the ship sails through the sky, Captain Katarina hanging from the rigging, relishing the feel of the wind whipping through her hair. It is all her crew can do to stop the sails breaking free of the rigging in the face of the howling crosswinds.

And then you see it! Zephyrus is carrying the *Tempest* and everyone on board straight into the broiling maelstrom of massing storm-clouds directly ahead. There, amidst the black thunderheads is the brass fish you saw all those days ago, after the devastation of Vastarin. Balthazar Sturm's Weather Machine looks huge up close! Its crystal eyes are observation domes, its fins and tail, steering sails and a vast rudder. In the side of the elementally-powered vessel you can see an access hatch with a railed balcony before it. Turn to 363.

239

Putting your eye to the viewing lens of the telescope you gasp in wonder at the way in which distant objects that would be invisible to the naked eye are pulled forwards into perfect clarity. It does not take you long to realise that the telescope is pointing over the border with Lendleland and into the kingdom of Femphrey. With only a few minor adjustments you are able to pick out the devastated village of Vastarin, its inhabitants hard at work repairing the damage done by the storm. And then you catch sight of something else, several leagues north of Vastarin, something that gleams like gold amidst the mass of anvil-headed thunderclouds. Carefully turning a knurled brass ring, you pull the object into focus … and can hardly believe your eyes.

There, at the eye of the storm, is a giant fish, made of wood and brass and sailcloth. Its huge tail is a rudder, its fins immense wings, its glittering crystal eyes viewing bubbles. You weren't seeing things after your battle with the Ice Elemental back in Vastarin; there really was a huge, fish-shaped flying machine! (Regain 1 LUCK point.) But how could a creation of wood and metal like that ever fly? There must be some manner of sorcery involved. And then the bizarre vessel is gone, swallowed by the storm. After experiencing such an incredible revelation, will you:

Take a closer look at the plans?	Turn to **289**
Descend to the bottom of the tower and explore the basement levels (if you haven't done so already)?	Turn to **160**
Quit the tower altogether having seen enough?	Turn to **398**

240

'If you're thinking of travelling by mine-cart, then you're a bigger idiot than I thought you were and you'll be on your own from here on in!' Brokk snorts. Now return to **290** and make your choice, but if you choose to travel by mine-cart you must remove Brokk from your *Adventure Sheet* and will not be able to consult the Dwarf again as you continue to explore the mine.

241

Ducking in under the goliath's guard you punch its chest-plate which springs open to reveal a set of three barrel tumblers, each bearing the numbers 0 to 9. You only have one chance to turn the tumblers to the correct setting. If you know of such a code, add 100 to the number and then turn to that paragraph. If you know of no such code, the Juggernaut knocks you clear with one sledgehammer blow of its iron fist. Lose 3 STAMINA points and return to **262** to finish the fight with the steel giant.

242

The hideous behemoth lurches towards you, its towering mass writhing with tentacles and snapping crustacean claws. You now suspect that you know what it is ... They are so rarely seen that they have acquired an almost mythical status. They are frightening, intelligent, ten-legged creatures that are found nowhere else on Titan. To some they are the Decapi, to others they are the Old Ones, but to those unlucky few who actually encounter them, it is enough that they are horrors of the abyss!

Once again you are fighting for your life. If you survive your encounter, this will be one battle that you will remember for the rest of your life.

ABYSSAL HORROR   SKILL 10   STAMINA 12

If you lose an Attack Round roll one die and then consult the table below to see what damage you suffer. (You may use LUCK to reduce any damage caused in the usual way.)

Dice Roll	Attack and Damage
1–2	Crushing claws – the creature strikes you with one of its snapping pincers. Lose 2 STAMINA points.
3–5	Tentacle twist – the monster grabs you with a rubbery tentacle. The tentacle only inflicts 1 STAMINA point of damage, but for the next Attack Round you must fight with your Attack Strength reduced by 1 as you fight to free yourself from its clutches.
6	Snapping beak – if the horror already has a hold of you it drags you into its beaked mouth and bites down hard; roll one die and lose that many STAMINA points. However, if the monster doesn't already have you in its grasp roll again on the table for damage; if you roll 6 a second time then the creature bites you as described.

If you manage to defeat this nightmarish monster, you are at last able to make it to the Sunken Temple. Turn to **222**.

243

As you rummage through the books and papers on the map-desk, you hear a strange clanking of gears and hissing of pistons, and a hideous-looking creature emerges from behind the books on a shelf in front of your face. It is a disconcerting amalgam of metal and clay-like flesh. It looks like a tiny horned and winged devil, but half of its head is exposed metal, one wing is a folding construction of leather and brass and one leg and one arm are entirely metallic. Your continued presence within Balthazar's Sturm's own cabin has attracted the attention of one of his curious technomantic creations. You are going to have to fight the Techno-Homunculus.

TECHNO-HOMUNCULUS   SKILL 9   STAMINA 6

If you destroy the part-mechanical, part-magical creature, at your final blow the Homunculus disintegrates in a dramatic explosion of sparks, many of which fall onto the papers filling the cabin, which then catch fire. The way to the other wooden door is now blocked by quickly rising flames. (Add 1 to your DAMAGE score and make a note that you have started a fire on your *Adventure Sheet*.) Hurrying back out of Sturm's private cabin you decide where to go next. Turn to **54**.

244

Hearing the throaty roar of an engine, you spin round to see the Mole powering towards you, Brokk the Dwarf at the controls. His features are set in a grimace of intense concentration as he steers the tunnelling machine towards the Earth Elemental, the drill-bit screaming as it runs up to speed. And then the two behemoths collide – the giant of rock and stone and the contraption of brass and wood.

As you watch, the Mole's drill tears a massive hole in the Elemental's side. Roaring in fury, the giant grabs hold of the tunnelling machine in one hand and flings it at the wall of the chamber. The machine explodes in a cloud of wooden splinters and metal components, Brokk the Dwarf falling from the wreckage to land in an unconscious heap on the ground. His noble actions may have actually saved your life. If you come to fight the Earth Elemental in the near future, you may reduce its SKILL score by 3 points and its STAMINA score by 8 points. Regain 1 LUCK point and then return to **316** to decide what to do next.

245

The tunnel you are following eventually brings you to steps hewn from the rock that lead down into the very heart of the volcano. The steps bring you into a vast chamber. Beneath you is a vast lake of boiling magma. It is all you can do to not succumb to the exhausting heat of the chamber. The rock-cut stair-case comes to an end upon a spur of black rock that juts out over the seething lake. Another set of steps, like the ones you have just descended, leads down to the spur from the opposite side of the chamber. The spur feels hot beneath your feet. You approach the altar-like plinth of black rock that stands at the end of the spur, and see six curiously-shaped holes carved into the top of it.

Suddenly, the magma surges violently and a column of flame shoots twenty metres into the cooked air of the chamber. You recoil instinctively, throwing up an arm to shield yourself from the incandescent flames. Squinting against the blistering light you see the jet of flame widen and take on a roughly humanoid shape, like a genie of flame. A voice, like the blazing roar of a conflagration, echoes around the magma chamber. 'Who dares desecrate this sanctuary of the Fire God?' the Fire Elemental bellows, and you feel its unbearably hot breath on your face.

Speaking up confidently, you tell the Elemental your name, shouting to be heard over the roar of the flames and the bubbling of the magma, and go on to explain why you have braved the perils of Mount Pyre to reach the sacred shrine of the Fire God.

'You have the audacity to demand assistance from a true servant of the Burning One?' the Fire Elemental rages. 'Then you will pay for that audacity with your worthless life!'

You are going to have to act fast if you are to avoid being burned alive by the furious Elemental. If you have six Fire Crystals, turn the letters associated with them into numbers using the code A=1, B=2, C=3 ... Z=26. Add the numbers together and then turn to the paragraph which is the same as the total. If the paragraph does not begin with the words, 'Invoking the power of the God of Fire', or you do not have six Fire Crystals, turn to **214**.

246

The cavern opens onto another small cave, but what you see here sends a shiver down your spine. If there was ever any doubt in your mind that this place was the lair of some monstrous beast or other, it is gone now. In the centre of the cave is a nest, constructed from the bleached bones of dead animals – and some of them are human bones. The nest is as big as a hay-cart and slithering from it, blinking uncomfortably in the lantern-light, are four ugly reptilian creatures. Their bodies are black and scaly and they crawl towards you on four clawed limbs. There are also the nubs of wings growing from their shoulder blades, while their saurian heads are already full of razor-sharp teeth. The hatchlings squawk as they catch sight of you, sensing that another meal has just arrived. Moving with startling speed, the young Drakes dart across the cave and attack. As Sylas and the wolfhound take on two of the hatchlings, you are left to deal with the remaining pair.

	SKILL	STAMINA
First HATCHLING	7	7
Second HATCHLING	6	7

If you kill the young Drakes, turn to **32**.

247

Passing along a broad, stone passageway you emerge into a large circular chamber that forms the entire ground floor of the tower. The space is devoid of decoration but is littered with rubble and other rubbish – everything from twisted metal spars and joists to what looks like the remains of a Dwarven steam engine. On the opposite side of the chamber an archway leads to a spiral stone staircase. If the tower is going to provide you with any answers as to the origin of the devastating storm and the bizarre flying machine, you're not going to find them here. Determined to explore elsewhere, you start to cross the rubble-strewn chamber.

With a cacophonous crashing and clanging, the pile of what you had taken to be nothing more than scrap ironmongery starts to pull itself together and take on another, more obvious shape altogether. Gushing steam, with a loud hissing of pistons and the clanking of iron girder limbs, an incredible amalgamation of metal parts rises from amidst the rubble. Do you want to wait and face whatever it is that is taking shape (turn to **67**), or would you rather try to make it to the archway and the spiral stair beyond before the transformation is complete (turn to **197**)?

248

The stupid birds think you're after their food and aren't prepared to give up their feast without a fight. Flapping their wings furiously while screeching at you raucously, the vultures hop towards you, trying to peck you with their savage beaks or slash your flesh with their cruel talons. You must fight the birds two at a time.

	SKILL	STAMINA
First VULTURE	7	6
Second VULTURE	6	6
Third VULTURE	6	5

As soon as you have killed two of the birds, the last one takes flight, favouring survival over sacrifice. Turn to **228**.

249

The tunnel keeps curving to the left on its way down into the volcano until it finally comes to a dead-end within a small cavern. The walls of the cave are suffused with red light. Lying on the far side of the cave is the blackened skeleton of some large reptilian creature, although whether it is that of a Basilisk, a Salamander or something else, you do not know. Lying within the cage formed by the skeleton's ribs is a prism-shaped quartz crystal, which glows with the same lambent light as the cavern walls. If you want to venture into the cave to claim the crystal, turn to **269**. If you would rather retrace your steps to the last junction, turn to **319**.

250

The foothills of the Witchtooth Line rise up gradually before you. The mountain range that separates Femphrey from the Kingdom of Gallantaria to the north is a forbidding wall of black rock. Heavily laden rainclouds are massing over the jagged peaks, some of which are permanently covered with snow. You fancy you see a black, winged shape flapping over a spot a league or more to the west. You are going to have to watch yourself in this wild land. It is that afternoon that you reach the village of Clast.

During your travels, gossip and rumour keep making mention of this place. Rumour has it that the place has been decimated by a series of terrible earth-quakes. Gossip has it that they were caused by a foul-tempered Earth Elemental trapped beneath the mountains. But whatever the truth of the matter, there is no doubt that some tragedy or other has befallen Clast.

Everywhere you look you can see structural damage to buildings – collapsed roofs, slumping walls, broken timbers. One or two smaller hovels have collapsed altogether, while others look like they are about to go the same way. The villagers return your appalled gaze with wary looks of their own, as they go about repairing the damage as best they can.

As you wander through Clast you start to acquire a small following. Perhaps it is the magnificent sword sheathed at your side that has attracted them, but then again, it is possible that some of them recognise you. After all, the Hero of Tannatown is known throughout the kingdom of Femphrey and beyond.

It is not long before your presence in the village attracts the interest of the headman. He is a barrel-chested individual with a bristly red beard and muscular arms like sledgehammers. His leather apron, with its scorch-marks and soot stains, tells you that he is also the local blacksmith.

'Well, well, well. We are honoured indeed,' he says, regarding you with eyes narrowed. 'To have the Hero of Tannatown in our midst! I am Arturo the Ironsmith and you find yourself in the village of Clast. What can we do for you?' he asks suspiciously.

You see no reason to hide anything from this man, seeing as he might be able to help you, and so you tell him everything.

'Well, it sounds to me like the solution to your problem could be the saving of Clast as well,' he says at last. 'Further up into the hills lies the entrance to a

Dwarf mine. It's said that the Dwarfs found something buried down there, in the darkness deep below
the earth. Some say it was an Earth Elemental, some
say it was a Dragon, and some, a dread portal to the
domain of Demons. But whatever the truth of the
matter they shut down the mine, quick as you like,
and left. No one from Clast has dared enter the mine
to find out what's down there, but the tremors and
quakes have been getting worse in recent weeks, and
soon someone's going to *have* to go down.

'But if you're planning on mounting your own expe-
dition into the dark, I would advise you to take a
guide. One of the Dwarfs who used to work the mine
still lives in these parts. He's called Brokk and he
spends his days making beer now. He could be
persuaded to take you down into the mine, if your
money's good.'

You thank Arturo for his help. Will you set out for the
mine straight away, alone (turn to **190**), or will you go
in search of Brokk the brewer (turn to **57**)?

251

As the molten remains of the lava monsters sink back
into the scalding ooze, you jump from the last steppingstone onto the far bank of the hellish river.
Among a tumble of rocks you spy a crystal that shimmers with an inner fire. Looking closer you see the
letter L form within the flames. (If you want to take
the Fire Crystal add it to your *Adventure Sheet* along
with its letter.)

You decide not to dally any longer, in case more of the Magma Beasts emerge from the lava river, and enter the larger tunnel mouth. You have not gone far before you reach yet another junction. A narrower passageway leads off at right angles. If you want to follow this new route through the volcano, turn to **344**. If you want to continue along the larger tunnel, turn to **274**.

252

Making your way down to Chalannabrad's impressive docks you know something is wrong when you see the forest of masts over the rooftops of the buildings that surround the city's grand harbour. The docks are full to overflowing with all manner of ships, everything from merchant galleys slavers to freebooter galleons. There is usually a steady stream of vessels setting sail from here for the distant continents of Allansia and Khul, with just as many boats travelling to Chalannabrad from elsewhere around the globe – but not today. All of the vessels are in harbour and you cannot see so much as a schooner out at sea, beyond the grand harbour wall.

You soon discover why when you run into a salty old sea-dog, sitting on a jetty picking his teeth with a splinter from his wooden leg. 'It's the storms, see? There's more of 'em, and they're getting worse, threatening the seaways. And reports of Great Eel attacks are on the increase too. If you want to go to sea today – forget it!'

The day drags on, with you pleading with the sea-captains to take you out. You are beginning to despair that you won't be able to find anyone willing to help when you come across the redoubtable Captain Katarina. Her reputation is almost as widespread as yours, but she is particularly known for her reckless-ness. She looks every part the lady buccaneer, dressed in practical leather trews and a fine embroidered jerkin. A scimitar hangs from her sword-belt, her luxurious, long black hair is tied back in a ponytail with a ribbon of Khulian silk, and a patch covers the orbit of her left eye, taken in a battle with a Giant Crab.

You have nothing to lose in telling her of your quest, hoping against hope that she might agree to help you out of the goodness of her heart. 'I know the place you seek, and I'll take you there too,' she says. 'All I ask in return is half of whatever you bring back from the bottom.' Sounds like the best offer you're going to get so you agree; Captain Katarina's ship, the *Tempest*, sails with the tide.

You have been at sea for less than a day when a thick sea fog blows up as if from nowhere. It moves towards the ship with a sinister purpose until its sickly yellow, cloud-like mass threatens to engulf the *Tempest*.

Captain Katarina looks concerned. 'I've not seen the like before,' she says. 'That is no natural sea-mist. There's sorcery at work here, I'd swear it.' You know she's right; you can feel Wyrmbiter vibrating in its scabbard at your side, but what are you going to do about it? If you have Prospero Seacharmer with you, turn to **272**. If you have a Hunting Horn, and want to blow it, turn to **292**. If neither of these things applies to you, you have no choice but to face the unnatural fog with your sword drawn (turn to **332**).

253

As you lift the bell jar, you suddenly notice the lightning-flash patterns that adorn the butterflies' ragged wings, but by then it is already too late. As the innocuous-seeming insects beat their wings, a gale begins to blow in through the arched openings of the tower room. Within seconds a howling wind is circling the room, lifting the discarded jar, the plinth and even you into the air, whirling everything around together at the heart of the cyclone. In your helpless state you are hurled against the walls, floor and ceiling. Roll one die, add 1, and lose that many STAMINA points. (If it is Windsday or Stormsday, you suffer an additional point of STAMINA damage.) The butterflies eventually escape the room through the arched openings and only then does the wind die down again, leaving you to pick yourself up from the floor and struggle on up the tower. Turn to **281**.

254

This new tunnel twists and turns until you skid to a halt at the edge of a terrible precipice. The last of the stone bridge breaks away from the sides of the chasm and plunges into the lava river below – the level of which is much higher than it was the last time you were here. Your hopes of escaping this way are dashed in an instant. You have no choice but to turn back and go the other way, praying to the gods that an alternative escape route will present itself. Add 1 to your TIME TRACK and turn to **304**.

255

With a terrible screeching cry, a monstrous winged shape suddenly flies up from the gulf beneath the platform. It is almost ten metres in length, has two powerfully-clawed legs and an enormous pair of dragon-like wings. The black scales that cover its body shine with dark iridescence. You see now that the other end of the chain is secured to a clasp around one of the creature's hind-legs. The Wyvern is none too pleased to find you awaiting it on the platform and not its master, and screeching again it snaps at you with its fang-filled snout. Once again, you are forced to fight.

BLACK WYVERN   SKILL 9   STAMINA 10

As the Wyvern's movements are restricted by the chain, after you have fought three Attack Rounds you can escape back up the stairs. Turn to **285**.

256

You make it to the top of the stack without incident. Only you are not at the top. Instead you find yourself standing before a natural archway in the face of the stack. Cautiously you pass through it and enter a domed space within the rock itself. The wind blows in through other clefts in the rock and a worn set of steps, that appear to have been carved from the rock itself, leads to a dais of red sandstone. Standing on the dais is a robed figure, its hooded cloak billowing and flapping in the wind. The cowl of the robe hides the figure's face completely.

A woman's voice carries to you on the wind, barely more than a breathy whisper. 'What do you want with the Keeper of the Four Winds?' the voice demands. Will you reply that you come seeking aid (turn to **108**), or will you draw your sword and run at the cloaked figure (turn to **90**)?

257

Cautiously you approach the captain's skeleton, as defiant in death as he must have been in life. Your heart pounding its own tattoo of fear against your ribs, you carefully lift the key from around the captain's neck. But there was nothing to worry about, the skeleton does not come to life to exact its revenge and nothing else untoward happens. (Add the Golden Key to your *Adventure Sheet*, noting that it has 17 'teeth') You are now free to leave the captain's cabin, but will you explore inside the hull (turn to **217**) or leave the sunken galleon and make for the fissure (turn to **6**)?

258

Two doors lead off from the small top deck of the vessel, the one to the aft bearing the image of a snowflake, the door to the fore having a simplified picture of the sun cut into it. Choosing somewhere you haven't already been, will you:

Open the snowflake door?	Turn to **236**
Open the sun door?	Turn to **213**
Leave the top deck and explore elsewhere?	Turn to **391**

259

You enter an airy chamber at the rear of the vessel. A framework of timbers fills the space, to which have been attached various pulleys and a large windlass. Everything is connected to everything else by a complicated system of ropes. The groaning of wood and the creaking of ropes fills the chamber. As far as you can tell, this must be part of the *Eye of the Storm*'s steering mechanism. But what would be the best way to cause the most damage here? Will you find something to try to jam the windlass somehow (turn to 275), or cut the inter-connecting ropes with your sword (turn to 288)?

260

'I remember this place,' Brokk pipes up. 'We ran into an infestation of Iron Eaters down here. There was even talk of something bigger; something worse. I would suggest we get out of here as quickly as possible,' he says, pointing along the left-hand path at the crossroads. Now return to 310 and choose which way you want to go.

In a second, Wyrmbiter is in your hand again. With a bestial scream the Yeti shows itself. Teeth bared, the creature knuckles towards you through the drifting snow. As it closes on you and the Huntress, it rears up on its hind legs, to its full four metres, and beats its chest in a crude attempt to intimidate you – only it works!

Snarling, Fang throws itself at the hulking beast but, before your very eyes, the Yeti catches hold of the Cat in its clawed hands and hurls the Sabretooth over its back. Larni falls from the saddle with a cry, landing awkwardly in the snow, while blood pours from a savage wound in the Cat's side. Then the Yeti turns its attentions to you!

YETI   SKILL 10   STAMINA 12

Unless you are wearing a Sun Talisman, you must reduce your Attack Strength by 1 point for the duration of this battle. If the Yeti wounds you at all, roll one die. If you're not wearing a Sun Talisman, on a roll of 4–6 its chilling talons impart an additional 1 STAMINA point of damage, and on a roll of 6 will drain 1 SKILL point as well. If you slay the savage beast, turn to 374.

Its lantern-eyes blazing white-hot, the unstoppable machine strides towards you like some terrible, walking siege engine. Once again you are fighting for your life! Before battle commences, make any alterations necessary to the automaton's stats.

JUGGERNAUT   SKILL 11   STAMINA 16

If you think you know a way to deactivate the Juggernaut and you win two Attack Rounds in succession, turn to **241**. If not, or you never manage to win two Attack Rounds in a row, but you still win, turn to **156**.

263

You travel south for another day (move the Day of the Week on 1) without seeing any other signs of life apart from distant circling carrion birds. Having spent a night under the stars, not long after dawn you come upon the kind of feature that can't be missed – a massive fracture stretching for as far as you can see across the parched plain – the Screaming Canyon. Well is it so named, for the scouring winds that sweep across the Howling Plains are channelled through the maze-like chasms of the rift, producing eerie howls and screams, as if demons dwelt there. Something tells you that the aid you seek lies somewhere within this maze of branching gullies and ravines. Boldly you set off into the canyon. You have not gone far when you come to a parting of the ways between the towering cliffs. Will you take the left-hand path (turn to 303) or the right-hand route (turn to 283)?

264

Spurring their steeds forwards at a gallop, the two horsemen bear down on you, sabres in hand. You must fight them both at the same time.

	SKILL	STAMINA
First HORSEMAN	8	7
Second HORSEMAN	7	7

If you win and the battle lasted for 12 Attack Rounds or fewer, turn to 277. If it lasted for more than 12 Attack Rounds, as you are fighting the horsemen another patrol turns up. Turn to 205.

265

Warily, you step out onto the narrow bridge. You have taken only a few steps when you hear an ominous crack and feel the rock shift beneath you. Without a second thought you start to run, not daring to take your eyes off the archway ahead of you. You are still several metres from the end of the bridge and safety when it gives way altogether. With a herculean effort, you fling yourself forwards. Roll three dice. If the total rolled is less than or equal to your STAMINA score, you make the jump, landing on the far side of the bridge (turn to **185**). If the total is greater than your STAMINA score, turn to **225**.

266

You find Inigo Crank already outside the tower, waiting for you. He has his own pack stuffed with charts and a number of the models from his workroom.

'There's no time to waste, Sturm has several days' start on you,' the engineer states. 'He has bound four Greater Elementals within the Elemental Engine of his flying machine to provide it with its source of power and keep it up in the air. If you are going to have any hope of stopping Sturm and his Weather Machine, you are going to have to find the means to overcome those Elementals. Search in places where the four elements of earth, air, fire and water are in greatest concentrations.'

'And where's that?' you ask.

'Deep beneath the mountains of the Witchtooth Line, on the wind-swept Howling Plains, at the heart of Mount Pyre, the volcano that stands within the mountainous borders of Mauristatia, and deep beneath the Eelsea. Now hurry! The whole of Femphrey is in danger and you must get moving. I would come with you, only I think I'd slow you down.'

You agree with the old man – there's no time to lose – so where will you begin your search for the means to defeat Sturm's bound Elementals?

To the north, within the mountains of the Witchtooth Line?	Turn to **115**
At Mount Pyre, to the east of the kingdom?	Turn to **309**
To the south of Femphrey, on the wind-swept Howling Plains?	Turn to **83**
Beneath the Eelsea, beyond the western coast of Femphrey?	Turn to **13**

267

Sturm staggers away from you, little more than a blackened cinder now, and transforms again. He starts to grow, his skin hardening as he does so, until he stands before you as a three-metre tall behemoth of earth and stone. With a roar like a crashing land-slide, the Colossus stomps towards you. But how can you fight something made of solid earth? If only you could wash it away, as the sea eats away at the land …

If you have the Shell of the Seas and you know the name of a Water Elemental who could help you, turn it into a number using the code A=1, B=2, C=3 … Z=26. Add the numbers together and turn to the paragraph with the same number. If not, turn to **8**.

268

You have prepared carefully to defeat the crazed Elementalist and success could well be within your grasp. (Add 1 LUCK point, even if this takes your LUCK score beyond its *Initial* level.) However you still have to somehow gain access to Sturm's Weather Machine; how do you intend to manage such a feat?

If you want to use a Potion of Levitation, turn to **207**. If you know the name of an Air Elemental and want to call on it for aid now, turn its name into a number (using the code A=1, B=2, C=3 ... Z=26 and adding the numbers together), add 30, and turn to the paragraph with the same number. If you have the codeword *Susagep* written on your *Adventure Sheet*, turn to **128**. If not, but you have the codeword *Noollab*, turn to **149**. If you have none of these things, turn to **107**.

269

You creep into the chamber, the rock at your feet cracking with every footstep. Carefully you reach between the ribs of the scorched skeleton and withdraw the crystal. You almost jump out of your skin as the skeleton suddenly collapses around you, the bones clattering noisily against the rocks. You freeze, waiting to see if anything heard you. When nothing enters the cave to see what all the noise was about, you let out your pent-up breath in a great sigh and take a closer look at the crystal. It burns with inner fire, the flames forming a letter F. (Add the Fire Crystal and its letter to your *Adventure Sheet*.) Intrigued by your find, you leave the cavern and return to the last junction. Turn to **319**.

270

You set the last tumbler, close the chest-plate and take another wary step back from the iron man. The humming coming from within the golem rises in pitch and then, with a great deal of clanking and hissing of pistons, the automaton rises to its feet. It towers above you, the top of its head scraping the roof of the bilge-tank. And then it comes to a standstill again, although the crackle of caged lightning continues to blaze within its crystalline eyes. No matter what you do next – whether it is waving your hands in front of its face, giving it verbal commands, or even tapping it on the chest-plate – the golem remains motionless as if waiting for something. (Add the codeword *Notamotua* to your *Adventure Sheet*.) Keen to know what is needed to get the golem to move, you climb back up the rusty ladder into the main body of the strange ship, having to accept the fact that you'll just have to wait and see. Turn to **54**.

271

Muldwych the Mad Monk looks at your palms, in your eyes and even gets you to stick your tongue out and say 'Ahhh!'

'Well, it doesn't look good,' he says at last, with a despairing sigh. 'I see only doom ahead of you in your quest. Nothing but your doom. Doom, doom, doom!'

The doomsayer's words fill you with a cold dread and you start to doubt that you will ever achieve what you have set out to do. Lose 1 LUCK point. Muldwych has nothing more to offer and so you and the mad monk part company, going your separate ways.

You eventually make it through to the other side of the swamp. Finding the going much easier now, you follow dirt roads as they pass through apple orchards and carefully tended turnip fields on the way to Chalannabrad. Move the Day of the Week on 3 and turn to 50.

272

Standing at the prow of the ship, the sorcerer raises his hands in the face of the approaching fog and begins to weave his spell. As you watch, a set of malevolent features form within the roiling mist. A pained expression contorts Prospero's face as he battles the sorcery controlling the Fog Elemental. And then the battle is won, and the fog is gone, leaving the

Tempest free to continue its journey across the sea.
Test your Luck. If you are Lucky, turn to **359**. If you are
Unlucky, turn to **147**.

273

Another sloping passageway gives you access to one
final cave. It is circular and strewn with massive
boulders – slabs of rock that look like they have
been brought down by the endless earthquakes.
Crystalline seams within the walls sparkle with phos-
phorescence, strange light-emitting minerals bathing
the cavern in an eerie milky light. And something else
catches your eye as well; resting on a plinth of rock, in
the middle of the chamber, is a crude clay figurine.
Approaching the plinth you take a closer look. The
figurine is an ugly thing, no more than 30 centimetres
tall and curiously bound with bands of green copper.
Carved into the bands are the words, 'Break the
bonds that bind me'. Something tells you that you
have found what you have been seeking, but what are
you going to do with the statuette now? If you to
break the copper bands, turn to **316**. If you want to
take the statuette with its bonds intact, turn to **293**.

274

The passageway continues to broaden out until it
becomes the entrance to a vast cavern. Far above you,
the rocky roof of the chamber is thick with smoke,
and the reason for this becomes clear when you catch
sight of a huge snaking coil of crimson-scaled flesh
slithering around an outcropping of igneous basalt.

You come to an abrupt stop and arm yourself. The rasping sound of the hard scales against the rock pillar is suddenly drowned out by a terrible roar. From around another outcrop appears the monster's head. It is that of a great Wyrm. As the monster comes at you, belching flame and smoke, you see that the rest of its body is that of a huge serpent at least fifteen metres in length. Leathery black wings unfold from its back, to frame its horned head. If you want to try to run from the Firewyrm, turn to **294**; otherwise you have no choice but to fight it.

FIREWYRM   SKILL 9   STAMINA 11

If the Firewyrm wins an Attack Round, roll one die; on a roll of 5–6 it blasts you with flame, causing you 4 STAMINA points of damage. If you manage to slay the monster, turn to **314**.

275

Breaking off a convenient length of wood from the inside of the hull, you wedge the plank firmly between the peg-teeth of the windlass. The mechanism protests as it tries to turn and then gives up. You have successfully locked the *Eye of the Storm* on its current course. (Add 1 to your DAMAGE score.) Your work here done, you return to the stairwell. Turn to **54**.

276
'Zephyrus!' you scream as you plunge through the storm-clouds surrounding the doomed Weather Machine. Over the rush of wind in your ears you hear a hurricane roar, and then your body is being supported on a cushion of air. You are being carried in the gale-strong arms of an Air Elemental.

'You called and I have come,' the manifestation of the West Wind booms. 'Command and I shall obey!'

'Take me back down to the ground!' you scream at the top of your voice, over the howling wind, and in no time at all you are back on terra firma. Turn to **400**.

277
As soon as their masters are dead, the Lendlelanders' mounts flee, probably heading back to the encampment. A quick inspection of the barbarians' bodies turns up 2 Meals' worth of Provisions, 5 Gold Pieces in total and a large predator's Sabretooth Fang, tied to a leather cord; a hunting charm of some kind no doubt. (If you want to take the Sabretooth Fang, add it to your *Adventure Sheet*.) You don't want to hang around here for too long, in case another patrol turns up looking for the last, so, having done your best to hide the bodies of the horsemen behind a knotty bush, you hurry on your way again. Turn to **142**.

A day after leaving the slopes of Mount Pyre you find the air temperature dropping steadily, and the further north-west you travel, the more the landscape starts to look like it is caught in the grip of winter. Freak snowstorms – no doubt caused by Balthazar Sturm's ship – have blanketed the hills, valleys and forests in drifts several metres deep. You pass villages smothered in snow, icy rivers and frozen lakes. If you are not wearing a Sun Talisman, you must lose 2 STAMINA points from the effects of the biting cold.

As you battle on through the bitter weather, the wind begins to pick up, sweeping icy flakes of snow into your face. It is then that you hear a shrill whinnying. Looking up into the blizzard-wracked sky, you see a striking white horse, with large feathered wings, fighting to stay airborne as it comes under attack from a pair of scraggy creatures that are part bird and part reptile. Their scrawny wings and scaly bodies are rimmed with frost. They are trying to claw the Pegasus with their taloned feet as they peck at it with razor-sharp beaks. The white flanks of the Pegasus are stained red with blood where the bird-reptiles have already wounded it. If you want to help the Pegasus, turn to **340**. If not, you battle on through the blizzard, leaving the poor creature to its fate. Lose 1 LUCK point, move the Day of the Week on 1, and turn to **250**.

279

Hooking the grapple over a spike of rock, you let the rope drop over the edge of the cliff and warily begin your descent. The lower you go the hotter it becomes; sweat pours off your body. But that is the least of your problems. You suddenly feel the rope give and look up. The rope has caught fire above you and one by one the strands are burning through. You quickly start to ascend again but there is not enough time. The rope burns through completely before you can reach safety, dropping you into the bubbling lava lake below. In seconds there is nothing left of you, not even your skeleton, as Mount Pyre consumes you. Your adventure is over!

280

Hearing a crash behind you, you risk a glance over your shoulder, and see the hulking form of the Dreadnought tear the door to the chamber off its hinges and force its way inside. The steel-cased figure marches past you and with a roar of gears, launches itself at the Juggernaut.

Play out the battle between the Dreadnought and the Juggernaut, as you would any other battle, but first make any necessary alterations to the automaton's stats. This is going to be a truly colossal conflict!

	SKILL	STAMINA
JUGGERNAUT	11	16
DREADNOUGHT	10	12

If the Dreadnought bests the Juggernaut, the crackling blue light in its eyes dies, the Spark having burnt itself out. The iron colossus will not fight for you again (regain 1 LUCK point and turn to **156**). If the Juggernaut smashes the Dreadnought to smithereens, turn to **262**.

281

The staircase ends at the entrance to another tower room, again smaller in circumference to the one below. This room has no windows but you can see perfectly well thanks to the pulsing blue-white glow coming from a small brass and glass flask standing on a workbench amidst a nest of copper wires. These cables connect to a large sparking switch bolted to the opposite wall and currently in the on position. There is a crackling background hum of electricity and the room is thick with the burnt tin smell of ozone. To all intents and purposes it looks like someone has managed to capture lightning in a bottle.

By the light of the bound lightning you can make out an archway in the opposite wall that leads to another spiral stone staircase. Then you see something move. Several small, squat shapes are emerging from the shadows beneath the workbench and from behind banks of machinery. As they move within the sphere of the incandescent glow of the strange flask you see that they are no bigger than Dwarfs and appear to be entirely contained within leather overalls and brass helmets. From behind the tinted glass goggle-eyes of the helmets you can see the flicker of more trapped lightning.

It seems quite likely to you that if you are to enter this room and examine the flask or even if you want to cross to the staircase on the other side, you are going to have to fight these curious creatures. If you are prepared to do just that, turn to **311**. If you think you have seen enough you can either leave the tower (turn to **398**) or descend the staircase into the depths of the basement levels, if you have not already done so (turn to **160**).

282

Pulling yourself through the water with powerful strokes, you make for the temple. If you have the codeword *Retsnom* recorded on your *Adventure Sheet*, turn to **200** at once. If not, then the horror unfurls a tentacle, grabs you tightly around the ankle and in a flash is dragging you towards its gaping beaked maw. You have no choice but to fight. Turn to **242** and for the first Attack Round you must fight with your Attack Strength reduced by 1 point, as you are still in the grip of the beast.

283

The wind moans as it blows towards you along the chasm you are following. The wind gradually picks up until you round a large boulder to be confronted by a startling sight. There in front of you is a concentrated, swirling whirlwind of dust and sand, no bigger than you are. Without warning the dancing Dust Devil moves towards you and you find yourself having to fight the territorial air spirit.

DUST DEVIL   SKILL 7   STAMINA 6

If it is Windsday, increase the Dust Devil's SKILL score by 1 point and its STAMINA by 2. Due to its shifting, insubstantial form, it is very hard to actually harm the wind sprite; any successful strikes against it will only cause 1 STAMINA point of damage. If you defeat the creature you are able to continue on your way. It is not long before you reach another parting of the ways. Will you go left this time (turn to **208**) or right (turn to **333**)?

284

'Now you die!' Sturm screams, his voice the howling voice of the gale. You must fight the furious Maelstrom!

MAELSTROM   SKILL 12   STAMINA 10

If you reduce the Maelstrom's STAMINA to 3 points or fewer, there is an explosion of blinding white light accompanied by a clap of thunder. You are hurled backwards by the blast into a bank of machinery. Lose 3 STAMINA points and, if you are still alive, turn to **397**.

285

Standing outside the locked iron door you hear sounds of movement and angry muttering. It sounds

like there's someone trapped in the room beyond.
Will you:

Take the key from the peg on the wall
and unlock the door?   Turn to 335
Keep on heading down the stairs
(if you haven't done so already)?   Turn to 188
Head upwards again and explore
the rest of the tower (if you
haven't already done so)?   Turn to 220
Ascend the staircase and leave the
tower altogether?   Turn to 398

286

Two days of hard walking brings you within sight
of the walls of the capital city of Femphrey –
Chalannabrad! (Move the Day of the Week on 2.) You
have been here several times before, but the sight of
the city's open, tree-lined avenues, stunning parks
and monumental public buildings never ceases to
amaze. But you're not here to see the sights on this
occasion – you have a job to do. You waste no time in
making your way to the ancient and impressive
College of Mages – a building of soaring spires, sparkling crystal domes and myriad labyrinthine passageways hiding who knows what sorcerous secrets.
Being known to the Mages already – having completed a number of missions at their behest in the past
– you are soon granted an audience with the High
Council of Sorcerers, Spellcasters and Sages ...

Less than half an hour later, you are leaving the Council Chamber feeling furious and frustrated.

It was as if the Council didn't want to know about the potential threat to Femphrey, making it quite clear that they thought you were at best exaggerating and at worst making the whole thing up. But why were they so opposed to the idea of somebody manipulating the weather to further their own evil ambitions? Well let them think what they like; it's not going to stop you getting to the bottom of this threat to the kingdom.

As you stride away from the Council Chamber the door to the chamber opens and a youthful-looking mage with a neatly-trimmed goatee beard and wearing voluminous red robes embroidered with swirling golden comets steps out into the corridor after you. You recognise him at once. It is Matteus Charmweaver, a mage who you have worked with in the past – the last time, battling the Ogre Shamen of the southern Lendleland.

'I am so sorry, my friend,' he apologises. 'I can't believe the Council would treat you like that, after all that you have done for the College in the past. But it's because they're embarrassed. You see, they know who's behind the attack on Vastarin, but they don't know what to do to stop him.'

'Who is it then?' you ask.

'His name is Balthazar Sturm, and he used to be a

member of the College of Mages,' Matteus explains. 'He practised the path of the Elementalist, focusing particularly on meteorological magic, until he was thrown out for carrying out irresponsible sorcerous experiments, trying to combine magic and machinery. You might say that he left under a dark cloud, swearing revenge not just on the College, but also Chalannabrad and the whole kingdom. The truth is, from what you have told them and their own magical scrying, the Council suspect that Sturm is behind the attack on Vastarin, which means he's back and has begun to exact his revenge.'

'So how *can* he be stopped?' you press.

'Come with me,' Matteus says, mysteriously.

The mage leads you to his private quarters within the College where stands a stone bowl containing a pool of water, its surface as smooth and reflective as a mirror. Matteus intones an incantation and stares, unblinkingly, into the mirror-pool. You fancy you see images swirl and change within the water but you cannot clearly make out what they are. Eventually the pool clears again and Matteus looks up.

'There is no time to waste,' he states with cold finality. 'Sturm has created a weather-altering flying machine, and has bound four Greater Elementals within it to provide it with its means of sorcerous power. It is this craft that you saw within the eye of the storm. If you are to have any hope of standing against Sturm and stopping his Weather Machine, you are going to have to find the means to overcome these Elementals. You will need to search in places where the four elements of earth, air, fire and water are in their greatest concentrations.'

'And where's that?' you ask.

'Deep beneath the mountains of the Witchtooth Line, on the wind-swept Howling Plains, at the heart of Mount Pyre, the volcano that stands within the mountainous borders of Mauristatia, and deep beneath the Eelsea. I can offer you a little magical aid to help you on your quest, but there is precious little time to waste. The whole of Femphrey is in danger and you must be on your way as soon as possible.'

You can ask Matteus for help with one of the four elements, but which will it be? Will you choose:

Earth?   Turn to 306
Air?   Turn to 326
Fire?   Turn to 356
Water?   Turn to 376

Or alternatively, will you tell Matteus that, as there's no time to waste, you're ready to set off straightaway (turn to 395)?

287

You open the door and swim into what must have once been the captain's cabin – and he's still there! A skeleton, wearing a water-spoiled gentleman's jacket of crimson and gold and a bicorn hat, sits behind a heavy-looking oak desk, cutlass in hand. And there's something else striking about the skeleton – the large gold key hanging over his fleshless ribcage on a rusted chain. Everything else that might once have been of value or interest here has long since been taken by the sea. Do you want to risk lifting the key from around the skeleton's neck (turn to 257), or would you rather leave the captain's cabin and search the hull (turn to 217), or leave the wreck altogether (turn to 6)?

288

The keen edge of your blade makes short work of the ropes. Pulley blocks come crashing down and the windlass spins freely now that there is nothing to restrain it. The whole craft suddenly lurches sideways, throwing you across the chamber. You have deprived the helm of the means to steer the vessel. (Add 2 to your DAMAGE score and regain 1 LUCK point.) Your work here done, you return to the landing. Turn to 54.

289

It seems incredible, but the plans are for the most amazing flying machine. Its outer appearance is that of a huge fish but inside it is a complex mishmash of machinery and magic, containing devices with names like the Lightning Generator, the Burning Glass and the Elemental Engine. From what you can tell, spread out on the desk is the final set of blueprints for the incredible craft. (If you want to take the Blueprints add them to your *Adventure Sheet* along with the fact that they are version 13 of the plans.) Now will you:

Descend to the very bottom of the
tower and explore its dungeon levels
   (if you haven't done so already)?   Turn to **160**
Quit the tower altogether?   Turn to **398**

290*

The tunnel soon peters out at the edge of a towering precipice within a vast natural cavern. The rails continue, however, supported by a network of wooden scaffolding. Standing with its wheels still on the tracks is a mine-cart.

You would not like to try clambering over the rails and the teetering scaffolding to proceed any further, but it might be possible to travel onwards into the mine on board the mine-cart. It would be much quicker, for a start. If you want to do this, turn to **308**. If not, you will have to return to the junction and take the right-hand tunnel, by turning to **5**.

291

You grapple with the Giant, every muscle in your body aching with effort. Then you glimpse a gap in the Giant's defence. Hooking an arm around the back of one tree-trunk leg, you twist and shift your body weight. The Giant comes crashing down on the floor of the clearing with a great wallop that echoes through the forest. You step back, uncertain how the Giant will react to being defeated. Slowly, he sits up, a disgruntled scowl on his face.

'Now I see 'ow you did for old Gog Magog,' the Giant grumbles. 'Yoo really are a hero!' A broad, toothy grin appears on his face. 'If Cormoran 'ad to lose to anybody, I'm glad it was yoo.' And with that, you and the Giant Cormoran shake hands and go your separate ways. (Add the codeword *Naromroc* to your *Adventure Sheet* and regain 1 LUCK point.)

You keep on walking for another two days (move the Day of the Week on 2), always keeping the great grey wall of the Witchtooth Line ahead of you. Turn to **250**.

292

Making your way to the prow of the ship, you put the horn to your lips and blow. A booming note sounds across the waves. By the time it hits the approaching fog bank, it has become a deafening blast that tears apart the magical bonds providing the Fog Elemental with its sinister sentience. You take the horn from your lips and the note dies, but the Fog Elemental has been dispatched. The *Tempest* is free to continue on its journey across the sea. *Test your Luck*. If you are Lucky, turn to **359**. If you are Unlucky, turn to **147**.

293

As you pick up the statuette, with its primitive brutish features, you notice that a single word has been carved into its base: *Arkholith*. It is then that you feel the first of the tremors. You turn from the plinth and run for the exit. But before you even reach the tunnel mouth, with a sharp cracking of stone two of the large boulders dotting the cavern break apart, the shattered rocks becoming parts of a crudely humanoid body. Cracks in the boulders yawn open and you see hard mineral teeth within the rocky maws, while nuggets of quartz become sparkling eyes. If you are to escape this sacred place of earth power, you are going to have to fight the Boulder Beasts together.

	SKILL	STAMINA
First BOULDER BEAST	8	11
Second BOULDER BEAST	8	10

(If today is Earthday, add 1 point to both the monsters' STAMINA scores.) Although their rocky hides will blunt an ordinary sword, Wyrmbiter's enchantments mean that you can injure the Boulder Beasts as normal. However, if you fight them using a crushing weapon, such as a Warhammer or Mace, every blow that connects will smash their bodies for 3 STAMINA points of damage. To swap Wyrmbiter for a crushing weapon, if you have one, you must forfeit one Attack Round, during which time both the Boulder Beasts will get in an unopposed strike.

If you destroy these elemental monsters, the spirits inhabiting the boulders are banished back to the Elemental Plane of Earth, their rock bodies shattering into myriad shards. (Add the Clay Statuette to your *Adventure Sheet*, along with its name, and regain 1 LUCK point.) With the way ahead clear, you carefully make your way back out of the caves. It is then the seismic tremors return with a vengeance! Turn to **10**.

294

The instant you turn your back on the Wyrm it blasts you with its superheated breath. Lose 6 STAMINA points. (If you have a Dragon Tattoo or a Dragon Shield, are wearing a Wyrmskin Cloak or you drank a Potion of Fire Protection before entering the Fire Tunnels, you may reduce this damage by 2 points.) If you survive this roasting, you run for cover within the narrower passageway. Turn to 344.

295

You find the path you are following now curves around to the right, and rises as it does so. It is not long before you come to a dead-end within a high-roofed cave. The rocks in this chamber are black with soot and sulphurous fumes rise from bubbling mud-pools in the cave floor, and you are not alone. Hissing in anger at your having invaded their territory, a number of large sulphur-yellow lizards haul themselves out of their hot mud baths, determined to drive you away. These creatures are Salamanders – not the small amphibious type but the large, carnivorous lizard kind, creatures with a taste for cooked meat. They cook the flesh of their prey themselves – with their own fiery breath! You must fight the Salamanders two at a time.

	SKILL	STAMINA
First SALAMANDER	6	6
Second SALAMANDER	6	5
Third SALAMANDER	5	6
Fourth SALAMANDER	6	7

If any of the Salamanders wins an Attack Round, roll one die. On a roll of 6 the creature has spat a great gobbet of flame at you (lose 4 STAMINA points instead of the usual 2). If today is Fireday, the Salamander will use this attack on a roll of 5 or 6. If you defeat the Salamanders, you beat a hasty retreat from their cave before any more can turn up. Turn to **339**.

296

Although you may have discovered various intriguing clues during your exploration of the Lightning Tower, you still don't really have any idea who was behind the attack on Vastarin and so you have no choice but to travel to Chalannabrad for answers. The trek back over the border and into Femphrey is uneventful but time-consuming. Move the Day of the Week on 2 and turn to **286**.

297

Some sixth sense sets your hackles rising and, reacting on some instinctive level, you duck, successfully avoiding the swiping claw that makes a grab for you out of the blizzard. Suddenly the hunters have become the hunted. Turn to **261**.

298

You have rushed to complete your quest and defeat the insane Elementalist, but you could still triumph. However, if you are going to stop Sturm, you are going to have to get on board his Weather Machine first – and how do you plan to do that?

If you want to use a Potion of Levitation, turn to **207**. If you know the name of an Air Elemental and want to call on it for aid now, turn its name into a number (using the code A=1, B=2, C=3 … Z=26 and adding the numbers together), add 30, and turn to the paragraph with the same number. If you have the code-word *Susagep* written on your *Adventure Sheet*, turn to **128**. If not, but you have the codeword *Noollab*, turn to **149**. If you have none of these things, turn to **107**.

299

Holding the length of rope in one hand, you spin the grapple in the other and then let go. The barbed iron head clatters against the rock-face on the opposite side of the chasm and becomes snagged on a ledge. Having tested the rope to make sure that the grapple will hold, with a bold leap into the unknown, you swing across the chasm to land safely on the other side. After some judicial tugging, the grapple comes free again and you proceed on your way. Turn to **185**.

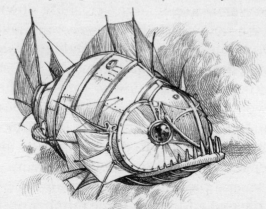

300

As you approach the maw from the other side, you see that one of the 'teeth' of the rock mouth is made from a clear quartz-like crystal. Intrigued you risk snatching the crystal from the rocks. Looking more closely, you see that it burns with inner fire, and that the flames form the letter H. (If you want to take the Fire Crystal with you, add it and its letter to your *Adventure Sheet*.) It is then that you realise that the scalding flames are no longer venting. Seizing the moment, you run back through and head on along the tunnel. Turn to **245**.

301

Swimming up to the statue you tug at the trident, but it is locked within Hydana's stony grasp. You pull harder, bracing your legs against the statue. Suddenly something begins to give – but it's not the trident. The huge statue of the Sea God starts to topple towards you and you only just manage to swim out of the way before it comes crashing down on the sand-strewn floor of the temple sanctum. Before you can do anything else, a deep rumbling reverberates throughout the temple, and pieces of the structure shake loose, tumbling slowly through the water around you. You have desecrated the Sea God's temple and incurred his wrath. (Lose 2 LUCK points!) You have no choice but to try to escape as the building collapses around you. As you swim for the surface, several pieces of falling masonry strike you. Roll one die and add 2; this is the number of STAMINA points' damage you suffer. If you are still alive, if you have the codeword *Retsnom* recorded on your *Adventure Sheet*, turn to **358**. If not, turn to **318**.

302

Descending the iron steps into the bilges, you are soon standing knee-deep in stinking, rust-coloured water. The putrid smell of the stagnant water that has dripped down through the ship to collect here is truly nauseating. If today is Stormsday, turn to **320**. If not, turn to **336**.

303

The sun continues to beat down as you make your way along the gorge. You have not travelled very far before you reach another fork in the path. This time will you head right (turn to **208**) or left (turn to **178**)?

304

The tunnel continues to ascend until you enter a spectacular cavern filled with huge crystalline growths, sparkling with a rainbow of colours. The whole cavern is shaking apart as the volcano starts to erupt, crystalline structures the size of standing stones crashing down from the roof in front of you. It is going to be a challenge to make it through this cavern unscathed, and then your heart sinks; you can see no other way out of this cavern. It is a dead-end! (Add 1 to your TIME TRACK.)

At that very moment, just when you are thinking you are doomed, another giant slab of quartz breaks free of the ceiling and smashes into the wall of the cavern. Daylight suddenly floods the crystal cave as a gaping hole appears in the side of the volcano. Without daring to delay a moment longer, you sprint for the opening.

How long has it taken you to get to this point? If your TIME TRACK is 4, regain 1 LUCK point and turn to **388**. If your TIME TRACK is 5, turn to **323**. If your TIME TRACK is 6, turn to **353**, and if your TIME TRACK is 7, turn to **373**.

305

Taking on a Giant unarmed was a bold move, but was only ever really going to go one way. The bout has barely begun before you find yourself lifted high into the air and then tossed across the clearing to land in an uncomfortable heap several metres away. Roll one die and lose that many STAMINA points, but no fewer than 2, and lose 1 LUCK point. The Giant, having proved itself, leaves you where you are lying and stomps off through the forest, muttering something about being ready to challenge the new chief. Having recovered your own equipment you limp off through the forest.

You keep on walking for another two days (move the Day of the Week on 2), always keeping the great grey wall of the Witchtooth Line ahead of you. Turn to **250**.

306

Matteus takes an earthenware bottle from a shelf and hands it to you saying, 'This is a Potion of Giant Strength. Earth Elementals are the most belligerent and strongest of all Elemental-kind. If you ever come up against one, you'll be glad you had this about you, but use it only in the most extreme circumstances.'

If you wish, you may drink the Potion of Giant Strength before any battle. It will raise your SKILL score by 2 for that one battle and the damage you cause by 1 point. Add the Potion of Giant Strength to your *Adventure Sheet* and turn to **193**.

307

Keeping low, ducking down behind any piece of cover you can find, you slowly advance on the horsemen's encampment. Once or twice you come rather too close for comfort to running into a mounted patrol and at one point you even have to double back a short way to avoid being spotted. But all this stealth pays off in the end, as eventually you find yourself sneaking past the animal-hide tents into the camp itself.

Taking even more care now, you make your way deep into the heart of the camp – past corrals of horses, blacksmiths sharpening weapons and armourers tending to the marauders' equipment. You round the side of a tent and freeze. Twenty metres ahead of you, you see a much larger and more magnificent tent. In front of its open door, flanked by guards, resplendent in his red lacquered leather armour and dragon-helm, seated upon his blackwood throne, is the leader of this massing army – the barbarian horde's Battle-Khan. Across his knees rests a keen-edged sabre and he is staring imperiously ahead at the war preparations taking place within the camp.

You know a little of the marauder tribes of the Lendleland plains and you know that their Battle-Khans are proud men, whose lives are ruled by a strict warrior's code. If you could face this warrior in single combat and shame him, by defeating him, you might be able to stop the planned invasion before it has even begun. It would be a bold move to challenge this Battle-Khan but from what you have seen with your own eyes, it would appear that Femphrey's borders are at risk of a harrowing by these battle-hardened tribesmen.

If you want to reveal yourself and challenge the Battle-Khan, turn to **348**. If you would rather quietly slip away from the marauder's encampment and continue on your way south, turn to **328**.

308

Fastening your lantern to the front of the truck, you clamber into it and use your sword to get the cart moving. As soon as the rails run over the edge of the precipice they slope downwards and the cart picks up speed. Suddenly a junction appears in the line ahead, with one route bending round to the left while the other branch turns right. You suddenly realise that there is no obvious way of steering, other than with a shift in bodyweight.

Choose which way you want to direct the cart – either left or right – and then roll three dice to test your STAMINA. If you roll less than or equal to your STAMINA score you succeed in directing the cart the way you want it to go. If you roll greater than your STAMINA score, roll one die again; if the number is odd you go left, if it is even the cart turns right. So, which way did you go in the end?

Left?   Turn to **122**
Right?   Turn to **138**

309

A day on from leaving the southern limits of Femphrey (move the Day of the Week on 1), the heat has only intensified. The sun blazes down from a sky devoid of clouds. You pass through a landscape that should be lush meadows and rolling farmland, but which is instead a drought-ridden desert. The ground is parched and cracked. River beds are dry and the wind sweeps eddying dust clouds before it.

One of these dust clouds resolves itself into a caravan of carts and wagons, being pulled by horses and oxen. A rag-tag band of dejected-looking people trudge along the road after it. You appear to be the only person travelling into this blighted area; everyone else is leaving it!

You ask a downcast farmer what has happened to force them to leave their homes and villages. 'Can't you tell?' he replies abruptly. 'It's the drought, isn't it? All our crops have failed. We have nothing to eat. There's nothing for us there anymore. Our only hope is to go elsewh–'

The man suddenly breaks off as the ground starts to shake. A moment later, the shuddering passes. 'What was that?' he asks, shooting you an anxious look. Another tremor ripples through the bone-dry ground beneath your feet and the road surface splits open. *Test your Luck*. If you are Lucky, turn to **346**. If you are Unlucky, turn to **218**.

310*

You come at last to a crossroads. From here you can either go left, along a damp tunnel (turn to **399**), right, along a dusty corridor (turn to **227**), or straight on, following a slimy-walled tunnel (turn to **327**).

311

Don't you just hate it when you're right? As soon as you step over the threshold into the room, the curiously clad creatures waddle towards you. As you draw Wyrmbiter from its scabbard, you notice that each of the strange beings has the word 'FULGURITE' etched onto a brass plaque on the front of their overalls along with a number. You are under attack from Fulgurites Seven, Nine and Ten. Within the confines of the cluttered laboratory you can manoeuvre yourself so that you face your attackers one at a time.

	SKILL	STAMINA
First FULGURITE	6	4
Second FULGURITE	5	5
Third FULGURITE	6	5

If you defeat all three, make a note of the numbers of the Fulgurites you have fought and then turn to **351**.

312

Boldly you leap onto the first of the steppingstones. You reach the second just as easily. You are getting the feel for this now; the third doesn't cause you any trouble at all. But it is as you are about to step out onto the fourth steppingstone, that you notice a disturbance in the flow of lava, and something monstrous emerges from within it. You unsheathe Wyrmbiter as the creature continues to rise from the lava river, standing three metres tall, knee-deep in the oozing magma. The creature appears to be formed from molten rock and yet where it is now exposed to the air it is starting to cool, forming a crazed, rocky black hide. Do you want to stand and fight the hardening Magma Beast (turn to **191**), or do you want to attempt to evade it by leaping across the last of the steppingstones (turn to **231**)?

313

The hunter, who introduces himself as Sylas, decides that it is best if you set off on your beast quest without further delay; the first to return with the prize wins the reward after all. All manner of fell creatures are known to make their lairs within the crags to the north of Eerieside, in the marshes to the east, and even within Lake Eerie itself. But where would the Stormdrake have its haunt, if it really does exist?

Once you are out in the wilds, well beyond the town, you put your tracking skills to good use. *Test your Skill*, subtracting 2 from the dice roll if you possess a

Sabretooth Fang. If you succeed, turn to 357. If you fail, turn to 195.

314

You have won a mighty victory indeed. Regain 1 LUCK point. Within the Firewyrm's lair, you find the charred remains of its previous victims – the charred skeletons of mountain goats and Salamanders that it must have picked off from the slopes of the volcano, and even some human bones. Among these burnt relics you find a handful of Gold Pieces (roll two dice and add 6 to discover precisely how many), a Warhammer, still clenched in the heat-fused hand bones of a dead Dwarf, and two curious crystals. Each glows with an eerie inner light, and they feel warm to the touch. As you pick them up, the flickering flames inside each appear to form a different letter – A and S. Having taken what you want from the Firewyrm's lair (making sure that you note it down on your *Adventure Sheet*), as the cavern is effectively a dead-end, you return to the last junction you passed and follow the other, smaller tunnel deeper into the volcano. Turn to 344.

315

Stepping out onto the gangplank, you leap off the end. You drop like a stone into the sea and the waves close over your head. The weight of your armour and sword drag you down towards the submerged reef. Your lungs begin to ache until, unable to fight the urge any longer, you take a gulping breath. But what's this? Miraculously you are still able to breathe – just as you had hoped. You breathe a sigh of relief and moments later your feet touch the seabed.

You quickly look around you. The sunlight penetrating the water is muted at these depths but, as your eyes become accustomed to the reduced light levels, you find that you can see well enough. Behind you the reef itself rises back up towards the surface and you can see the underside of the ship's hull above you. Not many metres ahead is the edge of the continental shelf, and beyond that nothing but the gloom of the ocean depths. To your right you can make out the holed wreck of a galleon, while to your left you can see that the seabed is riven by a great fissure. Deciding that you are unlikely to find the temple beyond the edge of the continental shelf, will you make for the wreck (turn to **337**) or the rift (turn to **6**)?

316

You prise the copper bands open with the tip of your sword and feel the first of the tremors almost immediately. The rock begins to shake beneath your feet and at the same time, as if in sympathy, the statuette starts to vibrate in your hand. You drop the ugly clay figure on the floor where it cracks open and immediately starts to transform. It swells until it is the size of a man, but it doesn't stop there. It continues to grow, taking on the form of a massive stone giant, its hide formed from grating slabs of rock.

You have unleashed an Earth Elemental on the world!

(Lose 2 LUCK points.) The strength of the tremors increases and pieces of rock break from of the roof to come crashing down around you. You back away from the plinth as the Elemental continues to manifest before you, and then turn on your heel and run. There is no way can stand and fight the Earth Elemental here, with the cave shaking apart around you.

You race back through the caves as fast as you are able, until you fly out of the cleft into the huge chamber where the caves meet the mine. The ground continues to shake at the approach of the Elemental. Earth Elementals are notoriously bad-tempered and evil-natured creatures and this one, having been trapped beneath the earth for Throff knows how long, is hungry for revenge. Two huge hands, with fingers like spears of rock, grasp the cave mouth and tear the fissure open, and the Earth Elemental enters the chamber. It looks like a giant composed of rock and earth. The Elemental raises its fists in anger and bellows its fury to the world. The roar, like the crash of a rockslide, echoes from the chamber walls, the subsonic waves causing more rocks to tumble down from the roof and splash into the lake.

If you have the codeword *Enihcam* written on your *Adventure Sheet*, turn to **244**. If not, what are you going to do now? Will you:

Use the Spark of Life, if you have it?	Turn to **92**
Drink a Potion of Giant Strength, if you have one?	Turn to **81**

Prepare to fight the Earth Elemental?   Turn to **61**
Keep running?   Turn to **42**

317

The deck of the sunken ship is deserted ... or at least that's how it appears at first. Then you notice the dark shapes circling in the water above. The forbidding silhouettes are unmistakeable – Hammerheads! And the sharks have seen you too. With a flick of its sickle-shaped tail, one of them makes its descent. The other quickly follows. Amidst the masts and the kelp, fight the Hammerheads one at a time.

	SKILL	STAMINA
First HAMMERHEAD	7	8
Second HAMMERHEAD	7	7

If you kill the sharks, the only place that might be worth exploring is whatever lies beyond the door to the forecastle at the prow of the ship (turn to **287**). If you would rather not hang around any longer on deck, in case something else spots you there and considers you a potential meal, you can either swim down into the hull (turn to **217**), or quit the wreck altogether and make for the rift (turn to **6**).

318

Your head breaks the surface and you breathe normally again. You soon find yourself back onboard the *Tempest*. If you have a shell with you, turn to the paragraph which is the same as the number of spines on the shell.

⚅ ⚃

'Did you find what you were looking for then?' Captain Katarina asks, but before you can answer, the hard-bitten buccaneer turns to the matter of her money. 'So, what treasures did you recover from the ocean depths? Did the sea give up its bounty?'

Did you recover any treasure from the reef or the rift? If so, turn to **69**. If not, turn to **88**.

319

After only a short distance, the new tunnel ends at another T-junction. It feels as if the dry air of the Fire Tunnels is getting hotter. For as long as you remain within the volcano you must reduce your SKILL by 1 point, due to the terrible heat. However, if you drank a Potion of Fire Protection before entering, if you are wearing a Wyrmskin Cloak, or if you have a Dragon Tattoo, you may ignore this penalty. Which way will you go now? Left (turn to **339**) or right (turn to **295**)?

320

The water suddenly convulses before you and a pile of stinking rubbish – bits of wood, discarded rags, strips of torn sailcloth, sheared metal components – rises from of the foul water. The rubbish has assumed a roughly humanoid shape and something like a mouth hisses at you from amidst the mound. The residual magical energy permeating the ship has also collected down here in the bilges and has animated the debris, furnishing it with a crude and malicious sentience.

DETRITUS   SKILL 8   STAMINA 8

If you reduce the magical rubbish heap's STAMINA score to 0, the esoteric energies holding it together dissipate and it crumbles back into the sloshing soup filling the bilges. Turn to **336**.

321

The instant you lift the shell from the plinth, you feel a commotion in the water around you and three figures appear in front of the statue of the Sea God. They look like women, although it is also quite clear that they are formed from seawater themselves. They watch you intently with eyes that glimmer like mother of pearl, and you hear them speak inside your mind.

'Why do you defile this sacred place?' the first asks.

'Who would dare profane the temple of the divine Sea himself?' asks the second.

'Speak now or forfeit your life to Hydana!' demands the third.

Do you want to try to explain your reasons for seeking the Sea God's aid (turn to 341), or will you simply draw your sword against them, so that you might take what it is you need (turn to 361)?

322

You set off up the slope towards the top of the rocky outcrop and the curious tower. As you look up at the tower, searching for any obvious signs of life, you see the V-shapes of birds circling the pinnacle far above. Only they're not birds. As you peer closer you see that they actually appear to be winged dogs, or perhaps wolves with wings.

A chill thrill of fear crackles down the length of your spine as you realise what these creatures are. Aakor were perhaps once ordinary wolves, before they gained their wings and their penchant for warm blood, and they have caught sight of you with their keen eyes. Steering themselves in your direction with their bushy tails, with a few beats of the broad, feathery wings sprouting from their shoulder blades, the pack swoops down on you, claws outstretched, fangs bared. Once again Wyrmbiter is in your hands. Exposed on the treeless escarpment, you will have to fight the Aakor all together.

⚀ ⚁

	SKILL	STAMINA
First AAKOR	7	8
Second AAKOR	7	7
Third AAKOR	6	7

As soon as you have killed one of the winged wolves, the other Aakor break off from the fight, howling, and soar away on the thermals to find easier prey. Add the codeword *Detnuh* to your *Adventure Sheet* and turn to **51**.

323

You had to double back once, on your flight through the Fire Tunnels which cost you dear in time. How quickly you made your run will be what decides whether you make it out alive or not. Roll three dice. If the number rolled is less than or equal to your STAMINA score, to **388**, but if it is greater, turn to **373**.

324

If you have the codeword *Knarc* on your *Adventure Sheet*, turn to **266**. If not, turn to **296**.

325

Taking the six-sided flask from your backpack, you ease it into the hollow inside the metal man's head. You then secure the lid again and take a cautious step backwards. Almost immediately blue sparks flash within the automaton's crystal eyes and a resonating hum fills the bilge-space – but that's all that happens. Obviously something else needs to be done for the golem to activate fully, something involving the numbered tumblers inside its chest. If you would like to try setting the tumblers to a particular number, turn to the same paragraph as that number. If you don't know which number to try you find that the top of the automaton's head is now locked and you cannot remove the Spark of Life again. Cross it off your *Adventure Sheet* and turn to **54** as you leave the bilges bitterly disappointed.

326

'Then I give you this,' Matteus says, taking a glass bottle blown into the shape of a man's face with puffed-out cheeks from a shelf. 'It is a Potion of Levitation. If you're going to be dealing with Air Elementals, it might be better if you can deal with them on their own terms.' Add the Potion of Levitation to your *Adventure Sheet* and turn to **193**.

327

You are proceeding along the passageway when you suddenly hear a wet splat on the ground behind you. Lying there on the floor of the tunnel is a strange, jelly-like creature. While you are distracted, looking at the curious tunnel dweller, another of the creatures drops from the ceiling right on top of you this time. The amoeba-like Iron Eater isn't interested in harming you, rather in consuming any metal you have about your person. But you are going to have to fight the Iron Eater anyway, if you are to save your precious equipment from being consumed.

IRON EATER   SKILL 4   STAMINA 5

If the monster wins an Attack Round, you do not lose
any STAMINA points; instead it eats one item of
armour (lose 1 SKILL point). When you have no
armour (such as chainmail, a shield or a weapon
other than Wyrmbiter, which is immune to the Iron
Eater's attack) left to eat the Iron Eater will fall from
you, its appetite satisfied for now. If you win an
Attack Round, you are able to dislodge the creature
and shake it onto the ground, where you can finish it
off with ease.

Once you are done battling the Iron Eater, you make
your way to where the tunnel ends at a natural chimney in the rock. There are no ladders or rungs ham-
mered into the rock to help you to descend. You are
either going to need to use a Rope and Grapple (turn
to 383), climb down using what hand- and foot-holds
you can find in the rock (turn to 347) or return to
the crossroads and (choosing a route you haven't
taken already) turn either left, along a dusty corridor
(turn to 227), or right, along a damp passageway
(turn to 399).

328

You suddenly feel very exposed as you turn and
attempt to retrace your steps through the camp. *Test
your Skill*. If you succeed, turn to 175. If you fail, you
are surprised by the appearance of a guard patrol
(turn to 348).

329

Sensing danger, you leap from the road, and behind the natural barrier formed by a tree. A volley of arrows embeds themselves in the bark on the other side. Your heart pounding in your chest, you unsheathe your sword.

'Call yourself a hero, hiding behind a tree like a gutless Goblin?' a harsh voice calls from elsewhere within the wood. You would know that voice anywhere; it is Varick Oathbreaker. His long-held rivalry has finally spilled over into outright aggression.

Boldly, you step from behind the tree, weapon in hand. Varick is advancing on your position with his gang of cut-throats in tow. 'Now who's the coward?' you throw back, turning the insult back on the rogue. 'Five against one's hardly fair, is it?'

'Who cares?' Varick spits. 'Way I see it, you've done me over one too many times. Who cares about fair?'

'I meant, it hardly seems fair on you,' comes your retort. 'I could take on these dogs with one hand tied behind my back.'

With growls of anger, Varick Oathbreaker and his band of brigands attack! You must fight them two at a time. However, Varick himself will only join the battle right at the end.

	SKILL	STAMINA
SCARRED RUFFIAN	7	7
BRUTAL BRIGAND	6	6

HIRED THUG	7	6
LUMBERING LOUT	6	7
VARICK OATHBREAKER	8	10

If you defeat your rival and his ruffian gang, turn to **371**.

330

You have sacrificed thorough preparation in your haste to put a stop to the crazed weather-mage's plans. It is unlikely that you will complete your quest successfully, as you are poorly-prepared. (Lose 1 LUCK point.) And if you are going to stop Sturm, you are going to have to get on board his Weather Machine first. How do you plan to do that?

If you want to use a Potion of Levitation, turn to **207**. If you know the name of an Air Elemental and want to call on it for aid now, turn its name into a number (using the code A=1, B=2, C=3 … Z=26 and adding the numbers together), add 30, and turn to the paragraph with the same number. If you have the codeword *Susagep* written on your *Adventure Sheet*, turn to **128**. If not, but you have the codeword *Noollab*, turn to **149**. If you have none of these things, turn to **107**.

331

Do you have the codeword *Notamotua* recorded on your *Adventure Sheet*? If so, turn to **280**. If not, turn to **262**.

332

As the relentless mist engulfs the ship you strike out with your enchanted blade. A malevolent face forms within it and coiling tendrils of fog coalesce into pseudo-tentacles that writhe towards you as the Fog Elemental fights back.

FOG ELEMENTAL   SKILL 7   STAMINA 10

If you reduce the Fog Elemental's STAMINA score to zero, the chains of sorcery holding the misty manifestation together are broken and it dissipates, leaving the *Tempest* free to continue its journey across the sea. *Test your Luck*. If you are Lucky, turn to **359**. If you are Unlucky, turn to **147**.

333

The first sign you have that something might be amiss up ahead is the large number of carrion birds in the sky above the ravine you are now following. And then you see it; lying face down on the ground is the carcass of a partially-armoured warrior. The dead man's pack lies abandoned beside him. Two crude feathered arrows protrude from his back. You don't know how long he's been here, but it's been long enough for the vultures to start on him. Three of the ugly birds are pecking the flesh from his bones. As you approach, all three turn to look at you and issue harsh, squawking cries, warning you not to get too close. Do you want to approach the body with the intention of grabbing the dead man's backpack (turn to 248), or would you rather leave the vultures to their meal and continue on your way without disturbing them (turn to 148)?

334

You soon find yourself being booed out of town, simply because you cannot make it rain, even though you never claimed that you could, when, quite obviously, nobody else can either. Irritated and annoyed, you leave Quartz, but the villagers' derision has shaken your confidence. Lose 1 LUCK point. You continue walking south-west for two more days (move the Day of the Week on 2), until you enter the desolate borderlands of the Howling Plains. Turn to 83.

335

Preparing yourself for whatever might be hidden behind the door, you confidently place the key in the lock and turn it. Your hand on your sword, just in case, you throw the door open. You are slightly surprised to see a gaunt-faced old man wearing a grubby robe and with a shock of wild grey hair peering back at you from behind a pair of pince-nez spectacles. The old man is obviously being kept here against his will but he appears to have been locked inside his own study. He is sitting at a work-table surrounded by ink-stained charts and plans, as well as a number of miniature wood and wire models of everything from flying machines to siege weapons. In fact, on hearing you unlock the door, he has armed himself with a hand-held loaded ballista. For a moment the two of you regard each other suspiciously until you reassure the man that you mean him no harm and a broad, relieved grin spreads across his face.

'By all the gods, am I pleased to see you?' he declares, excitedly jumping to his feet.

'Who are you?' you ask. 'And what are you doing locked in here?'

'Oh, I do beg your pardon,' the old man gushes. 'I was just so relieved that you weren't *him* that I completely forgot my manners. My name is Inigo Crank,' he says, holding out an oil-stained hand. You shake it uncertainly and introduce yourself. 'Ah yes, I've heard of you,' he goes on. 'Wasn't it you that scuppered the War-Tower of those Brician Battle-Lords?' You confirm that it was. 'Good job with that spanner, by the way. Anyway, where was I? Oh yes, you asked me what I was doing locked in here. Well, it's all down to that traitorous turncoat Balthazar Sturm isn't it?'

'Balthazar Sturm,' you say. 'I've never heard of him.'

'No, I'm not surprised, cocky young upstart that he is! He once studied at the College of Mages in Chalannabrad, under the great Elementalist Nimbus Cloudchaser, until he was thrown out for his irresponsible sorcerous experiments. Of course I didn't know that when I met him, did I? He conned me good and proper too. Had me convinced that he was a generous benefactor, funding my work, but in the end it was only so that he could steal it and use it to further his own insane plans of conquest and revenge! Only kept me alive in case something went wrong with that precious weather machine of his, didn't he? Calls it the *Eye of the Storm*, he does.'

Confused, you stop the man mid-rant and ask him, 'What plans for conquest and revenge?'

'Sturm wants revenge on the College of Mages and the whole of Femphrey. He has somehow managed to combine his elemental magicks with my machines to create a vessel through which he can alter the weather to a catastrophic degree, everything from causing floods, to creating a blizzard one minute and a crop-withering drought the next. Even an army that tries to stand against him will be powerless, for who can fight the weather?'

You tell Inigo that you have sworn to hunt down the source of the storm that devastated the village of Vastarin and, now that you know who is behind it, you will make it your personal quest to track Sturm's craft and thwart his evil schemes. Hearing this, the old man's grin broadens.

'That's excellent news!' he crows. 'But if you're to succeed where even an army could not, you're going to need some help. But there isn't time to stop and discuss it now. Let's get out of this place first, unless there's something I can help you with quickly.'

During your exploration of the tower you may have collected some unusual items. Each of these has a number associated with it. To ask Inigo about any one of these items, simple multiply its number by 10 and turn to that paragraph. You may have also fought some of the tower's guardians, which also had numbers associated with them. To ask about them, add their three numbers together and turn to the resulting paragraph. When you are done asking questions, turn to **365**.

336

You suddenly notice something lying amongst all the rubbish that has also collected here. Dragging sodden pieces of mildewed sailcloth out of the way, you uncover what looks like an artificial man made out of metal. Perhaps it is some kind of golem. You jump back, half-expecting the thing to come to life, but it remains exactly where it is, washed by the lapping bilge-waters. If you want to make a closer inspection of the artificial man, turn to **385**. If not, there is nothing else for you here, so you climb back up into the vessel above (turn to **54**).

337

The wreck looms out of the murk ahead of you, strands of kelp rippling like sails from its broken masts, moved by the undersea currents. The ship is listing slightly on its starboard side, the prow pointing out over the edge of the void. You can see a massive hole in its hull – quite possibly the reason why the ship sank in the first place – and wonder what it is that could make a hole that size. Do you want to enter the wreck through the hole in its hull (turn to **217**), or would you rather swim up to the deck (turn to **317**)? Alternatively you could leave the wreck well alone and head for the fissure in the seabed (turn to **6**).

338

As you advance into the snowy wilderness, the blizzard blows with even more force, as if the snowstorm was trying to stop you from finding the Yeti. *Test your Luck.* If you are Lucky, turn to **297**. If you are Unlucky, turn to **183**.

339

The tunnel starts to bend around to the left and with every step you take you feel the air getting hotter. It is not long before you discover the reason why. You find yourself standing on one side of a narrow natural rock bridge that spans a crawling lava flow far below. The heat here is almost unbearable. On the other side of this crevasse another carved, black stone archway opens onto another tunnel. If you are going to get any further, you are going to have to cross this fire chasm, but how are you going to do it? Will you:

Use a Rope and Grapple, if you have one?	Turn to **299**
Drink a Potion of Levitation, if you have one?	Turn to **367**
Proceed with caution over the bridge?	Turn to **265**

340

The Pegasus is desperately trying to fend off its attackers, but the battle is taking place high in the sky above you. The only way you are going to be able to help is if you have a Bow, a Crossbow, a Blunderbuss, or a Potion of Levitation. If you have one of these and want to use it, turn to **89**. If not, you have no choice but to battle on through the blizzard, leaving the Pegasus to its fate; move the Day of the Week on 1, and turn to **250**.

341

Patiently you tell the watery women about the bound Elementals and your quest to defeat Balthazar Sturm's Weather Machine. The Naiads are elemental creatures themselves, daughters of the ocean, but they have little interest in the problems of 'dry ones'. You try to make them see that Sturm's meddling with the weather will ultimately affect the seas as well, but are your arguments convincing enough? If you are wearing a Coral Crown, turn to **381**. If not, you must *Test your Luck*. If you are Lucky, turn to **381**; if you are Unlucky, turn to **361**.

342

Putting the Hunting Horn to your lips, you blow hard. A single sonorous note blasts from the end of the horn, swelling in power and volume the further the vibrations travel. Discordant harmonics become audible and the monster starts lashing its head from side to side in pain. Encouraged by the Stormdrake's reaction, you take a deep breath and blow again. The booming soundwaves buffet the monster which shrieks as the power of the Hunting Horn blows it backwards. And then the monster is tumbling away from you through the sky, unable to fight the power of the Horn. With the storm-clouds starting to clear from around the huge flying fish as well, you decide to make the most of the opportunity and, your heart in your mouth, make the ultimate leap of faith ... Turn to **14**.

343

Heading away from the mine, you follow the foothills as the Witchtooth Line curves south-east. A day into the latest leg of your mammoth journey (move the Day of the Week on 1), the air temperature drops rapidly and you find yourself travelling through a landscape that looks like it has been caught in the depths of winter.

The chill, biting wind picks up and you find yourself in the grip of a ferocious blizzard, but you press on through the whiteout regardless. Going is slow and you can see only a few metres ahead of you. With the sun hidden from you, as well as any major land-marks, you have no idea whether you are still travel-ling in the right direction. (If you are not wearing a Sun Talisman, you must lose 2 STAMINA points from the effects of the biting cold.)

You have been travelling like this for an hour or more when you see a large shadowy shape through the whirling snow ahead of you and you hear a woman's voice, as sharp-edged as the wind, call, 'Who goes there?'

Do you want to respond by calling out your name (turn to 352), or by drawing your weapon, in readi-ness to defend yourself (turn to 389)?

344

You stumble down the steep slope of the tunnel, deeper into the heart of the volcano. The air is so hot now that your throat burns with every breath. For as long as you remain within the Fire Tunnels, reduce your SKILL by 1 more point due to heat exhaustion. However, if you drank a Potion of Fire Protection before entering, or if you have a Dragon Tattoo, you may ignore this penalty. However, a Wyrmskin Cloak cannot provide you with the protection you need here. An opening appears at the end of the tunnel and you emerge into another cross-passageway. At this T-junction, will you go left (turn **245**) or right (turn to **364**)?

345

Skipping across several boggy channels onto another path, your change of route steadily leads you way off course. Before you know it, you are deep within the stinking swamps, but you are not alone. Roll one die and consult the table below, to see what it is that has tracked you through the marsh.

Dice roll *Encounter*

1   A pack of mangy swamp-dwelling rats have caught your scent. Their voracious appetites impel them to attack. Fight the rats as if they were one opponent.

SWAMP RATS   SKILL 5   STAMINA 10

2

A pair of Swamp Goblins has found your trail. They try to ensnare you within their net. *Test your Skill* and if you fail, reduce your Attack Strength by 2 for two Attack Rounds as you fight your way free. The Goblins attack together with their bone-tipped spears.

	SKILL	STAMINA
First SWAMP GOBLIN	6	5
Second SWAMP GOBLIN	5	5

3

As you wade on through the stinking fens you become the target of a swarm of stinging marsh Thornflies. It is impossible to fight them off and you are bitten over and over again. Roll one die and lose that many STAMINA points. If you roll a 6 you must also lose 1 SKILL point as you are stricken with Blood-fever.

4

You pass a stagnant pool which is home to a Spit Toad. The man-sized amphibian shoots a jet of acid at you as you come within range. *Test your Skill* and if you fail lose 2 STAMINA points, as the acidic spit hits you. You must then fight the huge toad.

SPIT TOAD   SKILL 5   STAMINA 6

5

You are surprised when you come across a rotten log covered in fungi with fat stems and red-veined caps that are each as tall as a Dwarf. You are even more surprised when these gigantic toad-stools shuffle from their place on the log towards you, sinister fungal faces appearing within their stem-bodies. The Fungoids attack you by blowing toxic spores into your face, which in turn clog your lungs and irritate open wounds. Fight the strange carnivorous mushrooms as if they were one creature.

FUNGOIDS   SKILL 6   STAMINA 9

If you lose more that 6 STAMINA points in your battle with the sentient fungi, you must also lose 1 SKILL point as their toxic spores hamper your breathing.

6   False alarm! There's nothing after you.

If you survive all that the swamp has to throw at you, you eventually make it through to the other side. Finding the going much easier now, you follow dirt roads as they pass through apple orchards and carefully tended turnip fields on the way to Chalannabrad. Three days later the brilliant white buildings of the city are within sight. Move the Day of the Week on 3 and turn to **50**.

346

The ground shudders again, and this time it feels like an earthquake! Great rents open in the parched ground as a number of monstrous worm-like creatures burst from the waterless soil. Each of them is the size of a hay-cart, and looks like a cross between a white caterpillar and a maggot. As the farmers do their best to fight off the hungry Tremor Worms you defend yourself as one of them lurches towards you, its eyeless head swaying, mandibles strong enough to bite through plate armour snapping hungrily.

TREMOR WORM   SKILL 7   STAMINA 9

If you kill the worm, turn to **11**.

347

Trying to spot handholds with only the light of your lantern, swinging from where you have secured it to your backpack, is hard enough but on top of that the rock is wet and slippery. Your heart pounding within your chest, you continue your descent into darkness. *Test your Skill*. If you are successful, turn to **383**. If you fail, turn to **366**.

348

As soon as they clamp eyes on you, the guards spring into action. Quickly surrounding you, they waste no time in taking you prisoner. Turn to **19**.

349

You have saved Femphrey – and possibly the rest of the Old World – from Balthazar Sturm's insane dreams of conquest, but have paid the ultimate price in doing so. As the *Eye of the Storm* disintegrates in the sky above you, and the conjured storm blows itself out, you plunge to your death. Your adventure is over!

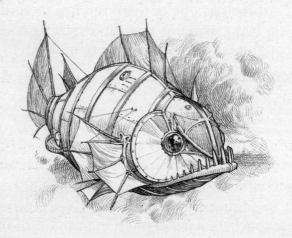

350

You are ready to face Balthazar Sturm at the heart of the storm – but how well have you prepared for this moment? Of the following four locations – the Witchtooth Line, the Howling Plains, Mount Pyre, and the Eelsea – have you visited:

One?	Turn to **330**
Two?	Turn to **298**
Three?	Turn to **268**
Four?	Turn to **237**

351

As you land your killing blow against the last of the Fulgurites the light in its goggle-eyes dies, its leather suit deflating as if there was never anything inside it at all. Now that you have rid the room of its guardians will you:

Take a closer look at the flask?	Turn to 377
Continue on up the tower?	Turn to 392
Descend the staircase into the depths of the tower (if you haven't done so already)?	Turn to 160
Leave the tower altogether?	Turn to 398

352

Shouting your name into the blizzard you hear the woman come back with, 'The Hero of Tannatown, slayer of the Crimson Witch?'

'The very same,' you reply and then wait with bated breath to see what will happen next.

A moment later, a large Sabretooth-Cat pads out of the snowstorm towards you. Its pelt is almost as white as the snow, except for the addition of grey tiger stripes. But more remarkable than the creature itself is that sitting in a saddle strapped to its back is a woman, wearing the practical leather armour of a huntress. She carries the tools of her trade about her person; a bow and quiver full of arrows are slung across her back, while a saw-toothed blade hangs in a scabbard from her belt.

She regards you with an expression approaching awe on her face. 'To think that I should run into a legendary adventurer like you, in the middle of a blizzard,' she says. 'It must be fate. Perhaps it was destined that we should hunt the beast together.'

What beast, you wonder, and who is this woman anyway? So you ask her.

'My name is Larni,' she explains, 'and I have travelled far in pursuit of a monstrous and dangerous predator – a Yeti. This freakish weather has brought it down from its home among the glacial peaks of the Cloudcap Mountains. I have been hired to track the beast down and slay it, before it slaughters another herd of cattle or terrorises another farmstead. I was onto its trail at last when this blizzard blew up and Fang here,' she says, patting the neck of the Sabretooth affectionately, 'lost its scent. But if you were to join us in the hunt, I am sure that the three of us together could run it to ground in no time. You will help us, won't you?'

If you agree to help Larni and Fang hunt the Yeti, turn to 382. If not, you tell her that you are already set upon a quest to bring an end to the weather that brought the snow-beast down from the higher slopes in the first place, and continue on your way alone. By the time another day has elapsed the snows are but a memory. Move the Day of the Week on 1, and turn to 189.

353

You went the wrong way more than once in your flight from the volcano, but will these errors prove fatal? Only luck can save you now! *Test your Luck.* If you are Lucky, turn to 388. If you are Unlucky, turn to 373.

354

There is still one more obstacle for you to face before you can leave the tower. Standing in the centre of the rubbish-strewn workshop level is a towering metal figure. Its body is a rattling steam engine and you can see the incandescent glare of chained lightning behind a scorched glass plate in the middle of its chest. The same furious light crackles within the behemoth's glass eyes, while flaring metal chimneys protruding from its shoulders puff smoke and steam into the room. Steel-claw fingers reach for you as the Steam Golem takes its first clanking step forwards. Not for the first time you thank the gods that Wyrmbiter is an enchanted weapon that can cut through metal as easily as it cleaves through flesh.

STEAM GOLEM   SKILL 8   STAMINA 10

If you manage to destroy the colossal magical automaton, turn to 324.

355

Perhaps there is something you can do to help. Borrowing the fastest horse in the village, you gallop away from Tumbleweir northwards. It wasn't far from here that you encountered the Giant, Cormoran. As you ride over the crest of a ridge you catch sight of the Giant as he lumbers over the moors looking for sheep. It's time to call in a favour.

Turning the panting horse around, you gallop back to Tumbleweir as fast as you can, Cormoran keeping pace with long lolloping strides. As soon as you can see the lake and the village, and the dam that separates the two on the verge of collapse, you don't need to explain yourself any further but simply point.

Cormoran stands on the eastern spur, next to the dam. To awed gasps from the bewildered onlookers, the Giant raises his tree-trunk club above his head and brings it down hard on the top of the escarpment. The waterlogged hillside gives way and slides down into the valley, tonnes of rock and mud creating a second supporting wall in front of the dam.

Tumbleweir is saved! The slumped hillside will hold the waters of the lake back until someone can be found who can solve the problem of the sluices-gates satisfactorily. (Regain 1 LUCK point.)

Two days later (move the Day of the Week on 2) the rain has stopped, and you reach the edge of the wilderness known the Howling Plains. Turn to **83**.

356

'Take this,' the mage says, handing you a small flame-shaped bottle of red glass. 'It is a Potion of Fire Protection, made from the secretions of Giant Fire

Salamanders and ground dragon's scales. It will prove invaluable if you're to brave the Fire Tunnels of Mount Pyre.' Add the Potion of Fire Protection to your *Adventure Sheet* and turn to **193**.

357

Your hunt for the Stormdrake takes you into the rough terrain north of Eerieside, until you reach a tall crag that looks down over the now-distant town, with an ominous-looking cave – like a great fanged maw – near its summit. It is too late in the day to attempt an assault on the peak now so you build a fire and settle down for the night, the wolfhound keeping watch over you both.

Come the dawn (move the Day of the Week on 1), you start to climb the peak. Using goat-tracks and knotty bushes to aid your ascent, you all make it safely to the top. And here you stand, facing the forbidding cave mouth. The entrance at the peak is huge, certainly big enough for something the size of a dragon. Cautiously, swords drawn and lanterns lit, you, Sylas and the dog enter the echoing darkness beyond.

The gaping cave-mouth leads to a broad tunnel that descends through the crag. At the bottom you find yourself in a huge echoing chamber. Two more massive tunnels, really just off-shoots of the main cavern, lead away to left and right. The air is redolent with the stench of rotting meat. Do you want to explore to the left (turn to **378**), or the right (turn to **246**)?

358

As you kick your way towards the surface, a long, sinuous shape rises from the reef below you – something large enough to take down a sailing ship! The Leviathan has a rapacious appetite and it is determined not to let you get away a second time. Anglerfish jaws stretching wide, the sea serpent closes on you with a flick of its enormous tail.

LEVIATHAN   SKILL 10   STAMINA 20

If you manage to defeat this monstrous denizen of the deep, regain 1 LUCK point and turn to **318**.

359

After an uneventful night at sea, you rise the following morning to glowering overcast skies. (Move the Day of the Week on 1.) There is no land in sight, but the *Tempest* is at anchor. 'Is this the place?' you ask Katarina, yawning and rubbing the sleep from your eyes. You hadn't realised how much your quest has taken out of you.

'Not quite X marks the spot I'll grant you,' she drawls, 'but this is the place. We're anchored at the edge of Blackcoral Reef and rumour has it that down there, at the edge of the Devilfish Rift, lies the Sunken Temple of Hydana, God of the Sea. Some say that there was an island here once, until it was drowned by a tidal wave, others, that the temple's always been underwater. Many have come here looking for it, and few have found it. But even fewer have returned to tell the tale. But if there's anything that can help you gain mastery over a Greater Water Elemental, it'll be down there!'

Undaunted, you step up to the gunwale and make your preparations. You will have to leave your backpack behind. Although it's waterproof it wasn't designed to survive a journey to the bottom of the sea. However, you can still take your sword Wyrmbiter with you, along with two other items, which you carry about your person, but no food.

Your last act, before entering the ocean, is to make whatever preparations are necessary for you to be able to breathe underwater. Will you drink a Potion of Underwater Breathing, if you have one (turn to 315), put on a Breathing Helmet, if you have one (turn to 379), or call on the aid of Prospero Seacharmer, if he is with you (turn to 393)?

360

For two days you traverse the wildly varying terrain of Femphrey, passing from the rocky escarpments of the Witchtooth foothills, through ancient woodland, to gently rolling dales and scrubby plains. (Move the Day of the Week on 2.) And then you reach the Eerieside Marshes.

These foetid fens spread out from the eastern shore of Lake Eerie. It was from the depths of the vile lake that you recovered the dragon-slaying sword, Wyrmbiter. The swamps themselves are one of the few truly lawless areas of the kingdom. Wanted brigands have their hideouts within it, while in its deeper recesses, evil creatures dwell amidst its hidden bogs and deadly sinkholes. And yet the quickest way from the mountains to the coast and the docks of Chalannabrad is through its boggy bounds. Besides, what does a hero like you have to fear from a bunch of cowardly swamp-dwellers?

You are following a well-trodden path through the mist-shrouded marshes when you see a figure approaching you through the fens. This stranger is wearing a heavy habit of black sackcloth and leans on a long staff for support. The man is muttering to himself as black-winged carrion birds circle lazily overhead. If you want to continue on your current path, turn to **211**. If you would rather take another route through the mire to avoid an encounter, turn to **345**.

361

As far as the Naiads are concerned, you have desecrated the Temple of Hydana and such a crime cannot go unpunished. Shrieking, the three elemental creatures rush towards you, determined to drown you. Although they are only made of water themselves, they form icy talons at the ends of their fingers to use as weapons. You must fight all three Naiads at the same time.

	SKILL	STAMINA
First NAIAD	8	7
Second NAIAD	7	7
Third NAIAD	6	6

(If today is Seaday, add 1 to the Naiads' SKILL scores and STAMINA scores.) If you defeat the Naiads, you are free to take the Shell of the Seas (add it to your *Adventure Sheet*, noting that it has 12 spines) and, this part of your quest complete, you set off for the surface and the *Tempest* again. If you have the codeword *Retsnom* recorded on your *Adventure Sheet*, turn to **358**. If not, turn to **318**.

362

The magical energies that power the automaton-golem are tied directly to the elemental energies powering the *Eye of the Storm*. As a result, the DAMAGE you have done to the vessel has also weakened the Juggernaut. If you have to face the Juggernaut in combat, reduce its stats as described on the chart below.

Damage score	Effect on the Juggernaut
6–7	Reduce its STAMINA by 2 points
8–9	Reduce its STAMINA by 4 points and its SKILL by 1 point
10–11	Reduce its STAMINA by 6 points and its SKILL by 2 points

Now turn to **331**.

A shrieking, reptilian cry suddenly breaks across the heavens like thunder, and lightning explodes across the sky. Flying towards you out of the encroaching maelstrom is a creature from legend – the Stormdrake. It is said that when the Stormdrake flies, apocalyptic storms will assault the land, leaving waste and devastation wherever they go. The creature powers towards you on massive wings of taut black skin, thunder rumbling across the sky with their every beat. It is terrible to behold with its scaly black body, as long as a ship, and its huge saurian head. It stretches wide its jaws and another ear-splitting scream cuts through you. (If you have a Hunting Horn, turn to 342 at once!) The power of the storm blazes within the monster's black eyes and lightning crackles around its darkly gleaming claws. You understand what you are going to have to do if you are to ever board the *Eye of the Storm*, Wyrmbiter singing as you unsheathe your dragon-slaying sword.

STORMDRAKE   SKILL 11   STAMINA 14

(If it is Stormsday, increase the Stormdrake's SKILL score by 1 point and its STAMINA by 2 points.) As you are not alone, you get two strikes against the storm-bringer each Attack Round. As well as working out Attack Strengths for yourself and the Stormdrake, you must do the same for your companion, who has a SKILL of 10. This means your companion can injure the beast as well as you. However, if the Stormdrake wins an Attack Round, it focuses all its attentions on you – as the wielder of Wyrmbiter; roll one die and on a roll of 5–6, the monster blasts you with a crackling bolt of electricity from its lightning-sheathed claws, which will cause 4 STAMINA points of damage rather than the usual 2. If you manage to slay the raging Stormdrake, finding yourself directly over the brass fish, you make the ultimate leap of faith into the unknown … Turn to 14.

364

Rock formations in the roof and floor lend the tunnel the appearance of a gaping maw. Suddenly a gout of flame erupts from between the stone jaws as gas and flames vent from elsewhere within the volcano. You observe the bursts of flame for a few minutes, trying to see if there is a pattern, so that you can pass through when it's safe. However, as far as you can tell, there is no pattern. If you are going to proceed any further, you are going to have to pass between the jaws and risk being burned. If you want to pass between the stone jaws, turn to 384. If you would rather not tempt fate, you will have to go back the other way (turn to 245).

365

'Come on, it's time we were gone,' the old engineer hisses conspiratorially, 'before those damnable Fulgurites find us. It will only take a few minutes for me to pack my things, then I'm out of here. If I were you, I'd scarper too.' Add the codeword *Knarc* to your *Adventure Sheet* and then decide what you want to do next. If you want to escape from the mad weather-mage's lair yourself, turn to **398**. If you would rather explore the upper levels of the tower (if you haven't done so already), turn to **220**.

366

It was almost inevitable, given the conditions. Your hand slips from the narrow ledge that you were clinging to and you fall the rest of the way down the chimney. You land in an untidy, aching heap on the sandy floor of a natural tunnel that cuts through the bedrock of the mountains. (Roll one die and deduct that many STAMINA points; if you roll a 1 you will still suffer 2 STAMINA points of damage.)

And then suddenly, they're all over you – small, eight-legged, sharp-toothed monsters covered in bony-armour that helps hide them among the rocks of their subterranean home. Roll one die to see how many Grannits attack you. If you roll 1–3, you must fight four of the creatures; if you roll 4–6 you must fight six of them! However, due to the narrow confines of the tunnel, you fight them one at a time. Each of the Grannits has the following attributes.

GRANNIT   SKILL 4   STAMINA 3

If you defeat the nasty little critters, you hurry on your way before any more crawl out from under a stone. Turn to **80**.

367

You gulp down the contents of the potion bottle and immediately feel its effects. You rise straight up into the air. You only stop when your head hits the rocky roof above. (Lose 2 STAMINA points.) From there you manage to pull yourself across the roof of the chamber, using jagged stalactites to help you, over the lava river. It is not long before the potion wears off again and you return to the ground only now at the other end of the rock bridge. Cross the Potion of Levitation off your *Adventure Sheet* and turn to **185**.

368

You step through the door and onto the bridge of the *Eye of the Storm*. On its far side, the split-level chamber takes on the curved shape of the prow of the ship, two massive crystal observation domes making up most of the fore section, giving those on the bridge unprecedented views of the kingdom below. Banks of machinery line the walls and are being tended to by a team of bizarre-looking creatures. The size of Dwarfs, they are clad in sealed suits of stitched leather with all-enveloping brass helmets. Dazzling blue sparks of lightning flicker behind their goggle-eyes. These Fulgurites ignore you as they busily go about their work.

A network of pipes from the banks of machinery converges at a central control console that protrudes from a raised metal platform jutting out over the floor of the chamber. Standing before it is a tall, bald-headed man wearing a robe of ever-changing hues. The cloak turns a rich ultramarine and storm clouds sweep across the back of it. The next moment it becomes a rich orange and sunbursts bloom across the cloth. There is no doubt in your mind as to who this man can be.

Balthazar Sturm turns and fixes you with a furious glare. 'So there you are!' he bellows. 'The one who's been causing me so much trouble!'

'That's right!' you shout back, triumphantly. 'And now I'm going to put pay to your dreams of conquest once and for all!'

'That's what you think,' Sturm snarls, 'but I am Master of the Elements!'

'And I have dealt with your kind before,' you reply, unsheathing Wyrmbiter in readiness. 'It was I who banished the Bone Shamen of Bathoria and I who defeated the Crimson Witch. I don't think a Weather Mage is going to cause me any real problems.'

'Well, we'll just have to see about that, won't we?' he roars. His robes immediately turn a deep red and flames appear behind his eyes. 'Won't we?'

At that Sturm clicks his fingers – and immediately bursts into flames! As the fire consumes his body, his flesh becomes liquid fire. 'See how my anger burns!' Sturm roars, apparently none the worse for wear following his dramatic transformation, and stalks towards you. If only you could snuff out his flame as you might blow out a candle ...

If you know the name of an Air Elemental who could help you against this raging Human Torch, and want to call on it now, turn its name into a number using the code A=1, B=2, C=3 ... Z=26. Add the numbers together, subtract the total from this paragraph and then turn to this new paragraph. If not, turn to **112**.

369

Muldwych is full of gratitude for what you have done in saving his life. 'I owe you a great debt,' the monk says, 'one I can never fully repay, but let me do what I can – let me tell you your fortune.' If you want to have your fortune told, turn to **271**. If not, you and the mad monk part company and go your separate ways.

You eventually make it through to the other side of the swamp. Finding the going much easier now, you follow dirt roads as they pass through apple orchards and carefully tended turnip fields on the way to Chalannabrad. Move the Day of the Week on 3 and turn to **50**.

370
You set the tumblers, slam the Juggernaut's chest-plate shut, and then throw yourself clear, expecting the automaton to shut down at any moment. But something is wrong; the iron giant starts to speed up rather than slow down and then, in a whirl of wrecking-ball punches, the Juggernaut goes berserk. You entered the wrong code and now there will be no stopping the steel monster (lose 1 LUCK point). Return to **262** to finish your fight with the steel giant, adding 2 to its SKILL score!

371

In doing away with Varick and his gang, you have helped improve the reputation of adventurers across the kingdom. (Regain 1 LUCK point.) No wonder the brigands tried to ambush you, only Varick has anything of value; a sum total of 8 Gold Pieces, a large Ruby (worth 4 Gold Pieces) and a Healing Elixir (which will restore up to 4 points of STAMINA and 1 SKILL point when drunk).

Another two days takes you from the wilderness at the heart of the kingdom to the coast and the capital. Move the Day of the Week on 2 again and turn to **50**.

372

You tell Giles to get everyone out of the village and as high up into the hills as possible. You are sure that the dam is about to burst. And you are right. You are just helping the last mother, child and elderly relative to the top of the western spur that supports the dam when the ancient structure collapses. First it is only one plank of wood that flies free, a spout of water jetting from the face of the dam after it, then a piece of twisted pipework – and then the whole lot gives way.

An unimaginable weight of water breaks free from the dam, the force of the flood sweeping the entire village away in an uncontrollable torrent. With the rising water lapping at your heels, you scramble up the muddy bank as it starts to wash away beneath you. It is almost as if the water doesn't want you to get away – and it doesn't.

A serpentine creature, formed from the turmoil of white-water, emerges from the flood and hurls itself at you. Once again you are fighting for your life.

TORRENT   SKILL 8   STAMINA 10

If today is Seaday, add 1 to the Torrent's SKILL score and 2 points to its STAMINA, and if the Elemental creature injures you on a roll of 4–6 it causes 3 STAMINA points' DAMAGE (rather than the usual 2). If you defeat the creature, its watery essence rejoins the flood.

Although you managed to save the villagers, Tumbleweir itself has been destroyed. (Lose 2 LUCK points.) You leave under a cloud, quite literally, but within a day at least the rain has stopped. Another day after that, you reach the edge of the wilderness known as the Howling Plains. Move the Day of the Week on 2 and turn to **83**.

373

You spent too long negotiating the treacherous Fire Tunnels of Mount Pyre. Magma pours into the cavern behind you in a torrent before erupting from the side of the mountain with cataclysmic force. Nothing could survive being caught in the blast of an erupting volcano – including you! Your adventure is over.

374

With the Yeti dead, you tend to Larni and the Sabretooth. You offer up a prayer of thanks to the gods – both are still alive. Larni is most concerned at her companion's condition. Rummaging in the Cat's saddle-bags, she takes out a jar of salve and applies it to Fang's injuries. She then offers you the jar saying, 'It's a healing salve, from Ruddlestone. Please, use it on your wounds. It's the least I can do after all you've done for us.' (You may use the Healing Salve to restore STAMINA points up to half your *Initial* STAMINA score.)

Larni then takes a finely-crafted Hunting Horn from the saddle-bags. 'I'm afraid I cannot let you take the Yeti's pelt,' she explains. 'I need it to prove that the monster is dead, but please, take this instead.' (Add the Hunting Horn to your *Adventure Sheet*.)

As the Huntress sets about skinning the Yeti, you set off again through the snow-swathed landscape. With the snow-beast dead, the blizzard has blown itself out. By the time another day has passed the thaw has set in. Move the Day of the Week on 1 and turn to **189**.

375

After a day of foot-slogging under a blazing sun, that sits like a burning ball set within a sky the colour of baking sand, you reach a settlement of small houses. (Move the Day of the Week on 1.) At first you wonder if it is a mirage as it shimmers in the heat-haze. For hundreds of acres around, where there should be lush meadows and fields full of ripening corn, there is nothing but a dusty wilderness. It does not look like it has rained here for weeks. Your suspicions are confirmed when you follow the road to Quartz.

Standing at the centre of the village on the back of an open wagon, is a bizarre contraption. It is all brass pipes, spinning windmill vanes and whirling brass spheres. The machine is making quite a racket, pistons clanking and gears grinding. At its heart is what looks like a furnace which ultimately connects to a lightning rod that is pointing up into the cloud-less sky. A small but curious crowd surrounds the machine, watching its movements expectantly, as if waiting for it to do something startling. Watching the machine with equal anticipation is a tall man wearing gaudy multi-coloured robes and a red velvet top hat.

'And now,' you hear the showman proclaim, 'the moment you have all been waiting for!' He glances nervously at the azure sky above him. 'The moment my miraculous machine will bring the rains back!'

As far as you can tell the man is a charlatan; there isn't a cloud in the sky. You get the impression that he has taken the villagers' gold with promises of summoning the longed-for rains, but there's more chance of a shower of frogs than actual rain, considering how

⚃ ⚁

Balthazar Sturm has seized control of the kingdom's weather.

The hero in you cannot stand to see people being taken advantage of in this way, but then again, the quicker you stop Sturm, the sooner the kingdom's weather patterns will return to normal. If you want to intervene on behalf of the villagers and expose the fraudulent rainmaker, turn to **396**. If not, you leave Quartz behind and continue south-west into the baking borderlands of the Howling Plains. Move the Day of the Week on 2 and turn to **83**.

376

'I offer you this Potion of Underwater Breathing,' Matteus says, taking a sea-green glass bottle shaped like a fish from a shelf crammed with flasks. 'If you're going to look for aid against a Water Elemental at the bottom of the sea, you're going to need this.' Add the Potion of Underwater Breathing to your *Adventure Sheet* and turn to **193**.

377

You are about to pick up the flask when a thought hits you. You first pull the switch on the wall down, into the off position. The electrical hum dies, but the glow from the bottle remains. Picking it up, feeling its weight in your hands, you marvel at the retina-searing ball of lightning trapped within. A peeling label, written in a spidery hand, reads 'The Spark of Life'. If you want to take the flask, record the Spark of Life on your *Adventure Sheet*, along with the fact that the flask has 6 sides. With the flask stowed away inside your backpack, will you:

Ascend the new staircase to the next floor?	Turn to **392**
Descend the other staircase into the depths of the tower (if you haven't done so already)?	Turn to **160**
Leave the tower altogether?	Turn to **398**

378

The stench of rotten meat intensifies as you proceed through the cave, until you enter a smaller cavern piled high with bones. By the light cast by the lanterns, you see skeletons of all manner of creatures, from cows and human beings, to goblins and even that of a griffin, the meat stripped from all of them. Whatever it is that calls this place home, it is a voracious carnivore.

Always on the lookout, in case the hungry beast should return at any moment, you and Sylas carry out a quick search of the cave. As you suspected, whatever it is that devoured all these creatures, it has no interest in treasure. Among the bones you find ...

A Bag of Gems (worth 8 Gold Pieces)
A Warhammer
A Rope and Grapple
A Bow and quiver with 6 arrows
A Golden Bracelet (worth 5 Gold Pieces)
A bottle labelled 'Potion of Levitation'

Sylas suggests that you split the hoard you have recovered fifty-fifty, just as you would the reward for slaying the Stormdrake. Choose three of the things from the list (noting that you can only take one of the treasure items) and add them to your *Adventure Sheet*; the hunter takes the rest.

The Warhammer is not magical but it is a crushing weapon; if you hit an opponent with the War-hammer, roll one die and if you roll 5–6 it does 1 extra STAMINA point of damage. You may use the Bow once in each battle, before having to engage in hand-to-hand combat (as long as you still have arrows left to shoot); *Test your Skill* and if you succeed you cause your opponent 2 STAMINA points of damage.

With your new possessions safely stowed in your backpack, you return to the main chamber to delve deeper into the cavernous lair in search of the Stormdrake. Turn to **246**.

379

Trying to remember all the instructions Briny Deep gave you, you put the helmet on and connect the air supply from the tanks you are carrying on your back. You quickly realise just how much the helmet restricts your vision. The apparatus is also rather cumbersome, and although its weight will be reduced when you're submerged, it will still hamper your movements. For as long as you remain underwater, you must reduce your SKILL score by 1 point. In addition, the tanks attached to the Breathing Helmet have a limited amount of air in them. Keep a careful note of how many paragraphs you turn to while exploring the seabed. As soon as you exceed 16 paragraphs, you are forced to surface (in which case turn to **318** immediately); but for now, turn to **315**.

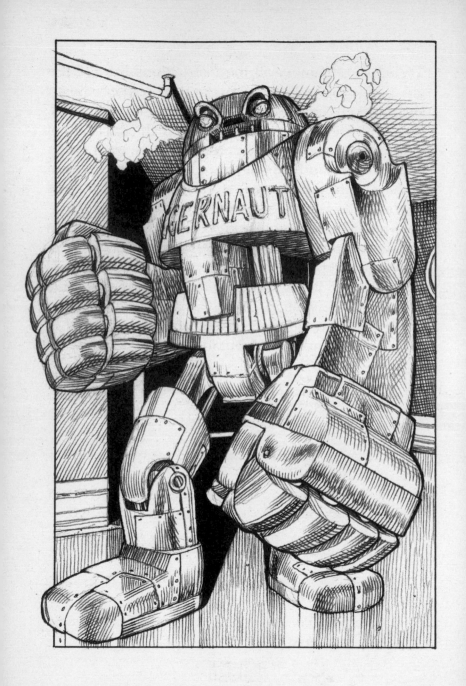

380

You open the door, and come face to face with a hulking mechanical giant, crafted from inter-locking steel plates. Its eyes are glowing crystals and on its chest-plate is inscribed a name: *JUGGERNAUT*. The door slams shut behind you and the lumbering metal colossus strides towards you on pistoning legs as steam boils into the air from the sides of its head. You see now that the iron giant is guarding another door on the other side of the chamber. If your DAMAGE score is 6 or more, turn to **362**. If not, turn to **331**.

381

'We appreciate your need,' the first Naiad says.

'And, as you come as a penitent, seeking our father's aid,' the second continues.

'We will give to you the Shell of the Seas,' the third finishes.

And with that, the three elemental women dissolve back into the sea, leaving only a parting farewell behind in your mind. 'May Hydana smile on your enterprise!' (Regain 1 LUCK point and add the Shell of the Seas to your *Adventure Sheet*, noting that is has 12 spines.)

With the shell firmly in your grasp, you set off for the surface again and the *Tempest*. If you have the codeword *Retsnom* recorded on your *Adventure Sheet*, turn to **358**. If not, turn to **318**.

382

Larni is delighted with your response. 'We should set off straightaway,' she tells you. 'This blizzard isn't going to bother the Yeti so we had best make our move and quickly.' You keep pace with the Sabretooth as its mistress searches for any signs of the beast; eyes peeled, you do the same. If you have a Sabretooth Fang, turn to **297**. If not, turn to **338**.

383

You make it to the bottom of the chimney in one piece, stepping down onto the sandy floor of what appears to be a natural tunnel this time, and not one carved out by the Dwarfs. Hearing a skittering sound you hold your lantern out before you and see what at first appear to be several rocks scuttling about the floor of the tunnel. But when one comes closer to the light to investigate, you see that they are not rocks at all, but stony-shelled crustaceans the colour of granite. And then there are more of the creatures scurrying towards you out of the darkness, chittering to themselves, intent on making a meal of you! Roll one die to see how many Grannits attack you. If you roll a 1, add one to the number so that you have to fight a minimum of two Grannits. Each of the nasty little critters has the following attributes.

GRANNIT   SKILL 4   STAMINA 3

If you defeat the vicious little monsters, you quickly hurry on your way. Turn to **80**.

384

Boldly, you leap through the open stone teeth of the fiery maw. *Test your Luck*. If you are Lucky, you pass through unscathed. If you are Unlucky you are caught in the middle of a fiery blast. Lose 4 STAMINA points. (If you have a Dragon Tattoo, or you drank a Potion of Fire Protection before entering these tunnels, you may reduce this damage by 1 point. If you have a Dragon Shield you may reduce the damage by 1 more point, and if you are wearing a Wyrmskin Cloak, reduce it by 2 points. All of these reductions are cumulative, so if you have the tattoo, drank the potion and have the shield, you can reduce the damage by up to 3 points.)

Beyond the maw, the tunnel winds onwards until it comes to an effective dead-end at a sheer drop, at the bottom of which lies a bubbling lake of magma. You cautiously peer over the edge and see a spur of black rock jutting out over the lava lake, which seethes with volcanic activity. You can see an altar-like block at the end of the spur. The heat is unbearable. You don't fancy the idea of trying to climb down the cliff face, burning your hands on the scalding rocks, but it might be possible using a Rope and Grapple. If you have such a thing, and would like to try descending the cliff, turn to **279**. If not (or you don't want to make such an attempt) you will have to pass through the maw again and return to the last junction, taking the other route through to the volcano's heart (turn to **300**).

385

The iron man must be at least three metres in height, even though it is currently lying prone within the filthy soup of rusty water. Its eyes are dull crystals and engraved onto its chest-plate is a name: *DREADNOUGHT*. As you run your hand over the engraving, the chest-plate pops open, revealing three tumblers bearing the numbers 0 to 9 on each one. It is then that you notice the top of the iron man's head is hinged. Levering it open you find a six-sided hollow space; its mechanical brain is missing. If you have something which you think might fit inside the iron man's steel skull, multiply the number connected with it by ten, deduct the total from this paragraph and turn to the new reference. If you don't have anything suitable, or don't want to use it here, you have no choice but to climb back up into the main body of the ship (turn to 54).

386

Having failed to find the mythical Stormdrake, you and Sylas make your way back to Eerieside. Even the wolfhound is quiet now, sloping along behind, its tail between its legs. The mood in the town is the same – none of the other hunting parties have found the any sign of the Stormdrake either.

'What will you do now?' Sylas asks, and you tell him that you need to push on to the Witchtooth Mountains. Bidding the hunter farewell, you go on your way. Two days later (move the Day of the Week on 2), you reach your destination. Turn to **250**.

387

The crawl-way opens out into a broad cavern, the roof of which appears to be supported by nothing but a few menhir-sized boulders. A pool of crystal-clear water has collected within a natural bowl in the rock, which sparkles and glitters with a rainbow of mineral deposits. If you want to pause to drink from the pool, turn to **132**. If not, turn to **171**.

388

You hurtle through the rent in the cavern wall, trip and roll headfirst down the side of the volcano. You bowl down the mountainside as Mount Pyre erupts with all the fury of the enraged Fire Elemental. You skin your knees and elbows on the rocky ground but, ironically, it is probably the fall that saves you from being engulfed by either the super-heated cloud of ash and rock debris or the lava that comes pouring from the wound in the mountain's side after it. (Lose 3 STAMINA points but regain 1 LUCK point.) The petrified stump of a burnt tree eventually breaks your fall. Scrambling to your feet again, you keep running, although exhaustion threatens to overwhelm you, determined not to let Mount Pyre catch you now …

If you possess a pair of Seven League Boots and would like to use them now, turn to **2**. If not, it takes you two days to return to the edge of Lake Cauldron. (Move the Day of the Week on 2.) The kingdom of Femphrey lies before you again to the west. Remembering that you can only visit each location once, where next will you travel to in your quest? Will it be:

The Eelsea?   Turn to **143**
The Witchtooth Line?   Turn to **278**
The Howling Plains?   Turn to **375**

Or, if you feel that you are ready, do you want to make your assault on Balthazar Sturm's Weather Machine (turn to **350**)?

389

For several long seconds you hear nothing, and then there is a sudden shout of, 'On, Fang!' and the shadowy shape leaps out of the gusting snow at you. It is a huge Sabretooth-Cat, its pelt almost as white as the snow, except for the addition of grey tiger stripes.

Sitting in a saddle strapped to the Cat's back is a woman, wearing the practical leather armour of a huntress. In her hands is a bow, with an arrow nocked to the string. As the Sabretooth bounds towards you snarling, she lets fly with the arrow. *Test your Luck*. If you are Lucky, the arrow misses you, but if you are Unlucky it finds its mark in your arm (lose 2 STAMINA points). The Huntress swings the bow over her shoulder and draws her saw-edged sword as the Cat slashes at you with its claws. You must fight the Huntress and her Sabretooth mount at the same time, and both of them to the death.

	SKILL	STAMINA
SABRETOOTH-CAT	11	9
HUNTRESS	10	8

Unless you are wearing a Sun Talisman, you must reduce you Attack Strength by 1 point for the duration of this battle. If you win, a quick search uncovers a Hunting Horn, a purse containing 7 Gold Pieces, and the Bow, along with its quiver of 6 arrows. You may use the Bow once in each battle, before having to engage in hand-to-hand combat (as long as you still have arrows left to shoot); *Test your Skill* and if you succeed you cause your opponent 2 STAMINA points' damage. Taking what you want, including one of the Sabretooth's fangs as a trophy if you wish, you leave the bodies to be buried by the snow and set off again through the blizzard.

The freak snowstorm blows itself out at last and you continue on your way again. By the time another day has elapsed the snows are but a memory. Move the Day of the Week on 1, and turn to **189**.

390

Quickly pulling out the Blueprints of the *Eye of the Storm* again, you find the schematics relating to the Elemental Engine. There is something here about the physical mechanism of the device although you understand very little of the principles behind it. However, you are able to work out enough to twiddle a few knobs here, pull the odd lever there, and shut-off several valves to cut power feeds to other parts of the ship. (Add 1 to your DAMAGE score.) However, if you want to do more, you are going to have to try something else. Will you:

Attack the Elemental Engine with your sword?	Turn to **47**
Take a Mace or a Warhammer to the machine, if you have one?	Turn to **82**
Try using a Spanner, if you have one?	Turn to **63**
Quit the Engine Room and explore elsewhere?	Turn to **126**

391

Choosing somewhere you haven't been to before, where will you explore next within the *Eye of the Storm*?

The top deck?	Turn to **258**
The middle deck?	Turn to **126**
The bottom deck?	Turn to **54**
The bilges?	Turn to **302**

392

The staircase leads to a wooden door that opens onto
the roof of the tower. The lightning conductor rises
up from the side of the building and past the top of
the battlements while steps ascend to a wooden platform which juts out over the edge of the tower and
the precipice below. What could that possibly be for?
Opposite you, another small turret projects from the
side of the main tower, its equally unassuming door
facing you. Do you want to:

Enter the turret room?	Turn to **209**
Descend to the very bottom of the tower and explore its dungeon levels (if you haven't done so already)?	Turn to **160**
Leave the tower altogether?	Turn to **398**

393

'Remove your boots,' the sorcerer instructs you.
Slightly bemused by this request, but trusting that the
wizard knows what he's doing, you do as you are
told. Stretching out his arms towards you, Prospero

begins to cast his spell. And then suddenly you are gasping for air – you can't breathe! Panicking, you put your hands to your neck and it is then that your fingertips find the gills behind your ears. And there's something wrong with your hands too; your fingers have become webbed – your feet are just the same. So that's why the wizard wanted you to take off your boots!

As long as you remain underwater, exploring Blackcoral Reef and the Devilfish Rift, the gills will remain, allowing you to breathe freely. You will also find that your webbed hands and feet will make it much easier to move around underwater. As a result, while you are beneath the sea, you may add 1 to your SKILL score, even if this raises it beyond its *Initial* level. But for the moment you are like a fish out of water. Gasping for air you run for the side of the ship, suddenly craving the cold, wet embrace of the sea. Turn to 315.

394

If you possess a pair of Seven League Boots and would like to use them now, turn to 2. If not, where do you want to travel to next in your search for aid against Sturm and his bound Elementals? Remembering that you can only visit each location once, will you head for:

The Eelsea?	Turn to 13
The Witchtooth Line?	Turn to 115
Mount Pyre?	Turn to 309

Or, if you feel that you are ready, do you want to attempt to reach Balthazar Sturm's Weather Machine at the eye of the storm (turn to 350)?

395

'Very well,' the mage replies. 'Then there is one more thing I can do for you. If you wish, I can cast a temporary enchantment upon your boots that will allow you to make one journey on foot in no time at all. Be warned, it will work only once. Would you like me to cast the spell?' If you would, turn to 153. If not, turn to 193.

396

'Don't listen to this charlatan!' you shout over the noise of the bizarre machine. 'Whatever he's promised you, he won't be able to deliver, and if you've paid him for his help, then I'm afraid he's robbed you too.' The showman's face has flushed as red as his hat – you've obviously hit a nerve. Various members of the crowd start to mutter amongst themselves and then their mutterings becomes angry jeers.

'Well, I'd like to see you do any better!' the Rain-maker suddenly shouts, challenging you. The crowd turns, almost as one, fixing you with angry scowls. 'Well, can you?'

Somehow you have become the subject of the villagers' frustrations now. But what can you do to make it rain?

If you have the Shell of the Seas, you will have a name associated with it. Turn this name into a number using the code A=1, B=2, C=3 ... Z=26, add the numbers together, triple it, and then turn to the paragraph which is the same as the total.

If you don't have the shell, but you do have the Spark of Life, you will also have a number connected to this item. Divide this paragraph's number by that one and turn to the new paragraph.

If you have neither of these items, turn to 334.

397

Looking up, you see the Weather Mage suspended in mid-air above the platform. His robe has become a deep blue, almost black, and flashes of lightning skitter across the fabric. His features are set in an arrogant grimace and the power of the storm burns within his eyes. His arms are stretched out from his sides and bursts of lightning arc between his hands. 'Now feel the full force of the storm!' Sturm roars sending a searing bolt of lightning into the deck plating at your feet. As the crazed Weather Mage swoops down at you, you have time to carry out one action (such as drinking a potion, changing your weapon or shooting a crossbow).

And then he is on you! In the battle to come, because Sturm is airborne you must reduce your Attack Strength by 1 point. However, if you just drank a Potion of Levitation you can ignore this penalty. If you are fighting him with your sword, every successful strike Sturm makes against you with his lightning blasts will cause 3 points of STAMINA damage as the electricity is drawn to the weapon and, from there, into your body. If you have another weapon with which to fight the mage (such as a Warhammer or a Mace) you will not suffer this additional damage, but to change weapons will take one Attack Round, during which Sturm will make an unopposed strike against you (for 2 STAMINA points of damage). Last of all, if today is Stormsday, increase Sturm's SKILL score by 1 point, and the damage delivered by his lightning bolts by an extra point. And now, at last, you meet your nemesis in battle.

BALTHAZAR STURM   SKILL 10   STAMINA 10

If you reduce the Elementalist's STAMINA score to 2 points or fewer, turn immediately to **56**.

398
You make your way back to the ground floor of the tower without incident. If you have the codeword *Rennaps* on your *Adventure Sheet*, turn to **324**. If not, turn to **354**.

399
The sound of a rushing torrent gets louder and louder the further you progress along the Dwarf-cut

passageway, until you emerge at the edge of a fast-flowing underground river. The only way onward appears to be over the lip of a waterfall a little further on to your right. If you want to clamber over to the edge of the waterfall and let yourself down into the darkness this way, turn to **9**. If you would rather return to the crossroads and turn left, following a slime-dripping tunnel, turn to **327**. If you want to go back and go straight on at the crossroads, along a dusty passageway, turn to **227**.

400

You have done it! The insane Elementalist Balthazar Sturm is dead and his Weather Machine destroyed. Femphrey is safe once again ... Or is it?

A rumbling sound, like distant thunder, causes you to look towards the horizon; what you see sends a shiver of fear down your spine. A great dust cloud is crossing the border from the kingdom of Lendleland to the south – a dust cloud thrown up by a vast horde of barbarian horsemen. The marauders are galloping towards you, the ground shaking at their thunderous charge. A tribe of Lendlelanders, allies of the insane weather mage, is making the most of the disruption caused by the *Eye of the Storm* and acting on their Battle-Khan's invasion plans. Could it be that you have defeated one evil, only for another evil to follow in its wake?

A vast shadow falls across the galloping horsemen. Some of them look up in fearful disbelief; horses whinny and shy, throwing their riders; others turn tail and flee back towards the border as the wreckage of the huge brass fish comes hurtling out of the sky towards them. The *Eye of the Storm* crashes down on top of the Lendlelanders, crushing men and horses beneath its burning hull. What remains of the Thundering Horde turns tail and flees in panic.

You have saved the day once again and thwarted an invasion of your homeland. Rightly are you known as the Hero of Tannatown, bearer of Wyrmbiter, and now Saviour of Femphrey … the Stormslayer!

THE END

CHOOSE YOUR ADVENTURER

Here at your disposal are three adventurers to choose from. Over the page are the rules for Fighting Fantasy to help you on your way. However, if you wish to begin your adventure immediately, study the characters carefully, log your chosen attributes on the Adventure Sheet and you can begin!

Gorrin Silverblade

Tomb-robber to some, bold adventurer to others, Gorrin Silverblade combines the skills of a thief with the strength of a warrior. The son of a blacksmith from Tannatown, he has a cunning mind and a strong right arm, both of which have served him well on many occasions, particularly when he's been up to his neck in trouble down some half-forgotten hole in the ground.

Gorrin has a happy-go-lucky temperament, his natural charm coming to his aid now and again on some rather tricky situations. Also skill with a sword is surpassed by only a few.

Skill	11
Stamina	18
Luck	9
Equipment	Wyrmbiter
	Lantern and tinderbox
	Hunting Horn
	Sun Talisman

Gold Pieces	16
Provisions Remaining	10 Meals
Day of the Week	Seaday

Aldar Ravenwolf

Aldar Ravenwolf grew up an orphan on the streets of Pollua, in Lendleland, after his merchant-trader parents were slain by Hobgoblins while crossing the Howling Plains. He eventually fled the city after killing a local gang-lord in a bar-fight and has wandered the Old World ever since finding work as a mercenary, protecting merchant caravans.

Aldar has always been careful with money, a habit instilled in him by both his parents and his destitute childhood, which means that he can always equip himself well in preparation for any adventure. His hardy constitution means that he can keep on fighting when others would have already given up the ghost.

Skill	9
Stamina	22
Luck	7
Equipment	Wyrmbiter Lantern and tinderbox Dragon Tattoo Hunting Horn
Gold Pieces	23
Provisions Remaining	10 Meals
Day of the Week	Stormsday

Erien Stormchild

Originally from a nomadic tribe of fur-trappers from the icy mountain passes of the Witchtooth Line, Erien Stormchild left her tribal lands for the plains of Femphrey in search of gold and adventure long ago. Blessed by Cheelah, goddess of luck, she succeeded in finding plenty of both.

Where others might rely on strength of arms, Erien puts her faith in magical charms and the absolute trust that her guardian deity will always watch out for her.

Skill	10
Stamina	16
Luck	12
Equipment	Wyrmbiter Lantern and tinderbox Sabretooth Fang Sun Talisman
Gold Pieces	19
Provisions Remaining	10 Meals
Day of the Week	Fireday

RULES AND EQUIPMENT

HERO FOR HIRE

Before embarking on your latest adventure, you need to establish your own strengths and weaknesses. You use dice to determine your initial scores. On pages 342–343 there is an *Adventure Sheet*, which you should use to record the details of your adventure. On it you will find boxes for recording the scores of your attributes. Record your scores on the *Adventure Sheet* in pencil or make photocopies of the sheet for use in future adventures. You can also download fresh *Adventure Sheets* from www.fightingfantasy.com.

Skill, Stamina and Luck

Roll one die. Add 6 to the number rolled and enter the total in the SKILL box on the *Adventure Sheet*.

Roll two dice. Add 12 to the number rolled and enter the total in the STAMINA box.

Roll one die. Add 6 to the number and enter the total in the LUCK box.

For reasons that will be explained below, all your scores will change during the adventure to come. You must keep an accurate record of these scores, so write small or keep an eraser handy, and never rub out your *Initial* scores. Although you may be awarded additional SKILL, STAMINA and LUCK points, their totals may never exceed their *Initial* scores, except on those occasions when the text specifically tells you so.

Your SKILL reflects your expertise in combat, your dexterity and agility. Your STAMINA score reflects how healthy and physically fit you are. Your LUCK score indicates how lucky you are.

Battles

During your adventure you will often encounter hostile creatures which will attack you, and you may choose to draw your sword against an enemy. In some such situations you may be given special options allowing you to deal with the encounter in an unusual manner, but in most cases you will have to resolve battles as described below.

Enter your opponent's SKILL and STAMINA scores in the first vacant Encounter Box on your *Adventure Sheet*. You should also make a note of any special abilities or instructions, which are unique to that particular opponent. Then follow this sequence:

1. Roll both dice for your opponent. Add its SKILL score to the total rolled to find its Attack Strength.
2. Roll both dice for yourself, then add your current SKILL score to find your Attack Strength.
3. If your Attack Strength is higher than your opponent's, you have wounded it: proceed to step 4. If your opponent's Attack Strength is higher than yours, it has wounded you: proceed to step 5. If both Attack Strength totals are the same, you have

avoided or parried each other's blows: start a new Attack Round from step 1 above.

4. You have wounded your opponent, so subtract 2 points from its STAMINA score. You may use LUCK here to do additional damage (see below).

5. Your opponent has wounded you, so subtract 2 points from your STAMINA score. You may use LUCK to reduce the loss of STAMINA (see below).

6. Begin the next Attack Round, starting again at step 1. This sequence continues until the STAMINA score of either you or your opponent reaches zero, which means death. If your opponent dies, you are free to continue with your adventure. If you die, your adventure ends and you must start all over again with a new character.

Fighting More Than One Opponent

In some situations you may find yourself facing more than one opponent in combat. Sometimes you will treat them as a single adversary; sometimes you will be able to fight each in turn; and at other times you will have to fight them all at the same time! If they are treated as a single opponent, the combat is resolved normally. If you have to fight your opponents one at a time, as soon as you defeat an enemy, the next steps forward to fight you! When you find yourself under attack from more than one opponent at the same time, each adversary will make a separate attack on you in the course of each Attack Round, but you can choose which one to fight. Attack your chosen target as in a normal battle. Against any additional opponents you throw for your Attack Strength in the normal way, but if it is greater than your opponent's, in this instance you will not inflict any damage. If your Attack Strength is lower than your adversary's, you will be wounded in the normal way. Of course, you will have to settle the outcome against each additional adversary separately.

Luck

At various times during your adventure, either in battles or when you come across other situations in which you could be either Lucky or Unlucky, you may use LUCK to make the outcome more favourable to you. But beware! Using LUCK is a risky business and, if you are Unlucky, the results could be disastrous.

The procedure for *Testing your Luck* works as follows: roll two dice. If the number rolled is equal to or less than your current LUCK score, you have been Lucky and the outcome will go in your favour. If the number rolled is higher than your current LUCK score, you have been Unlucky and will be penalised.

Each time you *Test your Luck*, you must subtract 1 point from your current LUCK score, so the more you rely on your LUCK, the more risky this procedure will become.

Using Luck in Battles

In certain paragraphs you will be told to *Test your Luck*, and you will then find out the consequences of being Lucky or Unlucky. However, in battles, you always have the option of using your LUCK, to inflict more serious damage on an opponent you have wounded, or to minimise the effects of a wound you have received.

If you have just wounded an opponent, you may *Test your Luck* as described above. If you are Lucky you have inflicted a severe wound; deduct an *extra* 2 points from your opponent's STAMINA score. If you are Unlucky, however, your blow only scratches your opponent; and you deduct 1 point *less* from your opponent's STAMINA.

Whenever you are wounded in combat, you may *Test your Luck* to try to minimise the wound. If you are Lucky, your opponent's blow only grazes you; deduct 1 point from the damage you sustain. If you are Unlucky, your wound is a serious one and you must deduct 1 *extra* STAMINA point than you would normally.

Remember: you must subtract 1 point from your LUCK score each time you *Test your Luck*.

More About Your Attributes

Skill

Your SKILL score may change occasionally during the course of your adventure, but it may not exceed its

Initial value unless you are specifically instructed to the contrary.

At various times you will be told to *Test your Skill*. The procedure for *Testing your Skill* works as follows: roll two dice. If the number rolled is equal to or less than your current SKILL score, you have succeeded in your test and the result will go in your favour. If the number rolled is higher than your current SKILL score, you will have failed the test and will have to suffer the consequences. However, unlike *Testing your Luck*, do not subtract 1 point from your SKILL each time you *Test your Skill*.

Stamina

Your STAMINA score will change a great deal throughout your adventure. It will drop if you are wounded in combat, if you fall foul of traps, and after you perform any particularly arduous task. If your STAMINA score ever falls to zero, you have been killed and should stop reading the book immediately. Brave adventurers who wish to pursue their quest must choose a new character and start all over again.

You can restore lost STAMINA by eating Meals or Provisions. You start the game with enough for 10 Meals, and during your adventure you will be able to obtain more. Keep track of how many Provisions you have left using the Provisions box of your *Adventure Sheet*: you may not carry more than 10 Meals at any one time. Each time you eat a meal you may restore up to 4 points of STAMINA, but you must remember to deduct 1 Meal from your remaining Provisions. You may stop and eat Provisions at any time except when engaged in battle.

Luck

Additions to your LUCK score come when you have been particularly fortunate or created your own luck by some action. Details are given, where appropriate, in the paragraphs of the book. As with SKILL and STAMINA, your LUCK score may never exceed its *Initial* value, unless the text specifically instructs you to the contrary.

Equipment and Gold

You begin your journey with some simple, basic equipment that you will need for the adventure ahead, along with a few more unusual items. You are dressed in leather armour and have a backpack to hold your Provisions, Gold Pieces and any treasures or other items you may find along the way. You also carry a lantern and tinderbox. To find out how many Gold Pieces with which you begin your adventure, roll two dice and add 12 to the number rolled. Note this total down in the Gold box on your *Adventure Sheet*. Your lantern should be noted in the Equipment box, as must any other useful items you may acquire on your quest.

As an experienced sword-for-hire you also have a number of unique items that have come into your possession during past adventures. The first of these is Wyrmbiter. Long thought lost, until you rescued it from the bottom of Lake Eerie, Wyrmbiter is a fabulous sword, worthy of a hero such as yourself. The blade is enchanted and so will harm the Undead, Demons, Elementals and other magical creatures. Also if you ever find yourself in battle with one of Dragonkind (which includes Dragons, Drakes, Wyrms and Wyverns) as long as you are using Wyrmbiter, you may add 2 points to your Attack Strength and increase any damage you cause by 1 STAMINA point. Add Wyrmbiter to the Equipment box on your *Adventure Sheet*.

You also have *two* of the four items listed below. You may choose any combination from the four, as long as you only choose *two*. Then add these to your *Adventure Sheet* as well.

DRAGON TATTOO   Covering almost all of your back is a magnificent tattoo of a mighty Red Dragon, with wings outstretched, something you had done on a whim during a stopover at the port of Harabnab.

HUNTING HORN   Made from the curling horn of some fabulous beast or other, you won this valuable artefact from a renegade duke of Gallantaria, after pursuing him for the bounty on his head.

SABRETOOTH FANG	As long as a dagger, and just as sharp, you wear this fang on a leather cord around your neck, a memento of a battle you fought with a Carnodon in the mountains of Mauristatia.
SUN TALISMAN	You wear this small golden talisman, which you recovered from a ruined tomb you stumbled upon on the borders of Kakhabad, on a chain around your neck.

The Day of the Week

As you would expect, in the Old World the passage of time is measured in days and weeks, with each week having seven days. The days of the week are as follows:

Day of the week	Name
1	Stormsday
2	Moonsday
3	Fireday
4	Earthday
5	Windsday
6	Seaday
7	Highday

You will also find these days listed on your *Adventure Sheet*. It is very important that you keep track of which day of the week it is during the course of your adventure, for such is the power of the elements and magic on the world of Titan that you will soon discover that different types of magic work better on the days associated with them than on the days linked to their opposing elements.

Before you start your adventure you need to determine which day of the week it is. Roll one die; your adventure starts on the corresponding day. So, if you roll a 1 it is Stormsday, but if you roll a 2 it is Moonsday (and so on). As soon as Highday has passed simply move back to the start of the week and Stormsday again.

In addition, for every day that passes you may automatically recover 1 STAMINA point without having to eat any of your Provisions, unless the text specifically tells you otherwise. You are such a practised adventurer, and renowned hero to boot, that it is easy for you to find enough to eat and sometimes people will give you a meal free of charge when they find out who you are.

Alternative Dice

If you do not have a pair of dice handy, dice rolls are printed throughout the book at the bottom of the pages. Flicking rapidly through the book and stopping on a page will give you a random dice roll. If you need to roll only one die, read only the first printed die; if two, total the two dice symbols.

FIGHTING FANTASY ADVENTURE SHEET

SKILL
Initial Skill =

STAMINA
Initial Stamina =

LUCK
Initial Luck =

ITEMS OF EQUIPMENT CARRIED

TIME TRACK

GOLD

DAMAGE

CODEWORDS

POTIONS

Adventurer's Name . . . .

DAY OF THE WEEK

🔵 **Stormsday**

🔵 **Moonsday**

🔵 **Fireday**

🔵 **Earthday**

🔵 **Windsday**

🔵 **Seaday**

🔵 **Highday**

PROVISIONS REMAINING

MONSTER ENCOUNTER BOXES

SKILL =
STAMINA =

SKILL =
STAMINA =

SKILL =
STAMINA =

SKILL =
STAMINA =

TURN OVER IF YOU DARE

EXCLUSIVE EXTRACT FROM

THE WARLOCK OF FIRETOP MOUNTAIN

Untold riches.
A warlock more powerful than you can imagine.
Are you brave enough?

Deep in the caverns beneath Firetop Mountain lies an untold wealth of treasure, guarded by a powerful Warlock – or so the rumour goes. Several adventurers, expert swordsmen like yourself have set off for Firetop Mountain in search of the Warlock's hoard. None has ever returned. Do you dare follow them?

Firetop Mountain is an imposing place, a dark lair full of wicked foreboding. You will do well to keep track of your progress for it is easy to get lost within the labyrinthine passageways that weave through the very rock of the mountain itself. This is the home of Zagor, a cruel sorcerer and the terror of the land of Allansia. To have any hope of succeeding, you must be both brave and skilful, for otherwise you will end up lost beneath the earth with only certain death to look forward to.

Your quest is to find the Warlock's treasure, hidden deep within a dungeon populated with a multitude of terrifying monsters. You will need courage, determination and a fair amount of luck if you are to survive all the traps and battles, and reach your goal of the innermost chambers of the Warlock's domain.

At last your two-day hike is over. You unsheathe your sword, lay it on the ground and sigh with relief as you lower yourself down on to the mossy rocks to sit for a moment's rest. You stretch, rub your eyes and finally look at Firetop Mountain.

The very mountain itself looks menacing. The steep face in front of you looks to have been savaged by the claws of some gargantuan beast. Sharp rocky crags jut out at unnatural angles. At the top of the mountain you can see the eerie red colouring – probably some strange vegetation – which has given the mountain its name. Perhaps no one will ever know exactly what grows up there, as climbing the peak must surely be impossible.

Your quest lies ahead of you. Across the clearing is a dark cave entrance. You pick up your sword, get to your feet and consider what dangers may lie ahead of you. But with determination, you thrust the sword home into its scabbard and approach the cave.

You peer into the gloom to see dark, slimy walls with pools of water on the stone floor in front of you. The air is cold and dank. You light your lantern and step warily into the blackness. Cobwebs brush your face and you hear the scurrying of tiny feet: rats, most likely. You set off into the cave. After a few yards you arrive at a junction. Will you turn west (turn to **2**) or east (turn to **8**)?

2

There is a right-hand turn to the north in the passage. Cautiously you approach a sentry post on the corner and, as you look in, you can see a strange Goblin-like creature in leather armour asleep at his post. You try to tiptoe past him. *Test your Luck*. If you are Lucky, he does not wake up and remains snoring loudly – turn to 9. If you are Unlucky, you step with a crunch on some loose ground and his eyes flick open – turn to 7.

3

The door opens to reveal a small, smelly room. In the centre of the room is a rickety wooden table on which stands a lit candle. Underneath the table is a small wooden box. Asleep on a straw mattress in the far corner of the room is a short, stocky creature with an ugly, warty face; the same sort of creature that you found asleep at the sentry post. He must be the guard for the night watch. You may either return to the corridor and press on northwards (turn to 6) or creep into the room and try to take the box without waking the creature.

If you want to try to steal the box, you will have to discover the full adventure in
The Warlock of Firetop Mountain.
Could it hold a valuable clue to the whereabouts of the Warlock's legendary treasure, or is it something much worse, something dark and evil that is kept in a box under guard for a good reason? Only YOU can find out.

4

You arrive back at the junction in the passage. You look left to see the cave entrance in the dim distance but walk straight on. Turn to **2**.

5

You charge the door with your shoulder. Roll two dice. If the number rolled is less than or equal to your SKILL score, you succeed – turn to **10**. If the number rolled is greater than your SKILL, you rub your bruised shoulder and decide against trying again. Turn to **4** to return to the junction.

6

Further on up the passageway along the west wall you see another door. You listen at it but hear nothing.

You have come as far as you can at this stage, adventurer, and the way beyond lies fraught with danger. Only the bravest dare to set foot inside the caverns beneath Firetop Mountain; only the best will come out alive. Vicious monsters and enemies await your next steps. Do YOU have what it takes to overcome the powerful Warlock and find the untold riches of legend?

7

The creature that has just awakened is an ORC! He scrambles to his feet and turns to grasp at a rope which is probably the alarm bell. You must attack him quickly.

ORC   SKILL 6   STAMINA 5

If you defeat him, you may continue up the passage – turn to 9.

8

The passageway soon comes to an end at a locked wooden door. You listen at the door but hear nothing. Will you try to charge the door down? If so, turn to 5. If you would rather turn round and go back to the junction, turn to 4.

9

To your left, on the west face of the passage, there is a rough-cut wooden door. You listen at the door and can hear a rasping sound which may be some sort of creature snoring. Do you want to open the door? If so, turn to 3. If you wish to press on northwards, turn to 6.

10

The door bursts open and you fall headlong into a room. But your heart jumps as you realize you are not landing on the floor, but plunging down a pit of some kind! Luckily the pit is not particularly deep and you land in a heap less than two metres down. Lose 1 STAMINA point for your bruises, climb out of the pit into the room and leave through the door, heading westwards. Turn to 4.

ONLINE

Stay in touch with the Fighting Fantasy community at www.fightingfantasy.com. Sign up today and receive exclusive access to:

- Fresh Adventure Sheets
- Members' forum
- Competitions
- Quizzes and polls
- Exclusive Fighting Fantasy news and updates

You can also send in your own Fighting Fantasy material, the very best of which will make it onto the website.

www.fightingfantasy.com

The website where YOU ARE THE HERO!